Dash of Love

The Sunshine Breakfast Club
(Book 1)

KARICE BOLTON

Copyright © 2022 Karice Bolton

Bulldog Press

Karicebolton.com

ISBN: 979-8-9851947-8-4

Interior: Adobe Stock © Aleksandr

Cover Design by Didi Wahyudi

Interior Formatting: BB Formatting Adobe Stock ©
Phoebe Yu

Edited by Valorie Clifton

DEDICATION

To my readers, friends, and family. Thank you for embracing my dreams.

Chapter One

Grace

The sun filtered through the lanky pine trees on the narrow country road where the posted speed limit was far too fast for any sane person's comfort level. With groves of pines and farms sprawled as far as the eye could see, I knew Buttercup Lake was where my daughter and I were meant to be for the summer.

This getaway would be the perfect way to spend time together. We could both remember what was important and try to figure out how to manage the future without the one stable force we'd been used to for as long as I could remember.

My husband.

Soul mate.

BFF.

I forced the lump down in my throat and gripped the

steering wheel as I glanced at my daughter. This summer was about healing, dang it.

She turned down the music on her earbuds and scowled at me for the intrusion. "What?"

"Nothing. I just love you."

Isabelle shrugged and adjusted her seat belt as she looked outside the passenger window.

"This should be a fun summer," I tried again.

She put her phone down. "For whom?"

My stomach knotted, and I let out a deep breath.

Since when did she start saying whom?

Never in a million years did I expect my little Isabelle to turn into the teenager of all teenagers. But the moment she'd turned thirteen and three-quarters, we'd become her nuisance.

We.

I kept in the silent tears and reminded myself that I was no longer part of a *we* with the love of my life by my side.

I was an *I* who was super single, supremely alone, and utterly confused. I needed answers. I needed time away.

A few days back, I found myself having a conversation with a squirrel in the park close to home. He looked like he'd lend an ear as long as he had an acorn in hand, and I needed someone to talk to. It was right after the school called about Isabelle again, and I went for a walk. Once I'd waited for the squirrel's response, that was when I realized I needed time away. His little, beady eyes met mine, and it was like he was letting me know this relationship needed to end.

Even the squirrel was letting me down gently. He even left a seed pod as a parting gift.

No doubt about it. I needed Buttercup Lake and the answers it might hold.

It had been sixteen months since Tim had passed away, and every single day, it felt like I relived the moment he fell to the turf and left us. He was playing soccer with his buddies, and it happened in a flash.

I'd been trying to pick up the pieces ever since, but it wasn't until I got that last call from Isabelle's school that I knew I needed to change our lives for the better. They told me she wasn't allowed to attend the school fair celebrating the last day of school, and I told them she didn't want to go anyway.

A completely mature response on my end.

But once I hung up the phone, I knew the only things that could possibly provide that solace I so desperately craved were Grandma Millie and Northern Wisconsin.

I'd spent countless summers riding my turquoise bike to the candy store, the dairy, and the ice cream shop, all sacred places before I'd hit the lake. To end the summer, I attended

Camp Buttercup. The lake was the one place that offered freedom no matter what was happening at home, and in my childhood, there was always something happening.

"Mom, watch out," Isabelle screamed and dropped her phone as a deer sprang in front of our Jeep.

Making sure no one was behind us, I slammed on the brakes. We slid to a stop as the deer stood in the road and watched us.

The doe's eyes connected with mine for a brief second before she bounded toward the woods.

"It's a good thing Great-Grandpa Renny isn't alive, or we'd be eating Bambi for dinner." Isabelle picked up her phone.

We traded a mischievous look, and we both started laughing, knowing she was right.

"It's going to be weird not having him at the house." Isabelle twisted in her seat to look at me as I started the car forward again. "He always sat at the kitchen table and grumbled about the ways of the world."

I nodded. "It is, but I know Grandma Millie will be so happy to see you."

"Hopefully, she doesn't die while we're there."

My heart stopped, and I glanced at my daughter, noticing a fresh glaze of tears surfacing. Izzy had experienced more loss in the last two years than any teen ever should, but that was how life worked sometimes, and I wanted to do everything in my power to show her that she had an incredible life ahead of her.

Yeah. We needed Buttercup Lake.

I spotted the tiny green sign welcoming us to the town of seven hundred and eighty people and let out a silent sigh and wondered why my husband had kept a key in an envelope with a woman's name scrawled on it along with the name of this town from our past. To say I was surprised to find something like that tucked in the back of his desk drawer was an understatement.

"Okay, Izzy." I slowed to the town's speed limit of twenty-five, and it suddenly felt as if we'd stepped back in time. "Here's to a summer to remember."

She removed her earbuds completely and slid them and her phone into her backpack.

"If you say so," she mumbled.

I reached over and squeezed her knee. "I know so."

"Isn't this where you and Dad met?" she asked.

A smile touched my lips, and I nodded, knowing she'd already heard the story countless times. "Yeah. We met the summer I turned eighteen."

"Dad said you were going with some other guy, but the

moment you met Dad, you dropped the other dude like a hot potato."

I laughed and nodded, remembering the very first night I'd met Tim. "It's true."

I was at Buttercup Lake with my summer friends. It was late at night. My boyfriend stood me up, and over walked Tim with a bouquet of roses.

"You know what sold me on your dad?" I asked, looking over at Izzy.

She was the spitting image of Tim.

"What?"

"His dimples." I grinned, turning down the street to Grandma Millie's. "The same dimples you have."

Izzy rolled her eyes, but a glimpse of a smile surfaced.

She sniffled. "I miss him."

"I miss him too, baby." I clutched her hand in mine as I drove with my left hand.

This was the most conversation we'd had in months, apart from my telling her we were going to Buttercup Lake for the summer and her tearing through our house in disgust over missing her friends for three months.

Truth be told, I wasn't certain the people Izzy had started hanging out with were actually her friends... more like she was their target so they could get what they'd wanted, whether it was fast food or a place to crash overnight.

I spotted Grandma Millie's white, turn-of-the-century house with daisies in the garden beds bowing from the breeze and orange lilies dotting the drive. Her big vegetable garden in the front yard had tall deer fencing, but she also had a little area just for the deer to graze in the far corner. Her original hope was that if she fed them what she'd wanted to feed them, they'd leave everything else alone. Judging by the deer fence, it still wasn't working how she'd planned.

"The shutters aren't yellow anymore," Izzy said, taking in her home for the next three months.

I smiled. "Nope. The green looks nice, though."

I glanced at my fifteen-year-old, going-on-thirty, daughter and wondered what could bring us back together. I prayed it was Buttercup Lake and being away from outside influences, but I just didn't know.

And the worst part was that I felt like I was disappointing Tim. Granted, he'd seen Izzy turn from the happy-go-lucky little girl to the woman with a mission before he died, but it had gotten so much worse since.

"Oh, there's Grandma Millie." I waved as I pulled into the gravel driveway.

She waved back and sat on the porch swing, which was now painted green to match her shutters.

Before I'd even turned off the ignition, Izzy had bolted from the car and run toward Grandma Millie, who stood up and opened her arms.

Seeing Izzy with her great-grandma warmed my heart. My grandma was the kindest, most loyal grandmother in existence. She never spoke an ill word about anyone, even when my parents forgot they had children—three of us girls, to be exact. She just stood quietly next to us and helped to raise us each summer.

I turned off the car and took a deep breath as the realization hit me. We were at Buttercup Lake. I'd given notice at my job as an administrative assistant for a frozen food company and moved us here for three months.

The thought suddenly terrified me. What had I been thinking? I crawled out of the car and saw Izzy chatting animatedly with Grandma Millie and remembered it all.

Healing.

Answers.

We both needed to mend our broken hearts, and there was something about this woman and this lake that made that possible.

But the other part of me worried that Tim had something hidden that I never wanted to find out, and it started with a woman named Tracy and a key to who knows what.

I let out a sigh and made my way to the porch, where Grandma Millie opened her arms for me next and motioned for her famous hug.

The moment her arms wrapped around me, it felt like I was seventeen again, and she was assuring me that going back home to my parents' would be okay.

I closed my eyes and hugged her back, smelling the lavender and rose that were so very familiar.

"It's good to see you, my little Grace." She hugged me again before stepping back. "You look good. Tired but good."

"I think you're being extra kind because I feel like a mess."

"Ah, nonsense." She winked at me and turned to my daughter. "Anyone who has this angel for a daughter isn't anywhere near a mess."

Izzy beamed, and I saw the little girl I'd grown to miss.

"Now, let's get you to your rooms." Grandma Millie clapped her hands before reaching the storm door and holding it open for us to go inside.

"I just assumed Izzy and I would share the guest room."

Grandma Millie chuckled and shook her head. "When you're fifteen, it's okay to want space. So, Izzy has the guest room, and you have my bedroom." She wandered down the hall to the kitchen.

The thought that I'd be displacing a woman nearing ninety for the next three months didn't sit well with me. While Izzy looked relieved, I followed Grandma Millie.

"That's really sweet of you, but I can't chase you out of your own room."

Izzy came into the sun-filled kitchen behind me. The bright white cabinets and pale yellow walls were exactly as I'd always remembered.

"Oh, sweetie. I'm rarely here any longer. I found a man."

My eyes widened as Izzy stifled a laugh.

"A man?" My brows rose. "You found a man?"

In a town this small, it wasn't easy to do.

She wiggled her white brows and nodded. "How do you think I got my shutters painted?"

Izzy's hands flew to her mouth. "Grandma."

"I second that," I teased, startled to see a vivid sparkle in her gaze.

Izzy grinned and patted my back. "And you thought we'd help Grandma through her own grief. I think she helped herself."

Grandma Millie nodded. "Just because I can't remember where I put my keys half the time doesn't mean I can't remember where a man's—"

I laughed, cutting her off. "Okay, then. Your bedroom it

is."

"Anyway, Grace." She smiled." You and Izzy can have the run of the place. As I said, I rarely spend that much time here now. Oh, and I got your old bicycle all tuned up. New tires, chains, whatever it was that Steve at the bike shop said it needed. I thought Izzy or you might like to be able to take it out to the lake like you used to."

My grandma's thoughtfulness always amazed me, but now wasn't the time to dwell on her kindness when I just found out my grandma had already found a man.

I fully understood that curiosity killed the cat, but I needed answers.

Grandma Millie poured us all a glass of her famous lavender lemonade.

"Thank you for the bicycle. But who's the lucky man?" I asked, taking a sip.

The recipe was deliciously sweet enough to cut through the dampness of the day but tart enough to taste refreshing. Izzy closed her eyes as she drank it, and my heart started to settle.

Grandma Millie looked mischievous. "Jackson Barry Locke."

I almost spat out the lemonade and found myself choking on her words.

Izzy glanced at me. "You okay, Mom?"

I nodded, dabbing my eyes with my sleeve. "Jackson Locke is my age."

I was certain this bypassed all cougar references and flew to new, unchartered territory.

"Psh." Grandma Millie laughed. "Not *your* Jackson Locke. This is his great-uncle."

Izzy glanced at me. "*Your* Jackson Locke?"

My hands fluttered in the air. "I dated Jackson before your dad."

I'd also met his great-uncle eons ago.

Izzy looked impressed. "The guy who stood you up?"

I was surprised I'd ever mentioned that part to Izzy.

Grandma Millie snickered, and I knew to be afraid of anything going on in her mind.

My daughter smirked. "So, the Locke men have a thing for the Bailey women."

"We are Henry women," I corrected.

"Speaking of Locke men, the other Jackson is back in town." My grandma looked at me over her tipped glass.

"Is he taking care of his great uncle?" I asked nonchalantly.

"Jackson Senior doesn't need anyone taking care of him. I would know." Grandma Millie was incensed. "But his older brother does need a hand, and Jackson came back to help him out."

"How convenient." I smiled, seeing the sparkle in her eye. "What's his name? The uncle?" I tried to shift the subject away from Jackson.

The last I'd heard, Jackson had gone on to some Ivy League school and played on the golf team just like he'd planned. After that, I never heard about him, mainly because I loved my life too much to care.

After all, he stood me up.

I looked over at Izzy, who was staring at a clump of green bananas.

It didn't matter what Jackson had been up to all these years or who he's married to now. What mattered was getting Izzy okay again. Getting me okay again.

"Carter Locke. He's nearly ninety-eight, but he doesn't look a day over eighty. All those men really weather well."

Izzy wiggled her brows and lifted her gaze from the bananas. "I had no idea my great-grandma was such a cougar."

"*Grrrowl.*" Grandma Millie wiggled her brows, and we all broke into laughter.

Trying to bring the conversation back to a reality I could handle, I took another sip of lemonade and let out a happy sigh. "So, this man of yours painted your shutters."

Grandma Millie's eyes sparkled as they connected with mine. A sweet-smelling breeze ran through the open kitchen door, and she shook her head. "No, actually, his great-nephew, Jackson, did the kind act. Jackson."

Izzy snorted and shifted her gaze to mine. "*Your* Jackson? The plot thickens."

I playfully scowled at my daughter and felt an amazing connection zip between us.

Grandma Millie didn't end it there. "Fair warning. There's a pretty good chance you're going to run into that man. He's a social butterfly since he got to town, and all I had to do in return for the shutters was promise my lemonade on demand." She winked at me. "So, he might stop by from time to time."

I choked down my lemonade and suddenly knew I'd made a terrible mistake in coming back to Buttercup Lake.

Chapter Two

Jackson

My fingers grasped the rogue blades of grass in my uncle's front garden bed, and I ripped them from the loose soil, banging the dirt from the clump before I tossed it into the compost pile.

"Looking good, Jackson." The words my Uncle Carter spoke made him sputter into a coughing fit. When he regained his breath, I looked up to see him grinning at me. "Only about forty more feet to go, huh? You know, I used to do that weeding in one afternoon." His blue eyes sparkled with a pride I'd never dare puncture.

Days ago, when I told him I'd planned to help with his yard, he'd mentioned how long it used to take him, and I mentally vowed I'd take three times as long. I had a pile of mulch delivered and ready to spread once I rid the garden beds of weeds and grass.

"I heard something about that." I smiled and bent down, reaching for a different clump of weeds. "I think I might have to take Millie up on her offer of lemonade. You want some too? I can dash up there pretty quickly."

I stood and wiped my forehead of sweat from the humid day. The sun shone brightly with brilliant blue skies, and while the temperature wasn't abnormally hot, the moisture in the air made it seem stifling and like I needed to jump in Buttercup Lake and soak the day away.

"You don't mind if I..." I pulled at the bottom of my shirt, and my uncle chuckled.

"Why not? Let's give the ladies in town something to talk about." Uncle Carter coughed and shook his head. "When I was your age, I went shirtless whenever I could. Did I tell you about my time as a lifeguard at the lake?" He burst into a fit of coughing as I threw my shirt on a small boulder.

"It never gets old," I assured him. I jogged over to my uncle as his fit of coughing calmed and handed him his glass of water.

As my uncle took the glass, I heard a woman screeching in terror in the distance.

"You hear that?" I asked, searching the neighbor's yard and up the street.

"Ah, just a fox. You know they sound like a woman

screaming, right? You couldn't have forgotten everything about living up north."

I laughed and shook my head as the screeching got louder, and I jumped off the porch to find the source, and right when I did, I couldn't believe my eyes.

A woman atop a turquoise bicycle was wobbling all over the road, desperately trying to control the hulk of metal and rubber underneath her. I ran to the road and watched with helpless dread.

"What in the world?" Uncle Carter mumbled.

As the woman careened down the gentle hill with absolutely no control but at a speed that was surely going to lead to a mountain of catastrophe on the pavement in front of us, I waved my hands frantically and tried to get her to steer toward our yard and the pile of mulch I'd just ordered.

Without warning, the woman's legs stuck out from the sides of her bicycle. She closed her eyes and turned the bicycle right to where I'd pointed.

I jumped out of the way as she drove by, squealing, eyes still pinched shut, with a beauty that dropped me to my knees.

This was no stranger.

The moment the front wheel hit the bottom of the mulch pile, the back end of the bike raised, and she flew into the pile of bark. The turquoise bike tipped over as I ran to help.

She didn't move. She didn't groan. She just stayed face down in a pile of red mulch. She was missing a flip-flop, her red shorts were a little shorter than I'd expected, which I didn't mind in the least, and her white tank top clung to her body. Her dark hair was in a messy bun, probably a lot messier since her bicycle tour, but I looked to see any sign of breathing.

I cleared my throat. "Miss, are you okay?"

A garbled and sexy voice erupted from the landscape material. "Mm-hmm."

I knelt down next to her. "Mind if I help you up?"

"I'd rather just stay here."

I looked up and down the length of her body. Not much had changed, and only in good ways. Her hips had more curves, her butt looked rounded and absolutely lush, and—

Uncle Carter's figure cast a shadow over us as I looked up to see him staring at me, unable to hide his smile.

"You gonna just keep her face down in a pile of mulch?"

"I asked her if she wanted up and—"

"I'm fine," her muffled voice appeared out of the wood chips. "Just need a minute to regroup."

Uncle Carter rolled his eyes and shook his head as he tightened his grip on his cane and made his way back to the porch.

"Listen, I really want to make sure you're okay. I can call for an ambulance if you think you might need one," I offered. "It was a pretty nasty spill."

"I've seen nastier," she mumbled.

"Of course you have." I bit my tongue from saying more and watched the female mannequin in front of me wiggle her bare foot and tense her shoulders.

"I'm perfectly fine."

She put both hands next to her head and lifted herself up to her knees. I couldn't help but brush a few pieces of wood chips from her cheek before she turned to look at me.

Shock darted through her gaze as she shook her head with a little gasp of air. A few pieces of bark fell off her lips as she spat at the sight of me.

I kept my expression void of emotion even though everything about the woman kneeling in front of me tore my heart in half just like decades ago. I propped myself up and stood, reaching for her with my hand. She scowled and nearly sprang to her feet. She looked like she was ready to fight me, and I'd just saved her life.

Well, technically, the pile of bark saved her life, but I'd pointed her to it.

She wiped her mouth and shook her head, looking completely dazzling in her red shorts and white tank. Pieces of bark clung to the knit fabric on her breasts, and I resisted the urge to wipe them away. The thought made me chuckle.

"What's so funny?" She eyed me carefully.

"Nothin'." I shook my head, noticing her gaze run down my chest. "Just not who I expected to pull out of my uncle's mulch."

She glanced down at her white top and started dusting the tiny shreds of wood off her, but most pieces stayed clinging to the fabric.

"Ouch." She waved her hand in the air. "Splinter."

I raised my brows, trying not to let Grace Bailey's allure dazzle me into confusion. She'd already run off with my best friend once. I didn't need her to start hitting on Uncle Carter just for fun.

"Should I call an ambulance?" I quipped.

"I'm fine. I'll be fine." The tartness in her words stirred up a little something that seemed like fun. "I need to get back to my daughter."

She bent down for her bike when I noticed the dangling chain and the popped tire.

"You're not going to attempt another ride on that thing, right?" I eyed the bicycle, remembering her on the same one so many summers ago. We'd meet at the ice cream store, which also happened to sell twenty flavors of popcorn, and sometimes we'd head off to the community pool or over to Buttercup Lake. It had been such a carefree time.

"Like you'd care . . ." Grace scowled, which looked absolutely adorable. "Jackson."

Ah, so she did remember me.

"I care very much, or I wouldn't have directed you to the pile of mulch. The spill could have been much nastier."

"So now you're a hero?" she asked wryly.

I detected a hint of a smile, but I was pretty sure I could turn it upside down really quick-like if I misspoke.

"No. Just a concerned citizen. Listen, I'm glad you're okay. I'd be more than happy to plop your bike in the back of my pickup and drive you to wherever you're headed." I licked my lips and saw Uncle Carter watching us. I couldn't strike out in front of my uncle.

My eyes ran down her bare skin, and I pressed my lips together to resist the urge to say what I really wanted to say

"What?" She folded her arms over her chest. "Haven't you seen a woman before?"

I scratched my jaw and laughed. "I haven't seen *you* as a woman."

She tapped her foot. "And why would that matter?"

"I suppose it doesn't."

My uncle snickered, and I noticed how long it had been

27

since he'd coughed.

"But what I was observing was that you have a lot of splinters, and the moment you run a towel over your body, you're going to feel like you slept with a porcupine."

"Thanks for your concern." She eyed the pickup in the driveway. "I'll be sure to tweeze them out before bathing."

"You know, you could just put a raisin over each one and stick a bandage over it," Uncle Carter hollered with no cough again.

And I started to wonder if he'd been waiting for me to finish his yard work before his bout with pneumonia ended.

Grace looked perplexed. "A raisin?"

"Yup. It dries out the skin and makes the splinter pop out. Potatoes work too. By morning, you pull off the potato, and the splinter's stuck right in it," he explained.

I wasn't sure I believed my uncle's home remedies, but Grace seemed intrigued.

"They look mostly superficial." I shrugged. "You could just get some duct tape and run it over your skin quickly. It should pull most of them out."

She turned her attention to me and then back to my uncle. "I'll be sure to try the raisins tonight."

"Good girl." My uncle waved and stood before heading inside.

I ran my hands through my dark hair and let out a sigh. "So, do you want to be your typical stubborn self and push your bike home, or would you like to be sensible and let me give you a lift?"

"What makes you think I'm stubborn?" She eyed me, and I was dying to know what was running through her mind.

Until she opened her mouth.

"You're the one I gave chance after chance to, and look where it left me."

I wasn't quite sure where that was, so I grinned. "You were stubborn back when we dated. What's that saying? A leopard never changes its spots?"

Her gaze ran up and down my body, and she pretended to look annoyed. But her soft brown eyes gave it away

"Would you mind at least putting a shirt on?" She moved her folded arms from her chest and put her hands on her hips for a change.

"Does my overt masculinity bother you?" I mused. "Or is it my overall sexiness and toned physique?"

She snorted and shook her head. "Is this what usually works in a small town?"

I laughed. "Beats me. I haven't been to a small town since I came back to help my uncle."

Grace nodded slowly. "I heard about that. It's really nice

of you to lend a helping hand."

"It's the least I could do. His brother is a little tied up with his own shenanigans."

"You mean Millie Bailey?" She smiled, and her cheeks flamed red. "Sorry. I just learned about my grandma's fling."

"Oh, Grace. I don't think it's a fling." He smiled. "Has she ever told you about their history?"

She frowned. "No."

"You should ask her."

Her frown deepened, which only made her cuter.

Okay, downright sexy with her short shorts and barely there tank.

"Why won't you just tell me?"

I shrugged, kind of liking that I had something to annoy her about. Of course, it didn't exactly equal being left in the dust by my girlfriend of four years and best friend of nine all those years ago, but I'd take what I could get at this point.

"Telephone games. Things always get screwed up in translation," I informed her.

She pressed her lips together. "Fine. What about that shirt?"

I smiled and nodded. "Right. I'll go grab it."

"Thanks," she grumbled and went to take a step, but she exhaled a wail, and I grabbed her before she hit the ground.

Her fists pounded against my chest, and she squealed in pain and frustration. "Let me go."

"Are you sure? Looks like you'll hit the ground pretty hard if I do."

"Just . . ." She rolled her eyes. "Fine."

"How about I carry you to my truck, get you tucked in, and then I'll come back and grab your bike?"

She let out a deep breath which skated across my chest, and I clutched her a little tighter.

"You don't have to *tuck me in*, and you still need a shirt."

I smiled to myself and ignored her direction as I hauled her over to the truck, opened it with one hand while balancing her in my other arm, and set her on the old vinyl seat.

The smell of the warm plastic in the old truck pushed me back a few decades as she scrambled to buckle herself in before I closed the creaky old metal door with a thud. She rolled down the window manually and watched me wander over to her bike.

I picked it up and made my way over to the bed of the truck and put it in the back.

"Shirt," she called out the open window.

I ignored her and smiled as I climbed into the driver's seat and turned the key in the ignition, bringing the old engine roaring to life.

"Your back is gonna stick to the seat, you know." She wouldn't look at me. "Just like it did when you were a teenager."

Before pulling out of my uncle's drive, I turned to look at Grace. "Would you mind telling me why you are obsessed with me putting my shirt back on? I'm a grown man doing yardwork for his ailing uncle. It's hot as a skunk's tail in summer, and if I remember correctly, I'm doing you a favor." I chuckled and put the truck into reverse. "So, avert your eyes if the bare-chested man that I am offends you."

As I got up to speed on the old country road, the wind blew through Grace's beautiful auburn hair, and the smell of wild honeysuckle filled the truck's cab.

"I assume you're staying at Millie's?" I asked.

"I am." She kept her gaze out the window.

"I might have to grab some of her lemonade."

"We drank it," she said flatly, and I struggled to hold in my laughter.

"Are you always this pleasant?"

A smile brushed her beautiful lips, and she turned to see me as I slowed down, approaching Millie's house.

"Fine. She's probably made more by now. You're more than welcome to come in and get some."

I slowly pulled the truck into the driveway and saw

Millie and a younger version of Grace wandering between the deer fencing where lush green leaves filled the air.

My heart froze.

Grace wasn't here alone.

She had her family with her.

Tim?

"You know, I think I'll take a raincheck on the lemonade." I eyed Millie in the garden waving at us. "Let me just get you to the door and—"

"Um . . ." Grace looked uncomfortable. "If you only get me to the door, I might have to crawl the rest of the way, so . . ."

"Can't . . ." I couldn't say it. I didn't want to bring up how Tim could carry her the rest of the way. But I was a gentleman. "Fine. Let me get your bike first."

I climbed out of the truck and jogged around back and picked her bike up out of the truck bed before propping it against the porch. Millie was making her way over to us as I pulled Grace from the truck with her bum ankle and hundreds of superficial splinters.

Millie put her hands to her mouth. "Oh, no. The bike?"

"I'm fine. I was just too hard on it."

"Steve at the shop is going to hear about this." Millie ground her lips together into a plethora of wrinkles and hot pink lipstick.

"It wasn't his fault. I was forcing the cruiser to think it was a street bike," Grace assured her. "I promise it's not his fault."

Millie eyed Grace's ankle, which now had a slight purple tinge and swelling and no flip flop.

"Where should I put her?" I asked Millie, who motioned for me to follow her.

I saw the girl in the garden look over at us and scowl. She started to make her way to her mom, but she thought better of it, and a slippery smile seemed to cover her expression.

She must have wanted me to meet her father.

I carried Grace up the steps and followed Millie into her house as she motioned for me to follow her down the hall through the kitchen and into the three seasons room where a floral couch was draped with a pink and grey crocheted throw.

I set Grace down gently and waited for Tim to come bounding out of a nook, ready to knock me out.

"Would you like some lemonade for your trouble?" Millie asked. "You know I owe it to you whenever you want."

I smiled and nodded. "I wouldn't turn it down."

She clapped her hands and nodded. "Splendid. I just made a jug. You can take it back to share with Carter."

I looked at Grace while answering Millie. "Thank you. I

know he would appreciate it too."

Grace feigned a dirty look in my direction, which only made me grin wider. "Need some ice for your ankle?"

"It's just a sprain," she assured me. "It's not my first bike accident."

"Okay. Fine. But do you need some ice?" I repeated.

Millie chuckled. "Of course, she does. She's just too stubborn to admit it."

"I'm not stubborn," Grace grumbled. "I just have a lot on my plate."

Millie stopped and turned to look at her granddaughter, and she smiled slowly. "You're absolutely right about that, my dear Grace. But I'm going to do my absolute best to make things right again."

I didn't know what all had transpired between the two women, but I did feel the love between them. I wondered if maybe things had changed since the last time I'd heard about Grace Henry, formerly Grace Bailey.

And maybe there was more behind Grace's trip to Buttercup Lake than I fully understood.

"Hey, Jackson." Millie motioned for me to follow her into the kitchen, which I quickly obliged. "You look great without a shirt on, by the way. The Locke men certainly muscle out well." I didn't allow myself to think about my older uncle without his shirt, but I took the compliment.

I snickered as I filled a plastic bag of ice for Grace and wondered if I was the only man in Millie Bailey's home, and if so, where was Tim?

As if on cue, Millie cocked her head and brought her mouth closer to my ear, even though she was a good foot shorter than me.

"Tim's not here, you know."

I shook my head. "I don't know much of anything, really."

"Tim passed about sixteen months ago." Millie traded me the jug of lemonade for the bag of ice as the shock spread through me.

I looked at Millie and shook my head. "I had no idea. I'm so sorry. Please . . . please tell Grace how sorry I am. I have to go."

Millie nodded as I bolted out of the house and to my truck. I set the jug next to me and glimpsed the young girl still in the garden, and my heart ached for my best friend of so many years ago. The family he'd left behind. His daughter.

The pettiness that caused us never to speak again.

I gripped the steering wheel so hard my knuckles ached as I reversed out of the driveway, and I knew coming back to Buttercup Lake had been a mistake. The thought of someone my age . . . gone . . . *poof* . . . leaving a beautiful wife and daughter. Two things I'd never had, and here he was, gone.

Life was so unfair. He shouldn't have been the one to go.

As I drove back down the country road, I spotted something on the road. Realizing it was Grace's other flip flop, I pulled over, hopped out of the car, and grabbed it for safekeeping.

I could deliver it another day, but today wasn't that day.

Today, I needed to get back to Uncle Carter, and get back to pulling weeds and the life I thought I knew before I saw Grace again.

The life I understood, where my trip to Buttercup Lake was nothing more than a sabbatical away from life to take care of my ailing uncle, not a reunion with the only woman who'd stolen and crushed my heart.

Chapter Three

Grace

"Boy, I need to take a few dating cues from you and Grandma," Izzy said, laughing.

I playfully scowled at my daughter and pretended to swat at her, nearly falling off the couch in the meantime. "I don't know what you're talking about."

The truth was that since I nearly crashed into Jackson, I couldn't get my mind off him. No man should look that good with a shirt off, especially at his age. And his eyes. And his smile.

My lips puckered into a pout of annoyance as I ran masking tape over my legs again for the remaining splinters from the day before.

"Sure, you don't." Izzy grinned. "I saw him carrying the damsel in distress."

Grandma Millie walked into the three seasons room with

a pitcher of iced tea, three glasses, and slices of lemon.

"What? No famous lemonade?" I teased.

"Your lover boy took my last batch. I need to go to the store and snag some more lemons. This is the last lemon we have."

I frowned as my daughter chuckled. "He's not my lover boy, and I don't want to make my teenage daughter uncomfortable."

Izzy laughed. "Since when have you ever cared about that?"

"Since we came to Buttercup Lake." I smiled as Grandma Millie handed us the ice-cold tea. "Delicious, and just as amazing as the lemonade."

Grandma Millie looked at my ankle. "How's your sprain?"

"Getting better." I closed the book I'd been reading on my lap and let out a happy sigh. "But I think being here makes just about anything bearable."

Izzy nodded in agreement. Her usually pale cheeks had a rosy glow from a day in the sun. Little freckles appeared across her nose, just like when she was a little girl.

Since her dad and I had moved into a condo in Chicago after she'd turned four, she rarely saw the sun. Tim wanted to be closer to where he worked and promised the parks would be even better than a yard. Maybe for some families that worked wonderfully, but for ours, we managed to stay indoors most evenings and weekends, which was also what made finding an envelope with a key and a woman's name so perplexing. We were always together. Well, apart from his travels for work. I suppose he could have gotten a lot accomplished during his work trips. The thought made my heart sink.

Grandma Millie eyed my book. "You know, I think I have just the thing for you to do in between crashing your bike and telling yourself you didn't notice how good-looking Jackson Locke is."

"Grandma, I came here to clear my mind and to focus on healing myself. I have a teenage daughter to raise. She's my sole focus." My heart started pounding inside my chest as if it might burst at the thought of it all.

"This might help the healing part." She eyed my book. "You like to read, right?"

"Of course."

"And you like to eat?"

I smiled. "Always."

"Then come with me to The Sunshine Breakfast Club. It's a fun book club with great food and a little bit of gossip. Usually, we meet once a week in the morning, but this week, we're meeting on Saturday night." My grandma sat on the ottoman and rested her hand over my daughter's leg.

My daughter perked up. "It sounds like a great idea, Mom."

I wondered why my daughter wanted to get me out of the house so badly.

"We've only been here a day. Is this your way of getting your mom out of your hair?" I teased.

Her expression turned serious. "No. I just think it would be good for you."

Grandma Millie turned to my daughter. "You could come too."

Izzy shrugged. "We'll see."

I chuckled. "I guess we will, but count me in, Grandma. Sounds fun for the summer."

Grandma Millie took a sip of tea and let out a sigh. "For the summer."

"Well, that's the plan." I eyed my grandma suspiciously.

"We'll see," she repeated her granddaughter's phrase, and I laughed.

Lizzy stood and took her empty glass to the kitchen as Grandma Millie studied me carefully.

"He didn't know about Tim."

"Pardon? Who?"

Grandma Millie looked around the sun-drenched room filled with stacks of books, flower paintings, and pressed flowers hanging on the wall, and she pursed her lips together before answering.

I craned my neck, waiting for the answer.

"Jackson," she said at last.

The mere mention of his name brought back all kinds of uncertainty and emotion. He stood me up on our last possible night together. He'd used me for years, knew what he could count on from me every summer when I'd return, and then essentially dumped me when things might get complicated.

I cleared my throat and shifted my leg, noticing my ankle wasn't as painful.

"Of course, he doesn't. Why would he? I mean, unless he reads Chicago's obituaries on the reg."

Grandma Millie shifted and let out an exasperated sigh. "I'm just saying, he seemed pretty choked up when I told him yesterday."

I nodded, trying to push away my own feelings. "I doubt I'll see him again, but I'll be sure to keep that in mind."

My Grandma nodded as my mind drifted back to Jackson. The last time I'd been in a man's arms was with Tim, and having Jackson not only have his arms around me but physically carry me into my grandma's home just seemed confusing. Albeit, a sprained ankle cleared things up pretty quickly.

Besides, we were merely two drifters passing through Buttercup Lake for the summer.

"My head hurts." I pressed my temples with my fingers and let out a groan.

The doorbell rang, and Izzy hollered that she'd answer it.

Things were so different in Buttercup Lake. If the doorbell rang back in the city and we weren't expecting anything, there would be no way that Izzy would be running toward the door.

We didn't hear much except a low murmur of voices before Izzy appeared, looking like a mischievous cat about to pounce on its prey.

"Mom, you have a visitor."

I cocked my head. "I do?"

"Yup." She popped the 'P' and continued to grin when I got a sinking feeling.

Jackson.

I slid my bum foot onto the ground and stood up slowly, gently adding pressure on my ankle. There was a slight ache, but nothing like earlier.

Shoot! I can walk.

"Thanks, sweetie." I limped toward her as she moved to

the side, and my hand grazed the top of her head.

"This time, he's wearing a shirt," my daughter whispered, and I couldn't help but laugh.

I made my way through the kitchen and down the hall to see the door wide open and Jackson standing with a large bouquet of flowers, an empty jug, and my missing flip-flop.

"Looking for a refill?" I asked, eyeing the container that once held my grandma's famous lemonade.

"Nah, I don't want to take advantage of Millie's offer. I'll be back plenty of times before the summer's over." Jackson shook his head, and a few stray pieces of dark hair slid down his forehead. "But I wanted to bring you these."

He pushed the large bouquet of flowers wrapped in beige paper into my arms and dangled my missing sandal in front of me, which I took and dropped on the floor next to its mate.

"Listen, Grace." He sucked in a deep breath, and his blue eyes locked on mine. "I'm so sorry about Tim. I just had no idea. I . . ." He dropped his gaze to the ground and shook his head. When his eyes returned to mine, I saw the kindness reappear that I'd fallen for so many years ago, but now sadness etched his eyes. "I can't even imagine what you and your daughter have been through. I wouldn't have given you such a hard time yesterday had I known."

A lump formed in my throat, and I pushed it down as

quickly as I could before it reappeared. The rawness of the loss suddenly felt ripe as Jackson learned that Tim no longer walked this earth.

I shook my head. "Please don't apologize. There's no way you could have known. It's been sixteen months, and I still don't believe it some days."

Jackson nodded. "I'll bet. I'm just so sorry. If there's anything I can do . . ."

"Thank you." I clutched the flowers. "You're wearing a shirt, so that's a start."

Jackson smiled and shook his head. "I seriously would have put it on in a heartbeat if I'd known."

I chuckled. "So my being a widow suddenly makes you more discreet?"

Jackson's grin lit up the porch. "I just don't want to add confusion."

My eyes widened in surprise, and I snorted. "Confusion? Because you're just such an exquisite male specimen, my poor fragile mind might—"

"Geez, Mom. Give the guy a break." Izzy's voice wrapped around me and wrestled me back to reality. My daughter looked at Jackson and smiled. "My mom isn't usually this ornery."

I stomped my good foot. "I'm not ornery."

"Mom," she warned.

"Izzy." My brow arched.

Both of hers raised, and then she added. "Are you going to formally introduce me to your first love?"

"Izzy," I repeated, but she just grinned.

She just grinned exactly like Tim when he knew he was right.

I let out a defeated sigh and smiled, bringing my gaze back to Jackson, who seemed to thoroughly enjoy this encounter.

"Jackson Locke, please meet my extraordinary fifteen-year-old daughter, Izzy Henry." I glanced at my daughter. "Izzy, this is Jackson."

"Your first love," she added again.

I shook my head. "I don't know about that. It was a long time ago."

"Mom, you're only in your thirties. You can't play the memory card yet."

Jackson's low, gravelly chuckle interrupted another joyous mother-daughter moment.

"For the record, your mother was my first love." His eyes moved from Izzy's to mine, and a weird flutter erupted in my belly.

"Until you stood her up," Izzy added.

Oh, score, my little Izzy.

Jackson smiled and nodded. "Like mother, like daughter."

"What can I say? She knows it's easier to be direct in this world."

Jackson's smile only widened.

"Here, I can take that to the kitchen." Izzy reached for the empty jug that Jackson had been holding and also grabbed my flowers.

"It was nice to meet you, Izzy." Jackson gave a quick wave as my daughter trundled down the hall to the kitchen, leaving Jackson standing at the front door with me.

"You too, heartbreaker," Izzy called back, and my eyes widened in horror.

He chuckled. "In all fairness, I think it's safe to say that you rebounded rather well from that night."

Ah, so he remembered leaving me in the dust.

"Oh, you mean the marriage, daughter, family thing?"

Jackson nodded, but the smile left his gaze.

My ankle started to throb, and I pointed at the rocking chairs on the porch. "I still have a bum ankle, but it's getting a lot better."

I scooted by him and sat on a rocking chair, feeling the balmy air embrace me as I propped my foot on the porch railing.

Jackson's eyes dropped to my crotch, and he scowled. "Grace, you have an issue."

"Huh?" I started to look down and groaned.

Jackson laughed. "You want me to get it or . . .?"

I smirked and shook my head at the ball of masking tape attached to my shorts. "Don't even think about getting that lucky, Jackson."

Jackson's smile only widened as I ripped the tape off. Even though he towered over me, he made me feel larger than life, even when I'd managed to walk into walls or fall down the stairs. Part of that could have been because I knew he'd always be there to pick me back up again.

Until he wasn't.

"What is it about you? Just having you within a mile radius makes me turn into a blithering klutz. I'm not usually like this."

"It's always been like that."

I rolled my eyes and laughed. "It really has." I needed to change the subject, pronto. Talking about the past could get us in a place neither wanted to be. "The paint job looks great."

Jackson stood next to the front door and gave a nod of his chin. His muscular body stretched as he reached for the top of the door frame. Every part of him looked as if he was ready to spring into action.

"I won't bite," I offered.

"I'm not sure about that."

Jackson was wearing a pair of jeans and a plaid shirt with the sleeves rolled up.

He looked good.

Really good.

"Oh, please. I'm as cuddly and sweet as they come."

"Well, the jury's out on that, but your daughter was a good character witness." He walked over and sat down next to me. "You do get a little ornery."

"I do not."

"I'm sure I must just bring the best out in you."

"I never expected to look like a clown out for a bike ride, while nearly crashing into my first boyfriend, and for added funsies, using a pile of mulch as a landing pad. To say I was mortified wouldn't give things an ounce of justice."

Jackson nodded and didn't say anything for a few seconds as I took a deep breath.

"My grandma had warned me I might bump into you, but I didn't expect to actually run you over."

Jackson clasped his hands in front of him and grinned. "I'm just glad I ordered that mulch, or things could have been a lot worse for you."

I nodded in agreement and dragged my gaze away. There was something so wonderfully familiar about seeing Jackson again. It was like the decades of absence between us had vanished.

"What have you been up to all these years?" I asked, tucking my one good leg under my bad one.

I noticed his eyes quickly run up the length of my leg and had to keep in a smile. Maybe I still had it, at least a little.

"PGA. That's pretty much been my life."

"As in golf? You're a professional golfer?"

He nodded. "Yup."

No wonder Tim hated to watch golf. Whenever a PGA tour would pop onto the television, Tim would dive for the remote and change the channel in an instant.

"Interesting."

"It has been, but I needed to take a break. Uncle Carter gave me a good excuse for a vacation."

"Pulling weeds is a vacation for you?"

The funny thing was that I believed it probably was a break for Jackson. He'd always been so focused on whatever his goals were that if he stepped away and did just about anything else, it would feel relaxing.

"At this point in my life, yeah."

"You've always been so intense." I frowned, trying to

wrap my mind around things. "So, you made a living playing golf?"

The familiar cocky grin I grew up with spread across his face as he nodded. "Yeah, but it's not as glamorous as it sounds."

My eyes lit up. "Indulge me."

"It's never-ending travel, long flights all over the globe, never the same place two weeks in a row, incessant crowds, constant negotiations with sponsors, practice sessions in between tournaments, no time for relationships, and exhaustion."

I stared at him. "I prepared charts so my bosses could sell more frozen vegetables to the masses."

"Oh." He nodded. "That's awesome. We need veggies in our lives."

"Do we, though?" I snickered.

"You kind of veered in the opposite direction of what you'd always told me about."

"You remember what I wanted to do?"

The dream I'd desperately clung to for my teens and most of my twenties had slipped so far away, I barely recalled it.

Jackson's tender smile arose as he nodded. "Yeah. I remember. I remember a lot of things."

I rocked a little faster and let out a sigh. "Tim didn't think it was a great idea, especially once I became pregnant."

Jackson's expression fell, and I had to look away.

I hadn't uttered those words aloud, ever. I thought of them all the time, but I kept them hidden.

It was true. When I married Tim, I'd put my dreams on a shelf, but I knew I didn't have to. I knew I could have done everything I'd wanted with my little Izzy on my hip, and I never understood why I'd listened to Tim.

"Wow, Grace."

I brought my gaze back to his. "That's what growing up does, right? We make decisions based on factors we hadn't yet figured into our childhood dreams."

His gaze narrowed. "No, I believe you could have done it all, Grace. I really do. It's not too late."

"Anyway, I quit my job and brought Izzy to Buttercup Lake for the summer because we both need a break. We need to regroup and figure out our new normal." I glanced over the porch to see a family of deer walking along Grandma Millie's deer fencing before heading to what she'd planted especially for them.

I let out an unintended sigh as Jackson's gaze caught mine.

"It sounds like we could both use a little bit of Buttercup Lake's magic again."

I grinned and rested my head against the back of the rocker and nodded, thinking about how different my life had become.

Chapter Four

Jackson

When I'd been at Millie's the other day, I noticed the grass had been getting a little long. I also noticed how damn sexy Grace Henry was limping around in a pink gingham top and white shorts and a ponytail propped high on top of her head.

But seeing the sorrow drip through her gaze as we spoke about Tim about did me in. It hadn't been my intention to intrude, but I had found her missing flip-flop, and flowers seemed appropriate.

And selfishly, there was something about her that drew me to her, just like when I was a teenager.

"You daydreaming about that Bailey woman like my brother?" Uncle Carter's voice sounded a little too chipper for a man with pneumonia, but something told me after two weeks, his lungs might be getting suddenly clearer.

"Yeah. Grandma Millie enters every thought I have."

Uncle Carter frowned and shook his head, hobbling toward the front porch with his cane. "Sarcasm doesn't do a soul good."

"But it makes a person feel better." I grinned as he turned to throw me a disgruntled look. "And for the record, her last name is now Henry."

Uncle Carter smiled and let out a sigh. "Yard looks great, Jackson. You've done a lot for me. I appreciate it."

"I needed the break."

"If breaking your back in my yard and helping me take a shower are your idea of a break, you might want to reconsider where you're at in life." My uncle grimaced and wandered outside.

I quickly followed him. "It has been great being back at Buttercup Lake, and you've been taking care of yourself. So what if I weeded a little or threw some mulch on your garden beds? It was only twice when you first got home from the hospital, and all I did was scrub your back and hand you a towel. You're quite capable."

"I know I am," he grumbled and looked out at his freshly landscaped yard. "But I still think you might want to focus on the state of your affairs."

I sat next to him and nodded. "I'll take that into

consideration."

"Have you ever been in love?" Uncle Carter didn't lift his gaze from the yard as he waited for my response.

"Once."

"And it was the Bailey girl?"

"Yup."

"But you've been with women since?" my uncle prodded.

"Enough."

"But never love again?"

I let out a deep exhale and kicked out my feet in front of me. "I'm on the road too much to be tied down."

My uncle chuckled. "That's very admirable of you."

"Ah, so you know a thing or two about sarcasm too."

My uncle brought his gaze back to me. "I know a thing or two about a thing or two, and I can tell you that love is a wonderful cure."

"A cure for what?"

"Sarcasm." He shrugged. "Cynicism. There's no room for it."

I laughed and shook my head. "I'll have to remember that on my next tour." I stood and stretched toward the ceiling of the porch. "I'm gonna borrow your mower and go cut Millie's grass."

Uncle Carter's brows rose a little quickly. "Oh, yeah?"

"Yeah."

"Since when did you have a real passion for turf maintenance?"

"It's the golfer in me," I assured him.

"If you run into my brother, let him know how much I appreciate his help during my fall and bout with pneumonia. Great guy, that brother of mine."

I laughed and shook my head. "See? You're an expert at sarcasm."

I trundled toward the garage and grabbed a couple of boards to drive the riding mower up to the truck bed. As I anchored them, I thought about what my uncle had said.

Would it look that obvious if I came to mow?

I shook my head and pushed the heavy mower toward the truck.

"Nah. Totally normal for neighbors to help neighbors, even if we aren't technically neighbors."

"Having a good conversation over there, buddy?" Uncle Carter hollered from the porch.

Had I not been in the middle of giving myself a hernia as I pushed the mower up the boards, I would have used my own version of sarcasm on my uncle.

Once I got the beast in, I shut the tailgate and slid the

boards next to the mower.

"Go get 'em, tiger."

I couldn't help but laugh at the same time a realization hit me. My life had suddenly become narrated by Statler and Waldorf from the *Muppets*, but I'd always had a fondness for the two cantankerous balcony dwellers.

As I pulled out of the driveway, my uncle waved and rested his head against the rocking chair as I left to possibly make a fool of myself.

I thought about Grace flying over her bike into the pile of mulch and smiled. "At least I'm in good company."

I didn't realize how fast I was flying down the country road until a police car chirped its sirens at me and the lights flashed behind me.

"Damn it. No good deed goes unpunished." I pulled over where the tall grass met the sandy dirt and turned off the engine. I didn't need to be single-handedly responsible for starting a fire in the Northwoods.

I looked in my rearview mirror as the officer sat in his car. After a couple of minutes, the officer strolled up to my open window and slid his sunglasses down.

"If it isn't *the* Jackson Locke." He smiled and shook his head.

His bright red hair and matching mustache gave him

away.

My eyes widened in surprise. "Nate? You're in law enforcement?"

"Pretty ironic, huh?"

"That's what my life is full of these days." I smiled.

"How've you been?"

I nodded. "Doing pretty fair. Can't complain. I came back to help Uncle Carter for a bit."

He laughed, knowing Uncle Carter could be a handful. "Yeah? How's that going?"

"Not too bad. I think he likes the company more than anything. Ever since Jackson started dating Millie, his social life shrank."

"Ah, true love." Nate shook his head. "Speaking of, I heard an old acquaintance is in town."

"Oh? Who?"

"Millie's granddaughter . . . Grace. Ring a bell?"

Now, this was the moment I could lie to a police officer and pretend I didn't know why that mattered or that I even knew, but with my luck, I'd need her for an alibi somehow and screw up my chances, so I did what any adult would do and gripped the steering wheel.

"I've run into her. Actually, I'm headed over there now to cut the grass."

Nate snickered. "Is that what they call it these days?"

"Some things never change."

He flashed a wry grin. "No, they don't. And on that note, did you know you were speeding?"

"I can't say that I did until I saw the lights behind me. I'm sorry."

"Consider this your warning, and next time, I won't be so nice." He smiled.

"Thanks, Officer." I grinned. "Maybe I'll see you around."

"I'm sure you will." He tapped the old metal truck and flicked his chin in Millie's direction. "Have a good one."

"You too."

I waited until he was safely in his patrol car and slowly pulled back onto the road.

Even though Uncle Carter's house and Millie's weren't that far apart in distance, the meandering country road made it feel like forever. Old and new farmhouses dotted the pastures and farmland, and then Millie's house came into view.

The back of Millie's property actually touched Buttercup Lake, but it had always been thick and overgrown. It was easier to just go down to the public beach, but if anyone ever wanted to tackle the thicket, it would be worth it.

As I slowed to turn down Millie's driveway, I spotted Grace's daughter yawning on the porch as she thumbed through a magazine. Grace was nowhere in sight.

I turned off the truck, and her daughter looked up, but once I stepped out of the cab, her daughter got a wicked grin on her face.

"Mom's not here. She went next door to have them test her nine-layer dip, and I think they want to set her up."

I scowled at the thought and grumped. "Nine layers seems excessive."

"It's delicious. Millie should be back any minute with more lemons if you're hoping for a refill."

"I just came by to do a quick once-over with my rider."

Grace's daughter scrunched her face. "Rider?"

"Riding lawnmower. I noticed the lawn had gotten a little long."

"Ah, interesting."

"Why's that?"

"No reason, but I'm sure my great-grandma will be pleased. Soon, you'll earn a spot at Sunday dinner," she teased. "I'm off to make a sandwich. Have fun spinning around the grass."

"Will do." I gave a quick nod and headed toward the truck bed, unloading the boards and securing them to back the mower down.

I heard the storm door smack shut and immediately wondered why the neighbors were trying to set up Grace. Didn't they know she needed to heal? Find out what her new normal would become? What she wanted to do with her life? She'd barely gotten to town, and Buttercup Lake was already trying to swallow her up like it had tried to do to me so many years ago.

But thankfully, I'd gotten away and carved out a great life.

That was the thing about people who had people. They always wanted everyone else to get their own people too. But maybe some of us just weren't meant to people.

As I sat on the rider and turned on the machine, I thought about my own dating life. It was pretty pathetic. After getting burned by Grace, I pretty much used my college years to focus on golf. Having my best friend steal my girlfriend also left a bad taste in my mouth for friendships too.

So was I guarded? Yeah.

Had it protected me so far? Double yeah.

I turned the steering wheel to the right and rode along the deer fencing that Millie had guarding her vegetables and flowers. A family of bunnies hopped into the woods, sprinkling Millie's property with half-eaten veggies, and my heart tugged for Grace again.

A family.

Hers managed to get blown up in an instant. I'd looked up information online to see what happened to Tim, but I didn't see anything listed in the obituary or donations specified other than to some rescue dog charity, which sounded more like Grace's idea than Tim's. He'd never reminded me of a dog person.

And Grace's daughter. She seemed so well-adjusted, even with something like that happening to her. She seemed like a great kid. Recently, I'd only run into mopey ones, so it was refreshing to get more than a few grumbles out at a time.

As I rode the mower and the smell of fresh-cut grass filled the air, the good times at Buttercup Lake started flooding through my mind. Since Grace and I didn't live in town, the summers I'd treasured were even more special.

When I stole the first kiss from Grace.

The first time we'd traded licks on each other's ice-cream cones.

Our first fight. Our first makeup session.

Our goodbyes every summer and our hellos when we'd return to Buttercup Lake every summer. The lake held such good memories, and then the camp at the end of every summer was just the topper.

I rounded the back of the house after mowing the side when Millie stepped onto the deck and waved with a glass of lemonade. I quickly turned the mower off and jetted across the turf.

"It's a bit muggy," she said, handing me the refreshment. "Lawns a passion of yours, Jackson?"

I took a sip and scratched the stubble on my chin and looked out toward the woods and thicket leading to the lake.

I hid a smile and took another drink before bringing my gaze back to hers. "Just thought I could lend a helping hand."

Millie grinned like she held some secret she was bursting at the seams to tell, but I didn't fall for the bait.

"I've been doing my grass for years," she said, smiling. "Must have slipped my mind."

"Must have." I took another sip as the ice clanked in the glass. "Grace's daughter told me that her mom was next door getting set up on a blind date or something?"

Millie's white brows rose, and she adjusted the pearls around her neck. "Could be. It's not my business. But she did make a great nine-layer dip for everyone to try."

"Sounds great. I'd better get back to mowing."

"Thanks, Jackson. And it's not my business, but I think she dreaded the thought of meeting anyone."

"Is he a local?" I asked.

She shrugged and shook her head. "Don't know, but I'm betting she'll be back before you finish the back. She knows I have a date with Jackson."

As I climbed back on the mower, I heard laughter float through the trees from the neighbors'.

"Must be having a great time," I muttered to myself and turned on the mower.

Just as Millie predicted, when I finished cutting the last row, Grace appeared at the back sliding door and poked her head out. She smiled and waved and closed the door.

Just seeing her made my day better.

I turned off the blade and rode the mower to my truck. Grace was sitting on the porch in a rocking chair, looking as incredible as ever.

"Hey, stranger," she called out.

I flashed her a smile and walked over. "How was your hot date?"

She laughed and continued rocking in the chair. "He was hot but taken."

I laughed. "Didn't they check on that beforehand?"

"He's an out-of-town relative, a brother. I don't think they knew, but it was sweet of them to think of me."

I nodded, leaning against the porch while trying not to let my relief show. "So, do you want to be thought of like that?"

Her eyes widened, and she straightened as the rocking chair stopped moving. "Like as a potential date?"

I nodded, and she let out a deep breath.

"I don't know. It's kind of weird, to be honest."

I watched her carefully, wondering if it felt as easy for her as it did for me.

"I can only imagine."

Grace's gaze quickly ran up and down my body, and I wondered what she was thinking.

A lot had changed since we'd last seen each other. We were kids turned young adults, that awkward stage where everything felt so new and exciting while also thinking we knew everything, which with Grace, I quickly learned I did not.

The storm door opened abruptly, and Grace's daughter came out with a plate of tortilla chips and dip.

She pushed the plate toward me. "For you."

"Me?"

"You didn't sound impressed, so I wanted to prove to you how good it is."

Grace stood from the rocker. "Not impressed?"

I chuckled. "It just sounded like a lot of flavors, and I see your ankle is better."

"I'm a super healer. Now, tell me your honest opinion

because I'll be taking it with me to the book club on Saturday night."

"Alright. Alright." I scooped some dip onto the chip and took a bite.

The flavors hit me like a firecracker inside my mouth. It was delicious.

"Amazing." I scooped up more dip. "Totally take this dip."

"Told you so," her daughter chided before spinning on her heels and going back inside. She reminded me of Tim.

"Teenagers." Grace grinned.

"I have to say that reminded me more of Tim and less about age."

Grace's smile widened, and she sighed softly. "I think you're right about that."

"I ran into Nate. Did you know he's a policeman now?"

Grace burst into laughter "Nate, as in the King of Practical Jokes?"

"Yup. I got pulled over coming here today."

"Why's that?" she asked, looking amused.

"I was speeding."

She eyed me curiously. "And why were you speeding, Jackson? Couldn't wait to see me again?"

I laughed and shook my head, wishing she weren't right.

Grace stood and walked over and lowered her voice. "Can I ask you a favor?"

"Shoot." The energy rolling off her was like a magnet for me. Exactly like I remembered when we were young. Whenever Grace was around, I wanted to be near her.

She bit her lip, scraping some of the soft pink lip gloss off her bottom lip as she exhaled.

"I found some things of Tim's, and I don't know what to make of them."

I cocked my head slightly. "Okaaay."

"I was hoping you might be able to shed some light or offer some male insight or . . ." Her face fell. "I don't even know, but I'm afraid of what I might find out, and I don't want to involve Millie or my daughter."

Intrigue slushed around with concern while worry filled her gaze as she added, "You're the only one I feel comfortable with. You know, no skin in the game. "

"Sure, Grace. Anything you need."

"Really?" Her expression relaxed slightly. "Even if it involves a shovel and a getaway car?"

I chuckled and nodded. "Just let me know what you need and when."

"Thanks, Jackson. I appreciate it." She looked around the front yard. "And the grass looks awesome."

"Thanks. I'd better get back to Uncle Carter, or he'll probably blow a gasket about not being fed on time."

Grace chuckled and nodded. "Thanks again for helping. When I'm done digging a little, I'll reach out."

"You don't have my number."

Grace snickered. "Something tells me you'll be around."

Chapter Five

Grace

I dug through my bag and grabbed the envelope that had my husband's handwriting on it and dumped the key onto the bed and slid out the piece of stationary with *Buttercup Lake* and *Tracy* scribbled on it.

Tracy.

My heart fell a little bit at the thought of Tracy. I didn't know any Tracy.

Was she nice? Did she know he had a family? My expression soured at that last thought. Tim had never given me any reason to not trust him.

"Hey, Mom." Izzy tapped on the door, and I quickly scooped the key and note back into the envelope before shoving them under a pillow.

"What's up?" I tucked my leg under me as I scooted back on the bed.

"Do you mind if we go to the lake today?" She looked down at her arms. "I'm as pale as Casper, and I'd like to have something good come out of this vacation to nowhere."

My brows arched in surprise. "And that counts?"

She nodded and shrugged.

I secretly reveled in the fact that my daughter finally wanted to head to the lake. It was something I loved to do growing up, and she hadn't shown much interest.

"Okay, then. Let's pack our bags and some snacks." Excitement pulsed through me as Izzy lit up. "I'll grab some towels."

Izzy nodded and bounded down the hall while I scanned my small selection of swimsuits in my underwear drawer. I reached for a floral tankini and a pair of pink shorts.

As I slipped it on, I heard Izzy chatting away with Grandma Millie, who was headed out to spend the day and evening with her boyfriend. I smiled to myself and let out a sigh.

Maybe things were just different at that age.

Right now, the thought of dating was terrifying. I wouldn't even know where to start. Would there be a dinner? Would Izzy come? How would our lives even begin to merge if there were actually fireworks? How would I deal with my pet peeves? How would they deal with their own?

The thought was not only paralyzing. It scared me right into the category of staying single forever.

As I put sunblock and the towels in my bag, Jackson popped into my head.

Of course, he wasn't wearing a shirt in this sneak peek of my imagination, which was really a little over the top.

The man played golf for a living. Why did he have washboard abs and a chest you could bounce a quarter on?

And most of all . . . why did I care?

I swung the bag over my shoulder and wandered down the stairs to see Grandma Millie and my daughter conspiring, which was nerve-wracking, to say the least.

"What?" I set the bag on the floor near the front door.

"Nothing." Izzy had a glow to her, which only deepened my worry.

Grandma Millie grinned at her great-granddaughter and tapped the couch. "I won't be home tonight, or tomorrow night, for that matter. I think you two are plenty settled in here."

Izzy chuckled and blew a kiss to her great-grandma, and I realized I was looking at twins.

Conniving, sneaky, twisted twins with an age gap of about seventy-some years, give or take.

"Make sure you wear plenty of sunblock." Grandma

Millie wagged her finger at Izzy, who nodded. "Your mom learned that lesson the hard way a few times."

Don't say it. Don't say it.

"In fact, one time, she wound up staying indoors for an entire week, and her boyfriend at the time . . ."

"Jackson," Izzy happily interjected.

"Yes, Jackson." Grandma Millie nearly lit up. "Had to come over and rub aloe on her back three times a day. And let me tell you, Grandpa Renny was not happy about this boy coming over and rubbing aloe on her back." She giggled, and so did I.

"But the only outfit I could wear was the bikini I got burned in because everything else hurt," I added in my defense. "So, I was very grateful for the help."

"And I had to explain to my husband that his hands felt like sandpaper and weren't going to help the healing, and I certainly didn't have time to soothe her skin, but Jackson had plenty of it." Grandma Millie grabbed her purse and kissed Izzy. "How'd we get on this topic, anyway?"

"You reminded me to wear sunblock."

"Ah, yes. Make sure you wear it unless you find a hot boy to rub aloe on you."

"No, Grandma Millie. That's not how it's going to work."

Grandma Millie snickered. "Well, Izzy could just have him rub the sunblock on instead. Then she wouldn't get burned. Anyway, have a good day at the beach."

Izzy's wry grin only grew once Grandma Millie shut the front door.

"Spreading aloe on your back every single day for a week?" She looked far too amused. "I bet he remembers that like it was yesterday."

I laughed and let out a blissful sigh. "I'd be surprised if he even remembers we were an item."

Izzy rolled her eyes and picked up her bag. "I already put in some water and crackers. Grandma Millie said they have a little shack that you can buy ice cream from, and sandwiches too."

"Then I guess we are set." I turned off a fan rotating in the kitchen and followed my daughter out the door with our bags.

"Is there really a slide?" Izzy asked as we made our way down the road toward the lake.

"Yeah. They had a slide and a diving board on one of the docks, but I'd like to think they've updated those from a couple of decades ago." I watched Izzy take in the same route I used to travel so many years ago and smiled even though a bit of heartache pressed deep into my chest as I thought about

Tim. He would have loved to have seen her here in our old stomping grounds.

I rested my hand on my daughter's shoulder as we walked along the gravel shoulder, and she looked up at me and smiled. "You were right, Mom."

I nearly fell over. "About what, in particular?"

"Coming here was better than staying in Chicago."

I squeezed her shoulder and dropped my arm down as we crossed the street to the makeshift parking lot. You'd never know from the street what kind of fun was hidden behind the thicket of elderberry and honeysuckle and a few red pines.

Izzy turned to look at me. "This is the beach?"

I laughed. "Just wait and see. It's another hidden gem of Wisconsin."

"If you say so."

"Oh, Izzy. I love you to the moon and back."

We jogged across the street and hit the gravel parking lot where the sounds of water splashing and kids squealing drifted through the air.

Izzy smiled. "That's sounding hopeful."

Cars and trucks were parked tightly in the square lot, and several families were hauling coolers and beach toys. A little beach shack with several colorful umbrellas lined the edge of the sand where the parking lot gave way to the beach.

"Wow." Izzy's jaw dropped open at the sight ahead of us.

The white sandy beach stretched around the lake as far as the eye could see. Camp Buttercup was across the water, where its own private beach had several beach chairs and umbrellas. It looked like it had been rented out for a private event. I glanced at Izzy and wondered if she might want to go this summer.

"Change your mind about spending the summer here?" I teased as several teenage boys played beach volleyball.

"It just might." She slid down her denim shorts and pulled off her white tank to reveal a cute bikini. I knew I had to bite my tongue about how small it was. She was a teenager. Bikinis were fine. Boys were fine.

From like ten feet away.

"You look cute. They'd be insane not to notice you." I grinned, hiding the worry of suddenly raising a teenage girl by myself.

Izzy's eyes connected with mine. "You think?"

I nodded. "I know."

Seeing the relief spread through my daughter made me realize just how much we needed to get away from the hustle and bustle of the city. Sure, Izzy had fallen in with the wrong crowd, but it was more like the wrong crowd had flocked to

Izzy. She never did anything intentionally rotten. Izzy just always happened to be the 'fall girl' for other people's shenanigans.

She gave me a quick hug, which completely stunned me, before whispering, "I like this side of you."

"Me too." I saw a line over at the beach shack with kids holding their parents' debit cards and nothing more than a wish for an ice cream bar sinking into their minds.

It was such a different life from what Izzy had grown up with, not better or worse, just different.

"You want some ice cream?" I asked, setting our bags down and tugging out the towels for the beach.

Kids screeched happily, running through the sand, kicking up a bit as they wove through the area we found.

"Nah. I'm good." Izzy plopped on the towel, kicked her sandals off, and started applying the sunblock.

She eyed the dock where there was a slide and the other dock where the lifeguard sat perched in the same chair I remembered. His skin was bronzed, his shorts were red, and he looked ready to lunge into the water at a moment's notice.

"Cute lifeguard," I whispered, reaching for the sunblock she'd tossed toward me.

She playfully swatted at me, pulling her knees into her chest. "Mom. You're so annoying."

"I think I remember being told that a lot back home."

She was quiet for a moment. "I'm sorry about all that."

My heart squeezed instantly. "You are?"

She nodded, resting her chin on her knees. "Yeah. Do you realize not one of my friends has texted me since everything happened at the school?"

"I had no idea." I opened a water bottle and took a sip.

Izzy let out a sigh. "I don't think they were ever my friends. I was just the scapegoat or their sugar mama."

I frowned, touching her cheek. But I knew not to say a word. This moment could turn instantly, and I felt it was important for her to come to her own conclusions.

She pushed her legs out in front of her and leaned on her elbows behind her before turning to look at me and smiled. "Did you do it with Jackson?"

I nearly choked to death on the water I'd just swallowed and wound up coughing up a lung instead.

Izzy giggled. "I take that as a yes."

"Izzy, don't you dare take my choking to death as a sign of anything."

"So, you're denying it?"

"I don't think I have to confirm or deny any of that with my teenage daughter."

"I'll find out one way or another." She chuckled. "I have

my sources, you know."

"I'm beginning to believe that." I eyed her and smiled.

A rogue volleyball rolled by Izzy. "Should I go give it to them?"

I hid a smile as I saw one of the teenage boys jogging toward us. He was paying absolutely no attention to where the ball landed and instead stared in Izzy's direction as if he'd just landed on Mars.

"I don't think you have to worry about that," I whispered. "Bogie at two o'clock."

Izzy glanced at the boy making his way over to us. A little gasp escaped Izzy's lips, and I kept my chuckle to myself.

The boy walked right by the ball and stood by Izzy. His body cast a shadow across Izzy and me as he smiled.

"I haven't seen you around before." He offered a cocky grin to my daughter, who in turn gave him one right back.

"Weren't you supposed to fetch something for your team, ball boy?"

The guy smiled and shook his head. "You're not from around here, are you?"

"Nah." She shook her head and turned her gaze toward the water.

My daughter had game.

Literal game.

And she was only fifteen.

He took a few steps back and reached for the ball. "Well, I hope I see you around again."

She brought her eyes back to his. "If you're lucky."

The guy laughed and nodded before jogging back to his waiting team.

"Wow, Izzy Henry." I whistled. "I could take a lesson or two."

She looked at me and smiled. "I don't know where that came from."

"Seriously? You never did that to a boy before back at home?"

Izzy shook her head. "No boys ever paid attention to me back there. I had plenty of fake conversations in my head, though."

My stomach squeezed for Izzy. "You know, I'm starting to wonder if you were happy in Chicago. I . . . we always thought you had a strong network of friends in grade school and middle school."

She shrugged. "They all got shipped off to a different high school."

I nodded slowly.

"And I had to make do."

I realized how seldom I'd had a real, meaningful conversation with my own daughter. Before Tim passed away, we were always busy with work, dinner, chores, homework, and a vacation here or there. We rarely managed to all eat dinner at the same time, and it was even rarer if it was something I cooked, but my hours were horrendous. I was at the beck and call of my entire team. Need a report at nine o'clock at night? No problem. Need a presentation built with ten minutes' notice before quitting time? You got it. I didn't plan on dinner, anyway. And Tim was just as busy. Plus, he traveled for work a lot.

My chest tightened at the thought of what his travel might have actually meant.

"You okay, Mom?" Izzy asked.

I nodded. "Yeah. Sorry. I just . . ."

"Drift off?"

I pressed my lips together and glanced toward the volleyball area. "You know, your admirer can't seem to stop looking in this direction."

"Yeah? Well, yours is coming over here too." She reclined and shut her eyes as I scanned the beach for any sign of Jackson.

She giggled. "Made you look."

"You are absolutely rotten." I chuckled and lay down

next to my daughter, realizing I could finally take that deep breath I'd been waiting for.

Chapter Six

Jackson

Uncle Carter felt he needed a day at the beach, and who was I to get in the way of a sick man's wishes? I just never expected the trek to be so tedious. We couldn't just take off for Buttercup Lake.

No, we had to go to the market and get chips, dips, salami, crackers, cheese, and the list went on. By the time we made it to the beach, the activities were in full swing. Paddleboarders canvassed the lake, a volleyball tournament was in win mode, and the ice cream shack had a line that stretched at least twenty people deep.

But the moment I set foot onto the sand, I remembered my summers here like they were yesterday.

I snuck my first kiss behind the beach shack, and it just so happened to be with Grace Bailey . . . err, Henry. And I still remember the electricity that shot through me when she wrapped her legs around my waist when we were bobbing in the lake after most everyone had gone home and the sun had nearly set.

"I reserved a table over here," Uncle Carter explained, motioning toward several covered picnic tables.

Surprise darted through me as I watched my uncle suddenly have a spring in his step. "You did?"

"Of course. You think I can get up and down from the beach chairs?" he grumbled as I hauled the large cooler and bag strapped over my shoulder.

"No, but I've been surprised at how much you've been able to do lately."

And it was true. Whenever I wasn't looking, Uncle Carter would sneak out to his garage and work on a few projects against the doctor's orders.

As I set the cooler on the picnic table, Uncle Carter let out a low whistle. "Well, would you look at that?"

I was almost afraid to, but I followed his gaze to see Grace Henry sunning on a striped beach towel with a pair of pink shorts and a white bikini top. I swallowed hard and looked away.

"I wonder if they're hungry," Uncle Carter took a seat on the picnic bench.

"They look like they're happy over there. In fact, I think

they're both sleeping."

As if on cue, Grace lifted her sunglasses and propped them on top of her head as she scanned the crowds before looking at her daughter.

Every damn inch of Grace was gorgeous. The way the sun touched her skin, the perfectly curved shape of her breasts under the fabric of her bikini, her hair swept into a ponytail.

"You want me to roll your tongue up for you before you go invite the ladies over for lunch?"

I scowled at my uncle when I saw a huge grin pinning his expression into complete mischief.

"You set me up?" I folded my arms over my chest. "You set me up."

Uncle Carter cracked his neck and shook out his hands. "Define set up."

"You knew Grace and her daughter were going to be here, and that was why you got the sudden hankering to leave the rocking chair on your porch."

His silver brows rose. "Is that an issue?"

"Well . . ." I glanced over at Grace. She was smiling and chatting with her daughter. "Maybe she doesn't want to be bothered and just wants to spend a day at the lake with her daughter."

Her daughter sat up, stretched her arms to the sky, and

tossed her sunglasses on the towel before hoisting herself up and wandering toward the lake.

"We can't let all this food go to waste. I won't allow it." Uncle Carter stood and popped the cooler open. "It would be rude not to invite them for a bite to eat." He looked over at me. "Go on. Seriously. Don't make me do something you'll regret."

I chuckled and shook my head in disbelief. The truth of it was that since seeing Grace nosedive into the pile of mulch at my uncle's house, I hadn't been able to get her out of my head. We had so much history, and I had so many questions.

The first being why?

Why did I get dumped for my best friend?

But then, none of those questions seemed to matter the moment I heard that Tim had passed away. It felt selfish to even wonder, and I felt even worse for wanting to be near her.

It didn't help that she wanted my help with something. The request almost seemed mysterious.

"I'm not asking you to get down on one knee," Uncle Carter continued. "I'm just suggesting that you do what any decent human being would do and offer them lunch."

I grinned at my uncle. "You won't shut up unless I go do it either, I imagine."

He opened a tub of Greek olives and smiled. "You

imagined correctly."

As I trudged through the sand, careful not to kick any up on sunbathers, I wondered what I would say to her when I finally landed near her towel.

But I didn't have to worry about it because before I even arrived, she turned toward me, and surprise washed over her face as a hand waved in the air.

"Hello, stranger." She grinned and took a deep breath, which made my eyes wander to her heaving breasts for a millisecond.

Who was I kidding? They weren't heaving, but they were beautiful.

"Funny meeting you here," she continued.

"I was thinking the very same thing." I glanced over my shoulder at Uncle Carter, who was watching us with eagle-eyed precision.

"I'm not sure whether I should be flattered or worried," she teased, patting the sand.

"Just what makes you think it was my idea?" I knelt down, and the smell of coconut drifted toward me, just like old times.

She laughed and looked toward the lake at her daughter, who was ankle-deep in the water with splashing kids all around her.

"I have to confess that somehow, my uncle knew you two would be here."

Grace smiled and bit her lip briefly as she eyed Izzy before bringing her gaze back to mine. "I did think it was kind of random that Izzy wanted to come to the lake today."

"My uncle had us stop at the market and buy enough food for the entire town if you and Izzy would like to join us."

Grace craned her neck around me to see my uncle undoubtedly staring at us.

"I think we would like that, Jackson." She waved at Izzy and pointed at the picnic area, and Izzy nodded back without budging. "She'll come when she's ready."

I stood and reached to help Grace up from her towel. "You can probably just leave everything there."

"You think?" She dusted some stray sand from her legs. "I always forget I'm in Buttercup Lake."

"It's kind of refreshing, isn't it?"

I couldn't even believe I was saying that. The truth was that I'd hated this place the moment I realized I'd lost my girlfriend to my best friend. It was like rather than blaming Tim or myself, I blamed the Buttercup Camp and the people of Buttercup Lake.

But the simpler times taking care of my uncle reminded me of what I'd been missing for so many years.

Grace held up her hands, and I lifted her easily as she sprang to her feet.

Keep your gaze up, Jackson. Be a gentleman. She just lost her husband, for shit's sake.

"You look like a robot," Grace told me. "You okay?"

She waved her hands in front of me, and I grinned.

"I hope you like hard meat and—"

"Jackson Locke, you're really something." She grinned, and I shook my head.

"Had you let me finish rather than traveling the way of the gutter, you would have heard the rest of the menu."

She chuckled and dropped her gaze to the sand as we navigated over to my peeping uncle.

"We have all the hard meats you can imagine, an endless cheese selection, smoked sausages, olives, and crackers."

"It wouldn't be Wisconsin without cheese and sausage, but you're getting pretty fancy," she teased as we made our way to my uncle.

"Hello there, Grace."

"Grace, this is Uncle Carter," I said as Grace gave a quick wave.

"Nice to meet you." She smiled at my uncle, who blushed on the spot. I think she'd actually met him a few times when she was younger, but I didn't want to point that out.

And I'd never seen my uncle blush. I didn't even think that was possible.

"You're so beautiful. I can see why my nephew has had a hard time keeping his head on straight."

I held my head in my hand and groaned. "Let me have a little game, would you?"

Uncle Carter flashed her a mischievous grin. "She knows you well enough to know there's not much cooking there."

I could always count on my family to keep me humble. There were times I wasn't sure that was always a good thing, but today, it would have to do.

"Truer words, Carter." Grace laughed and cocked her head toward Izzy as a boy walked up to her.

"Oh, geez. I think my daughter has a not-so-secret admirer," Grace muttered.

"Should I go scare him off, or . . .?"

Grace chuckled. "Can you imagine stomping over there and towering over that poor kid?"

"You mean like your Grandpa Renny did to me that first summer?"

She nodded. "Exactly like that, but it didn't work."

"No, it really didn't." I smiled, thinking fondly back to that day.

I should have been scared spitless, but being next to

Grace was worth every ounce of fear her grandpa pounded into me.

"I'm sorry to hear he passed away."

She smiled and nodded. "He was a good grandpa."

"A fine man, that Renny. Gone far too soon," Uncle Carter piped up.

"Too soon," I agreed.

"But hell. We're all getting up there, so who knows?" He popped open a beer and took a swig.

Grace chuckled and reached for some salami as she eyed her daughter, and I wondered if she ever thought back to us.

Chapter Seven

Grace

"Would you like to grab dinner on Saturday night? Be my plus one?" Jackson asked me as Izzy dried off with a towel and a piece of cheese hanging out of her mouth.

My chest tightened into a frenzied expectation of excitement, remorse, guilt, and worry.

And then I remembered I had a date with the Sunshine Breakfast Club.

"Actually, I'm headed to the local book club with my grandma. I'm supposed to make the dip."

"Way to sound sexy and available, Mom," Izzy smirked as she reached for an olive with Uncle Carter laughing.

I rolled my eyes at my teenager as her mystery man rolled up behind her.

Payback.

I turned back to Jackson and nodded before snagging

another piece of prosciutto, which happened to be a favorite of mine. "But I'm completely free on Sunday night. Grandma Millie is having her Sunday dinner at the house. Want to stop by?"

Jackson nodded, and I swore I saw a hint of relief dart through his gaze.

"Sunday dinner sounds incredible." He smiled just as Uncle Carter had his say.

"I'd like to believe I'm invited too." Uncle Carter barked from behind Jackson.

"Of course." I grinned, wondering what on earth it was like at their house on the daily.

Izzy's voice went an octave higher than usual, catching all of our attention as she shook her head. "I can't. I'm sorry. I have a book club to attend."

The teenage boy looked devastated and sucked in a deep breath right when Izzy continued.

"But you can come to my grandma's house for Sunday dinner."

"It runs in the family," Uncle Carter whispered under his breath.

The teenage boy's blue eyes lit up like he'd just witnessed a fireworks show, and I had to stop myself from grinning.

They exchanged numbers, and Izzy refused to turn around to look at any of us.

"Don't say a word. Not a single word." Izzy's voice was firm.

I swallowed down all the words and snuck a peek at Jackson, who looked utterly amused.

Jackson laughed. "Looks like you both have some reading to do."

Izzy turned and glanced over at Carter, who was putting food back into the blue cooler.

"I can help with that," she offered, and pride filled me to the brim.

It was like night and day since we'd arrived at Buttercup Lake.

"You've got an amazing daughter," Jackson whispered near my ear. "You and Tim have done an incredible job raising her."

His breath left a wave of tingles, and I closed my eyes to get my bearings. It didn't matter that he made me feel important or worth noticing.

This was ridiculous. There was absolutely no way we could start right where we left off all those years ago.

I blinked my eyes open to see Carter, Jackson, and my daughter watching me.

"Did you not drink enough water?" Carter's silver brows rose with merely a hint of concern.

"I . . . uh . . ." I nodded. "Yeah. Exactly. Too much salty stuff mixed with sun and no water."

Izzy's brows pulled together. "You drank like three bottles of water."

Jackson handed me another water, and even though I already felt waterlogged, I chugged it down to make a point.

And the point was that I could not, would not, should not fall for a man who had stood me up decades ago and was merely prancing around my old stomping ground.

Okay, he wasn't prancing. He had a confident stride and seemed very sure of his surroundings.

I let out a deep breath as Jackson scooted behind me, sliding his hands across my shoulders to get by.

I was left with electricity charging through me and my breath catching in my throat.

"I feel like an ice cream bar," Izzy announced, and Carter nodded.

"You know, I could use one too. My treat," he told my daughter.

"Perfect." Izzy looped her arm through his, which I knew was more to help him through the sand than anything, making me smile.

Jackson was right. We had done well with her.

"You two want any?" Carter asked over his shoulder.

I shook my head while Jackson nodded. "Something with chocolate."

Ugh. Chocolate. My nemesis.

I could eat pounds of it.

"Okay. Fine. Me too." I smiled and glanced at Jackson as Carter nodded approvingly.

Jackson was studying me, and a ripple of excitement ran through me, which was the craziest thing in the world.

I was thirty-five with no idea where my life was headed other than that Izzy was the most important thing in my world.

Buttercup Lake was supposed to be a calm and peaceful summer vacation with absolutely no blips in the road, and Jackson was a definite blip.

But I needed the topics between us to be safe. Not sexy at all.

Parents.

"How are your parents doing?" I asked.

His expression warmed and nodded. "They're doing really great, actually. I bought a little bungalow in the DR."

My brows rose. "DR?"

"Sorry. Dominican Republic."

I nodded and grinned. "Ah, yes. The DR."

He let out a gravelly chuckle which made my knees knock. "And the next thing I knew, they were retiring and never left."

I laughed. "Seriously?"

"Yup. It was meant as a vacation home for the family, but they took it to heart and never wanted to leave. So, they're very accommodating when I do make it down there."

I smiled. "Well, I hope they give you the big bedroom."

"Nope." He grinned, and my mind drifted to my parents and what a wreck they'd turned into. They were always one step close to the edge while my sisters and I grew up, but they definitely went over it once we were out of the picture.

"What are you thinking?" Jackson asked, folding his arms over his chest.

The way he looked at me made my entire body heat up, and I was suddenly at a loss for words.

So, I glanced toward the water and watched as the families and kids marched out of the lake and packed up to head home for dinner.

I took a deep breath and turned my attention back to Jackson. There was such an intensity about him as he watched me. But the one thing I didn't want to bring up to Jackson today was my parents.

"I'm thinking about how I never expected in a million

years for you to be at Buttercup Lake."

"Would that have changed your mind?" he asked.

"I don't know."

He nodded slowly and smiled. "Same."

My brows crinkled. "What do you mean? You wouldn't have come back if you knew I was here?"

Jackson's smile only widened. "I don't know. How we left things was kind of a sore topic for me."

My foot stomped unexpectedly.

"Wait. What?" My lips pursed together. "A sore subject for you? Imagine how I felt. I was the one who got stood up."

Jackson laughed and rolled his eyes. "Stood up? Please."

Fury danced through me. "What do you mean, please? You never showed."

He cocked his head and watched me. "What do you mean I never showed? I waited for hours."

I shook my head. "You know, it doesn't even matter. It was almost two decades ago. You have your version, obviously the wrong one, and I have mine, the truth."

Jackson straightened and took a quick step toward me. "Your version is not the truth, Grace. I waited for you and waited for you."

The closer he got, the harder it was to breathe.

Everything about Jackson was so commanding. The way

his shoulders molded into his chest and how his height nearly towered over me. He smelled like fresh soap and the outdoors. His heated eyes stayed on mine. He looked determined.

"Obviously, the years that have gone by have colored our version of the events." I swallowed down the uncertainty of my words.

Why was he so adamant that he'd waited hours? Why not just say I screwed up, and we could both move on?

"Grace, I didn't stand you up. You ran off with Tim." He drew a breath and slowly put his hands on my shoulders. "And you have Izzy and a wonderful family. It worked out how it was supposed to work out."

His eyes were filled with a gentle comfort that I needed to hear, but I also needed to say something.

"Thank you, Jackson." I sucked in a breath and saw Izzy and Carter making their way back to us. "But I didn't stand you up and just dash off with Tim."

Bewilderment dashed through Jackson's gaze as Izzy bounded in with my chocolate ice cream bar.

"We can save it for another time," I whispered to Jackson, who happily agreed as his uncle handed him his ice cream.

"This is the coolest place ever," Izzy said, taking a bite out of her ice cream bar.

"It's pretty special," I agreed.

"And just think. Some of us are smart enough to live here full-time," Uncle Carter added.

I smiled, having developed a fondness for Carter. He reminded me of my Grandpa Renny.

"Well, we'd better get going. This ice cream will give us exactly the energy we need for walking home," I told Carter and Jackson.

Carter beamed. "It was nice bumping into you."

I smiled and glanced at Jackson. "Yeah. It was nice bumping into you too."

"We just might have to bump into one another again, yeah?" Carter chuckled, and Izzy and I nodded in agreement as I put my bag over my shoulder and Izzy did the same.

"Good to see you, Jackson," I called over my shoulder. "I'll see you two on Sunday."

"Sunday it is," Jackson agreed, sounding slightly different from earlier.

Once we were out of earshot, Izzy took a lick of her ice cream and sighed. "What got into Jackson when we left?"

"You noticed?"

She shook her head and took another lick. "How could I not? Uncle Carter and I leave for ice cream with everyone all smiles and come back to Jackson's brows being furrowed and you ready to hightail it out of there."

I snickered and took a bite of chocolate. "You're far too wise for your years, Izzy."

"So, spill the beans." She looked up at me as we neared the road to cross.

"Why don't you tell me about the boy coming to Grandma Millie's?" I smiled and glanced at my daughter. Her dimples set deep into her cheeks. "I saw he tried again when you were in the water."

My attempt to change the subject failed miserably as soon as we reached the other side of the street.

"I'll tell you if you tell me," she countered.

I laughed, feeling the warm, balmy breeze coat my bare skin, and tried to fathom how life had wound me to this moment. I had my fifteen-year-old daughter quickly becoming a BFF. I was in a town that I dearly loved with my favorite Grandma Millie bouncing around the lake with a boyfriend. I'd lost my husband. I'd run into my first love. I had to read a five-hundred-page book about love and war by tomorrow so I could join a book club with complete strangers.

"Fine. Jackson and I have incredibly different versions of what went on the night I fell for your father."

"Or, as Jackson probably sees it, the night you broke up with him."

My gaze flashed to Izzy's, and I shook my head. "Have you ever thought about becoming a psychiatrist?"

She snickered and shook her head. "I'd make the most money from my family, and I'd feel guilty for charging any of you."

I squeezed Izzy into me as we trundled down the gravel toward the house and sighed.

"Anyway, he has it all twisted in his head that I stood him up." I shrugged, letting go of my daughter. "That he waited for hours for me."

"Isn't that what happened to you?" Izzy asked.

"Yup. So, either we will agree to disagree for the summer, or he'll realize I'm right."

"What if he's right?" she simply asked.

"He can't be right because I'm right. Only the person who got stranded is the person who can be stood up while the other person is busy doing that standing or gallivanting or whatever. The point is, he wasn't there."

Izzy chuckled. "Well, if the conversation with him went as well as it did with me, I can see why he looked a bit distressed."

"Okay, now tell me about your admirer. What's his name?" I asked, excited.

"Ball boy."

I snorted. "Seriously, Izzy? You didn't get his name?"

"His name is Ball Boy until I make sure he's worth knowing."

"Wow. I'm impressed."

We turned down the drive to see Grandma Millie sitting on the porch, rocking back and forth.

"Oh, I thought Grandma would be with her Jackson."

"Me too. I hope everything is okay."

Izzy and I sped up until we reached the porch where Grandma Millie sat. Her rocking slowed.

"Have fun at the beach?" she asked.

Izzy nodded. "Jackson is coming over for Sunday dinner."

"And so is Ball Boy," I added.

Grandma Millie pulled her brows together. "Ball Boy?"

Izzy nodded. "It's just some guy who was persistent."

"And pretty good-looking."

She shrugged, and I saw a blush creep up her cheeks.

Yup. Izzy was smitten.

"Well, good. That's what Buttercup Lake is known for."

"So, why are you home?" Izzy asked. "We thought you spent most nights at your Jackson's?"

"Oh, I'm going back." She nodded. "But I ate too many cherries and had the green-apple quickstep."

Izzy squinted her eyes and looked at me. "What's that?"

Grandma Millie started to answer, and I waved my hands at her. "Izzy doesn't want to hear about your bathroom escapades."

"It happens when you get old, and I didn't want to be at Jackson's house."

"Okay. Enough said." I chuckled as Izzy's expression turned horrified.

"The medicine should kick in, and I'll be back to watch our Friday night movie in no time," she assured me.

"Good to hear, Grandma." I chuckled under my breath. "The heat wore me out, so I might just take a nap."

"The heat or the drama with your first love?" Izzy chided.

Grandma Millie chuckled, and I realized immediately who had set us up.

"Wait a minute." I shook my finger at my grandma and chuckled. "You set us up."

"Izzy helped."

"Grandma," Izzy groaned. "Don't throw me under the bus. All I did was tell you my mom's favorite cured meats."

"Wow. I had no idea I would have to keep my eye on you two. Now, if you don't mind, I'm going to go upstairs and finish that book for tomorrow's meeting."

"You do that, dear," Grandma Millie chirped. "Your

daughter and I will just be out here gossiping about you and Jackson."

I smiled to myself and stomped up the stairs, knowing she was telling me the complete truth.

Chapter Eight

Jackson

I needed to know Grace Henry's story. Beyond the obvious that she married my best friend, what had she been up to all these years? Even more specifically, what happened that night she swears up and down that I stood her up? I was the one who got stood up.

I used the drill on the final bolt of the hammock my uncle suddenly needed installed on his back porch. How he thought he'd get in it or out of it blew me away, but I learned quickly to just follow Uncle Carter's orders. Besides, it gave me something to do other than find silly excuses to show up at Millie's house.

No, instead, these projects lent themselves to giving me plenty of thinking time, and I was pretty confident that wasn't helping either.

Because all I thought about was Grace Henry. What had

she been up to all these years? What were her plans? Was she going to stay in Wisconsin or go back to Illinois?

Why did it matter?

I gave one last rev to the drill and tightened the bolt.

"Okay, Uncle Carter. Another item checked off your honey-do list."

Uncle Carter grumbled as he stepped onto the back porch from his kitchen. "You know I could do this stuff myself."

"I know, Uncle Carter."

He took a few steps outside and bent over slowly, attempting to open up the netting of the hammock.

"Why's it so stuck together? How am I supposed to fit in that?"

"It spreads out."

"Like hell, it spreads out. I'm liable to fall straight on my ass and break a hip if I try to get in there like that. Can't you put it up so it stays wide enough for a grown man like me?"

"That's what your bodyweight is for."

He pointed at the rainbow-colored strings. "You do it."

I let out a heavy sigh. "Fine. Haven't you been in one of these before?"

"Yeah. When I was a kid."

"Fine. You just spread the rope out like this and put your butt down, kick your—"

"Howdy, boys. No one answered, but I heard voices out back."

Within a nanosecond, the hammock swallowed me up and rolled me out onto the porch like a caterpillar.

Grace gasped, and Uncle Carter snickered right before the hammock dumped me onto the porch with a thud.

"Oh, my gosh." Grace leaned down. "Are you okay?"

"Define okay," I said, attempting to untwist myself from the rope.

"Do you hurt?"

"Only his pride, I'm sure," Uncle Carter clapped his hands, laughing. "And you wanted me in this thing."

"You bought the damn thing," I said, trying to untangle myself from Satan's web.

Had it been any other woman I wanted to impress, I would have been mortified, but with Grace, it was like she already knew the mess I could be. She knew the goofy teen who had become the goofy golfer.

"Well, that little magic act makes me feel better about my bicycle acrobatics."

I smoothed my shirt and grinned. "Glad I could be of assistance."

"I just wanted to stop by and give you and Uncle Carter some fresh dip I made for the book club tonight, and I made some extra for you two."

I nodded, loving the fact that it was a book club, not a nightclub Grace was heading to for the evening.

She handed me the container and smiled.

"Thanks, Grace. That was really sweet of you."

Grace let out a deep sigh. "And I wanted to apologize to you."

I shook my head. "For what?"

"My wise teenager made me understand that while I may not agree with your version of events, I still needed to validate your account of things."

I really liked Izzy.

Lifting my chin slightly, I studied Grace. "That was painful for you, wasn't it?"

She smirked. "Quite."

I chuckled and nodded. "Listen, I think we have a lot to catch up on. Some stuff we don't ever have to touch, and other stuff we can rehash and reminisce. It's up to you, really. We're only here for a summer."

A shadow fell across her gaze, and my chest tightened. Had I said too much or too little? Was I pushing things too far?

"Did I say something wrong?" I asked.

She hugged herself and shook her head. "No. I guess.

Ugh. This sounds crazy, but I guess it just hit me that I really am only here for the summer."

I nodded, knowing what she meant. I enjoyed my career, but I was getting tired. My body was getting tired, not that falling out of a hammock helped.

But I'd often felt like I was missing things.

Coming back to Buttercup Lake showed me I was missing out on a lot more than I'd imagined.

"Yeah." I let out a sigh. "I'm sure it will fly by."

She nodded. "I knew we needed to come to Buttercup Lake. I just didn't know how much good it would do us so soon."

"I know what you mean. It's a special place."

"And running into you was a perk I didn't expect," she added.

"A perk?" I asked, surprised. I wasn't so sure I was in the perk category back at the beach.

"Definitely. You're oddly comforting."

I laughed. "Yeah. I get that a lot."

"You probably do," Grace teased. "I can only imagine how much comforting you do as a professional sports player."

"I'm not sure golf is quite like that."

Grace put both hands on her hips and rolled her eyes.

She was absolutely adorable in the sexiest way possible.

The way her little mouth curled into a pout made me want to pull her into my arms and kiss her.

"Please. You're the sexiest golfer I've ever laid eyes on."

"Am I the only golfer you've laid eyes on?"

She grinned. "There's that."

"Man, Grace Bailey. You still know how to drive me crazy." When I realized what I'd just said, I quickly tried to correct it. "Henry, I mean. Grace Henry."

She smiled and shook her head. "The crazy thing is that even though I married Tim at nineteen, I've always thought of myself as Bailey. Isn't that weird?"

I shook my head. "Not at all. It's the name you grew up with. The identity you built."

"It all went poof when I married Tim."

Her words surprised me, but I didn't want our conversation to veer off in the wrong direction.

"You know I got married because I was pregnant, right?" It looked like the words flew out of her mouth, and now she wondered how she could pull them back in. "Oh, my gosh. I can't believe I said that. I haven't told anyone that."

"I'm sure you loved Tim," I offered, knowing full well that she had.

She nodded. "Of course."

"Then the pregnancy just sped it along for you two.

That's all," I offered, hoping she'd jump on the subject and drop it.

She nodded. "No, you're right. I'm sure I would have married Tim regardless."

"See? There you go."

She grimaced. "I should not be talking about this with you. No way, no how."

I laughed. "And yet, I'm the lucky guy who gets to hear it."

"Okay, back to the swarms of women you managed to woo throughout your golfing career."

I scratched my chin and shook my head. "It really hasn't been like that for me."

"You're telling me that when you've been on a course, you haven't had a woman throw panties at the eighteenth hole or ask you to sign a boob?"

My mouth fell open before I started laughing uncontrollably. "Grace, I don't know what kind of golf tournaments you're watching, but they aren't any I've been to. Maybe I wouldn't be taking the summer off if I had that part to look forward to."

"The breasts or the panties part?" she teased.

I cocked my head and grinned. "You know I've always been a breast guy."

Her cheeks blushed. "Is it weird that I just get happy when I think about us?"

"Not at all."

The screen door opened, and Uncle Carter came walking over. "Sorry. I just had to grab some of this dip here so it doesn't spoil."

He tugged it out of my hands and turned back toward the house.

"How'd you know she brought dip?" I asked.

"I saw something in Grace's hands, and I heard her tell you. It's not rocket science."

I laughed. "You've been listening?"

"I haven't been listening. It's just impossible not to hear."

Grace grinned. "Well, what do you think, Carter?"

He chuckled. "About the panties or the breasts?"

"Either," Grace answered

"Don't let him fool ya. He's had plenty of women throw themselves at him. He's just never been interested or just lacks the ability."

"Thanks for that." I grinned as Uncle Carter went back inside.

"You have to love their honesty."

I laughed. "Do we, though?"

Grace leaned over. "My poor daughter had to hear about Grandma Millie having the green-apple quickstep."

"Oh, no." My eyes widened. "That's bad. I haven't heard that saying in ages."

"Yeah. Well, Izzy loves her great-grandma, but I don't think she feels like she wants to be included in all parts of her life. In fact, I probably shouldn't have passed that on to you, either. I'm so sorry. It's just like I feel like I can tell you anything, and I do."

"I like it."

Grace looked half embarrassed and half relieved. "You know what? It's just nice to have someone my age to talk to as well. Not that I'm not thrilled Izzy is finally talking to me again, but it's just refreshing to have someone my age."

Izzy seemed like the chattiest and sweetest teenager I'd met in a long time. It was hard to imagine that she didn't talk to Grace much.

"Was there an issue or . . .?" I hoped I wasn't prying too much.

Grace let out a sigh and shrugged. "I think it was just typical teenage stuff. It actually started even when Tim was around. We became a thorn in her side. Either we showed her too much attention or not enough. Sometimes we embarrassed her, and other times she never wanted us out of her sight. But since we've hit Buttercup Lake, I haven't seen any of that. She's just decent."

"What do you think about our families trying to set us up at the lake yesterday?" I asked.

Her expression fell. "You mean us both being there wasn't happenstance?"

"Uh, no. I don't think so." I wondered if I should have kept that to myself.

She burst into laughter. "No. I know it was a complete setup, which is funny because it's the second one since I've arrived at Buttercup Lake."

"Oh, yeah. I heard about the neighbor."

Grace nodded. "Yeah, the already very attached brother of our neighbor, but A for effort, I suppose. I'm starting to wonder if I just have a note on my forehead that says *I need a date*." She shivered. "Because I really don't."

"Duly noted." I let out a soft chuckle. "So, you're headed to the book club tonight?"

"Indeed, I am. I even finished the book. It was heart-wrenching."

"Yeah? Do you like to do that to yourself when you read?"

"Not normally, but this was worth it." Grace smiled, and I could see her relaxing more. "It even got Izzy. I heard her blow her nose this afternoon while she was reading it. But you probably just stick to *Golf Digest* or some jock thing."

I laughed. "A jock thing?"

She flashed a wicked grin. "You're a professional athlete. I can call you a jock if I want to."

"Grace, I have a bad feeling that I'd let you call me just about anything as long as it meant I got to be around you."

The words slipped out before I realized what I was saying.

Her eyes widened, and she took a step back. "I should probably get going, but I'll see you tomorrow for dinner."

She nearly tripped over her own two feet as I watched her flee our little chat, and I wondered exactly what had made her run.

"That Grace is a wonderful woman, Jackson. Mark my word. Any woman who knows how to make a dip like that is worth bringing into the family."

I spun around to see my uncle scraping up some dip from his plate after he wandered outside.

"If only it were that easy."

Chapter Nine

Grace

What had I been thinking to drop off some dip over at Carter and Jackson's house? It was like I was a glutton for punishment, and it screamed desperation and drove the wrong message home to Jackson.

That was for sure.

I should have just stayed home and cleaned up my old turquoise bicycle. It was time to retire the turquoise wonder and make it décor, and I was itching to start the project. It was a guilty secret I had, fixing up old things to make them beautiful again.

Not to mention, I was pretty confident I'd missed a splinter somehow because my left butt cheek was getting sorer by the day, and the heat wasn't helping it.

I fanned myself off as I stepped into Grandma Millie's house. She was at her boyfriend's house and planned to meet us at the book club.

"You look like you just stepped into a sauna. What happened to you?" Izzy nearly ran into me but stopped just short enough to see the beads of sweat rolling down my forehead and neck.

"I don't know." I shrugged. "Maybe it's menopause."

"Mom, you're only thirty-five."

"It can happen early."

Izzy smirked with a snicker. "I don't think it's menopause."

I laughed and folded my arms over my chest. "Then do tell. What do you think it is?"

"I think you just dropped an egg for Jackson."

My eyes widened, and I opened my mouth to say something to my daughter, but all I could muster was a grunt.

Her smirk only deepened. "So, I'm not wrong."

"Izzy, I don't know where you're learning this stuff, but it's completely inaccurate. Women don't just drop an egg because someone is good-looking."

"Ah, you agree he is attractive?" She folded her arms over her chest, and I suddenly felt like I was dealing with the Cheshire Cat perched high in the trees, ready and waiting to challenge my lack of a love life.

She shrugged. "I think he's cute. I can see why you fell

for him when you were my age. He has that young-looking face and seems to take good care of himself."

"I'm glad you approve," I said wryly. "Now, I just can't wait until Ball Boy shows up for our family dinner. The conversation will be so fun."

"Well, I won't get covered in sweat at the mere sight of him." Izzy chuckled as she turned up the stairs. "I guarantee you that."

"Don't jinx yourself. My genes are strong in you." I tapped her rear. "Now, grab your Kindle, and we'll get going."

"Fine." She happily stomped up the stairs, and I quickly went to the downstairs bathroom to wipe the dampness away and splash myself with cold water.

"Thank goodness for waterproof mascara," I muttered, thinking back to Jackson.

Did I really get all hot and bothered just by seeing him, or was it what he'd said to me before I nearly tripped over my feet to get out of there?

Probably both.

I dried my face off and wandered to the kitchen to grab the dip and chips for the club. Anxiety started to swell in my belly. I hadn't been out to a party for a very long time. Actually, the last time I spent with a lot of people was at Tim's memorial service.

Geez.

My shoulders slumped as I thought about the daze I'd lived in since he'd gone. Wake up, go to work, come home, check on Izzy, and fall asleep.

Start over the next day.

But not since I arrived here.

No. Things had started to change.

I noticed the smell of fresh-cut grass when Jackson mowed the lawn. I allowed the laziness of the summer breeze to dance with my skin when I was on the porch with my eyes shut. I tasted the simple sweetness of Grandma Millie's lemonade as it coated my throat.

Senses.

I finally remembered that I had the senses to enjoy life again.

Maybe it was as simple as not being in the same flat we'd bought together, anchoring the memories of the past with no hope for any new memories of the present, and certainly not the future.

I swallowed a lump as I put everything into a box, including my Kindle. Maybe, if luck were on my side tonight, the mysterious Tracy would show up and make my pursuit of information easier. It was a small town. Maybe the odds would be in my favor.

Izzy bounded into the kitchen with a new outfit on. She'd replaced her short shorts with a flowery sundress and sandals.

"You look cute."

She grinned. "Thanks. You look a lot less sweaty."

"Thanks."

"But you kind of look stressed."

Surprise covered my face. "Stressed?"

She nodded. "Everything okay? I was only teasing about dropping an egg."

I laughed and let out a slow sigh as we made it to the front door. "I was just thinking about our place back in Chicago."

She didn't say anything, so I looked over my shoulder.

Izzy had slowed, and she twisted her lips into a pout. "Do we have to go back there?"

"There as in our house, or there as in Chicago?"

She shrugged. "Both. Either."

"I don't know, Izzy. Our entire life is there. Our home, employment, friends, civilization . . ."

She shrugged. "Fine."

"That doesn't sound very fine."

"I don't like it there, Mom." She ground her teeth together and groaned. "Actually, I hate it there."

This wasn't the conversation to be having on the way out

the door to the Sunshine Breakfast Club, but if not now, when?

I set the box down on a table and reached for Izzy. "You hate it there that much?"

She stepped into my arms and nodded her head against my chest. "I'm sure it's great for some people, but I'm not one of them. There's so much pressure."

"Pressure?"

"To be cool. To be doing the latest trend or know what went viral or laugh at some prank." She took a step back out of my arms. "I don't have any true friends there. I know that now."

"But what about here? You don't have any here?"

"Yet," she corrected.

I smiled at the statement and nodded. "True. You've barely been here a week, and you already have a *friend* coming over for dinner."

"And there's so much to do. I can go to the beach. I can ride my bike or hike or just be me. I don't have to try to impress anyone."

"I resent that," I teased.

"What if we stayed here longer than the summer?"

It was something I'd let myself wonder more than a few times, but we hadn't even been here a week. I needed to work for a living, and this place wasn't exactly bustling with opportunities to fit my experience. Housing was scarce because it all went to tourists. There were many more cons than pros, but looking into Izzy's eyes made me realize I couldn't tell her no.

But I also couldn't tell her yes.

"We'll play it by ear," I offered. "Three weeks into this place, you might be bored spitless."

Her smile widened. "I doubt it. Just promise me you'll be open to the idea."

I nodded and gave her another quick hug before grabbing the box and heading out the door.

We piled into the car and made the short drive to the center of town at Buttercup Lake's Community Center. The words were splashed on the sign in bright turquoise lettering that looked like a day hadn't gone by since someone had touched up the paint.

That was something that I admired about Wisconsin. Everything was so tidy, fresh, and clean. There was a real sense of community pride that wove through the towns, streets, and homes.

The parking lot was nearly full, but I found a place in the back of the gravel parking lot.

"I think the entire town showed up to the book club. I

don't think I made enough dip."

Izzy shook her head. "I don't think so either."

"Oh, well. Live and learn."

I turned off the car as Izzy jumped out and grabbed the box out of the trunk while I fought with the seat belt.

When I freed myself and got out of the car, Izzy handed me the box.

"I highlighted so many passages," Izzy said.

"Yeah? That's awesome. I didn't think to do that."

Izzy gave me a funny look as we made our way into the building. Two double doors were propped open to reveal at least ten circular tables, mostly filled with people chatting away. I scanned the room and shook my head.

"Definitely not enough dip."

Izzy elbowed me and pointed to the other side of the room, where a banquet table with every kind of food imaginable was set out.

"Well, I guess we don't have to worry about not having enough food," I hummed, looking down at my dip.

"Come on. We need to find a place to sit before the seats are all taken."

I nodded and quickly followed my daughter to the banquet table and wedged my dip and chips next to a rather fancy spread of chicken skewers and peanut sauce.

I grabbed my Kindle and pushed the empty box under the table. "Okay, let's find a spot."

Izzy pointed at a table filled with older women that we quickly gravitated toward while I scanned the room for Grandma Millie.

We both set our Kindles on the table, and one of the women smiled at us. "That's thinking ahead. I always find these things yawners myself."

Izzy cocked her head in confusion, and I laughed. "It's our first time."

"Oh, really?" Another woman caught our conversation. "I've been to so many over the years, I've lost count, but what else is there to do on a Saturday night?"

I nodded and laughed. "Good point."

Izzy turned on her Kindle and glanced around the room.

"Mom, did you know Jackson was going to be here?"

My gaze snapped in the direction she was looking. "He never mentioned it."

I scanned the room and finally found him. "Well, there he is."

But he wasn't alone.

"Uh-oh," Izzy whispered.

"No uh-oh," I assured her. "He's a single man with lots of money and no ties to anyone or anything."

He draped his arm around a woman with a perky blonde haircut and sparkling blue eyes. She looked delighted with Jackson's arm draped over her.

"Typical," I muttered, not realizing it came out of my mouth. "I wonder when we start talking about the book."

"Hopefully soon." Izzy grimaced. "But I think he saw you."

I slid deeper in the chair and put my hand on my forehead. "Oh, great."

"Yup. He's coming this way."

I dropped my hand and sat up straighter as Jackson made his way over with a drink in hand. "Hey, you two. I didn't expect to find you here."

I cocked my head with uncertainty. Obviously, Mr. Golfer had one too many. "You knew I was coming tonight."

His brows pulled together in confusion. "No. I thought you were going to some book club or something."

The color drained from my face. "This isn't the book club?"

"Nope." He took a sip of his drink and his mouth puckered. "This isn't a book club, but it is a lovely reception celebrating Linda and Jim's wedding."

Music erupted from the DJ stand as the emcee introduced the newly married couple. I looked at my daughter, who appeared to be equally horrified and as ready to bolt as I was.

"How about that?" Jackson chuckled. "A couple of wedding crashers."

I turned to see him smiling and frowned. "Wait a second. When you invited me to dinner tonight, it was so you could have a date for this wedding?"

He laughed. "No. Not really. I might have dropped by for a little bit, but I would have made us some reservations on the lake or something."

"Sure, you would have." I laughed. "But if you don't mind, I need to get to the book club before it's over."

"Do you need any help finding it?" he offered. "I mean, I think it's safe to say you might."

I frowned but nodded.

As the music erupted and the bridal party started going crazy, Jackson motioned for us to follow him as we moved through the crowd with our Kindles looking like complete misfits. Once we finally reached the main hall, Jackson scanned a poster.

"How do you know your way around?" I asked since he didn't live here either.

"I spotted this sign on the way in," he replied.

"I know this sign wasn't here when we came in." I looked at Izzy. "Right?"

She shook her head. "I didn't notice it."

"It was here," Jackson claimed, not bothering to look at me.

Maybe the blonde caught his attention enough that I'd have the summer to myself.

"Okay, you're supposed to be in 103. The reception was in room 100." He scanned the hallways. "Must be that way." He pointed to the right.

"Thank you." I nodded quickly and reached for Izzy's hand just as she eyed Jackson.

"Enjoy your blonde," Izzy said over her shoulder, and my heart nearly dropped out of its chest as I squeezed her hand.

The moment we'd made it to the correct room, I took a deep breath and a group of about fifteen women turned toward the door. Grandma Millie stood up and scowled.

"Where's the dip?"

Chapter Ten

Jackson

I didn't know which was worse. The fact that Izzy and her mom thought I was on a date with my blonde cousin, who happened to be the bride's best friend, or the fact that I'd managed to send them on their way without correcting them.

I wandered back into the reception as the emcee was directing the bridal party to start grabbing the food when I noticed something that looked a little out of place on the banquet table. Nestled between floral arrangements, chicken skewers on a silver platter, and roast beef on a porcelain serving dish sat a red Melamine bowl of chips next to the same type of dish Grace had dropped off for my uncle and me.

Oh, no.

Grace forgot her dip.

I watched a groomsman pile a couple of scoops onto his plate and move on as I heard Grace and Izzy's voices behind me.

They were planning to steal back the dip, and they sounded far more adept than even my golf coach at the execution of plays.

As I watched the next groomsman pile another scoop of dip, I heard Izzy and had to keep from laughing.

"It's now or never, Mom. We've got to commit to this."

"Then now," Grace directed.

Without another second passing them by, Grace and her daughter snuck through the guests until they made it to the banquet table, where Izzy jumped the line and started talking to a bridesmaid while Grace reached under the table, grabbed a box, and plunked her famous dip and chips inside.

At this point, I couldn't stop laughing as I watched the bride and groom turn around to see Grace motioning for her daughter to follow her as she darted through the crowd of spectators.

"Thieves," the groom hollered as the guests turned to watch Grace and her daughter nearly make it to the door. "Close the doors."

Since I was the one standing near them, I knew that was my cue, but there was no way I could do that to the Henry girls.

"It's our dip," Grace hollered over her shoulder. "It was

by mistake."

As they made it through the doors, I couldn't help but be fascinated by Grace a little bit more.

She was funny, cunning, and charming enough that none of the men wanted to stop her or her daughter.

Murmurs filled the reception hall as the bride and groom scowled in my direction.

My cousin, Daisy, walked up to me. "Why didn't you stop those two?"

"It was Grace's dip. She just put it in the wrong room. They were headed to the book club."

"Oh, brother." Daisy rolled her eyes. "I'll calm the bride and have the emcee let the crowd know."

"Thanks." I nodded and suddenly wished I'd read the book that Grace and her daughter had. I wanted to be anywhere but here.

By the time Daisy made her rounds, the room was full of laughter, and the bride and groom seemed to enjoy that they'd be able to retell this story for years to come.

And I knew I'd never be able to get the images out of my head of Grace and Izzy stealing their dip from a wedding reception.

Kind of like I couldn't stop thinking about Grace flying off her bicycle.

But something told me she wasn't giving my falling out of a hammock a second thought.

Especially now that those two assumed I was with Daisy.

First of all, Daisy was in her late twenties. That age difference alone would do me in. There was a reason I needed a rest from golf. I was getting tired.

Or maybe I was just getting tired of golf.

No. That wasn't true. I loved golf and was even itching to go play a few rounds at Buttercup Lake Country Club. In fact, I was even thinking about trying to convince Grace and her daughter to come out with me to play too.

But something told me I wasn't about to be given the time of day by either Grace or Izzy.

And the thought nearly killed me.

"Are you Jackson Locke?" A woman around my age came over. "The golfer?"

"Yeah."

"Wow. My husband worships the ground you walk on. He's laid up from back surgery because he thinks he's the next big Locke, but if I could get your autograph, it would mean the world. I'm sure it would make him recover much faster." She handed me the cocktail napkin with the bride and groom's silver embossed initials.

I chuckled to myself as I thought about Grace and the

boob comment as I scribbled my name on the napkin.

Daisy came bounding over just as I handed my autograph to the woman.

"Mr. Celebrity strikes again." Daisy giggled as the woman walked away.

"Hey, can I ask a favor?"

"Sure!"

"Would you mind sneaking out with me for a few minutes to explain that you're my cousin?"

Daisy shrugged. "Why?"

"Well, I think Grace and her daughter think I was hitting on you."

She looked like she wanted to vomit, and I rolled my eyes.

"I know. I understand, but you don't have to be so over the top."

Daisy laughed and shrugged. "Sorry. Just a natural reaction."

"But will you?"

Daisy narrowed her eyes at me. "Wait a second. Is this the Grace who stood you up all those years ago and then went off with your best friend?"

I nodded slowly. "Yeah. It's her."

"And you haven't slugged the guy? And why would it

even matter if she thinks you're banging your hot cousin?"

A few people at a table next to us glanced in our direction.

I lowered my voice. "Grace's husband passed away. She and her daughter came here to escape it all."

She crossed her arms over her chest. "Don't you think she might need time?"

I straightened and nodded. "Absolutely. I'm not trying to rush anything or even pretend that something is going to happen, but I don't want her thinking that I'm flirting with her one day and then—"

Daisy winked at me. "Ah, gotcha." She looked around the room. "I doubt they'll miss me."

"Thank you." I squeezed her arm quickly as we made our way out of the wedding reception and down the hall to the book club, where we heard a chorus of women laughing their heads off.

Of course, I could hear Grace's laughter ring above the rest.

Damn.

I knew why I loved her then, and it was getting harder to ignore now.

The door was open, and Millie spotted me from across the room.

"Grace, I think you have a visitor," Millie nearly hummed.

All eyes turned to Daisy and me while Grace pretended to stare at her Kindle. Izzy elbowed her mom, but she wiggled away.

"Tough crowd," Daisy whispered. "So, what is this?"

"We are the Sunshine Breakfast Club." A woman closest to the door informed my cousin. "We come for good food, drink, and plenty of books."

"Throw in a little gossip and match—" Grandma Millie started, but someone stepped on her toe to hush her.

"Oh, sounds like fun," Daisy said.

"Loads of fun." Millie eyed Daisy. "Haven't I seen you around town?"

Daisy nodded. "Maybe. I only moved here a couple of weeks ago from Washington."

"Oh, yeah?" Millie pried. "And you've already found our most eligible bachelor, Jackson Locke?"

The room of women gasped, and Grace's head lifted for Daisy's response.

"Well, being that he's my cousin, I don't really think of him as much of a catch."

The women erupted into laughter.

Bringing Daisy with me to sort this mess out was perfect.

Until . . .

"My cousin just wanted to bring me over to clear things up between Grace and himself. In case there was a misunderstanding and she thought that I was his latest fling and . . ."

"You've said plenty," I whispered to Daisy.

She stopped and smiled while Grace looked over at me. Grace's gaze locked on mine, and it was as if I had gotten hit by the bicycle she'd been riding. So much emotion swirled through her eyes, and I even detected a hint of a smile.

If she didn't care, she wouldn't care.

But she did.

I ripped my gaze from hers when I noticed several of the women getting antsy. Their book was calling.

I smiled and glanced at Grace again, but this time her gaze was solely focused on her Kindle.

"I'll let you all get back to your night. Sorry for the intrusion. Hopefully, you enjoyed Grace's dip. She brought some over earlier, and it was delicious."

The women muttered and looked around as if they'd just been handed gossip on a platter as Grace flashed her gaze to mine.

I smiled before spinning around and heading back to the wedding with my cousin.

"You like to stir the pot," Daisy said, shaking her head. "I had no idea."

"Only with Grace."

"Payback?"

I shrugged. "Maybe."

"You still have feelings for her?"

I pressed my lips together and drew in a breath. How did I answer that without sounding like a crazy man, or worse yet, pathetic?

I ignored the question as I let myself get lost in thought and imagine what the rest of the summer might be like with Grace Henry wandering in town, and all I had to do was remember her snatching her dip from the bridal party, and I knew I was in for a treat.

Chapter Eleven

Grace

"Imagine a lost love torn away during war and finding him when you're ninety." Mandy, who was the one who'd picked the book, clutched her chest and swooned a little in her chair.

Grandma Millie rolled her eyes and laughed. "I'm waiting for my mystery next round. This was just a disaster waiting to happen. I mean, two ninety-year-olds? Are they gonna walk down the aisle?"

The entire room turned their attention to my grandma, knowing she was full-on dating in the same age bracket.

Grandma Millie scowled. "What?"

"What about you and Jackson?" Mandy looked incredulous. "You two aren't exactly recent college grads, and neither of you can keep your hands off one another."

Grandma Millie's lips pursed. "It's different. We're

mature. We're young for our age. These two in this book acted like they belonged in a geriatric facility for the last fifty years. It was like they forgot what it was like to live."

"So, it's the characters you took issue with." Mandy tried to keep the topic on course.

My daughter chuckled, and I tapped my knee to hers. She hadn't seen Grandma Millie on fire, and I didn't want us to be the ones to trigger her.

"All I'm saying is me and my Renny had the most amazing years raising our kids and helping with our grandkids. We lived tremendously, and this act two for me is no different from the rest of my life. I didn't suddenly morph into a new person." Grandma Millie tapped my leg with her hand. "I did so good that this one wanted to come back with her own daughter for the summer. Where were all the relatives in this book? What other stories filled their lives before they were both widowed?"

Mandy smiled and nodded. "I see your point. I'm just a hopeless romantic."

"And on that point, should we try setting up that sweet girl, Daisy, next?" Grandma Millie's eyes sparkled.

"How do they know she wants to date?" I asked my daughter.

"All I'm saying is that I think we ought to convince her

to join our club, and maybe Mr. Right will pop into town." Grandma Millie winked, and muttering erupted around us.

I laughed and shook my head. "Is that how it works? You all get busy, and matches are made?"

"Sometimes," Mandy said, nodding.

Grandma Millie chuckled. "More like miracles happen."

Everyone started to break for snacks, and it appeared my dip from the reception was a big hit.

One of the women my age scooped some of the dip onto her plate and looked at me. "Great dip. I have to confess that somehow, this group of ladies has a knack."

My brows raised. "For what?"

"The Sunshine Breakfast Club manages to meddle in covert ways." She took a bite of her chip. "And the next thing you know, you've found the man of your dreams."

I laughed. "Speaking from personal experience?"

"Sure am." She smiled as I piled my plate with the dip and some miniature pecan pie rounds.

Izzy was chuckling with Mandy and Grandma Millie, which was somewhat concerning.

"That sounds like a story in itself," I said.

"It is." She nodded. "My name is Abby, by the way."

"Nice to meet you."

"So, I've heard that you used to spend all your summers

here with Millie."

I smiled and nodded, glancing at my daughter with the other two women.

"I did. It was wonderful." I turned my attention back to Abby. "Some of my best memories are here at Buttercup Lake."

She let out a happy hum. "I feel the same since I came to town."

"When was that?"

"Well, oddly enough, I came to town with my now ex, who was working on some forestry project, and when it came time to leave, I gave him a big wave and changed my number."

"Ouch."

She chuckled. "For him, but he was a complete jerk. I'd actually started coming to the book club while we were dating, and I found the strength I needed to kick him to the curb from these ladies." She glanced at Millie. "Especially from your grandma."

I let out a blissful sigh and nodded. "She has a way about her."

"She really does."

"Anyway, Mandy's nephew was newly single and in town to visit for the holidays. So the next thing I knew, I was eating Thanksgiving dinner at Mandy's lovely home, and by Christmas Day, Elijah and I were inseparable."

"Our first official date was a snowmobile ride, and once we reached the ice shack, I knew I was in love."

"Wow. That's impressive." I nodded in admiration.

I think I secretly wished it were that easy for me. Well, it kind of was with Jackson, but I had to warm up to Tim, and I did. But guiltily, I knew I had meant Tim to be my rebound, but he was so kind and loyal. I fell hard, but it wasn't instantly. Thanks to Jackson standing me up, I had insecurity issues.

"Yeah. I thought so. But anyway, you must come to our Buttercup Lane coffee shop."

My brows furrowed. "The town has a coffee shop now?"

She clutched my wrist with her free hand. "Have you not been to the downtown yet?"

I shook my head. The only downtown I knew from Buttercup Lake contained the town grocer, which happened to be attached to the gas station. There was an ice cream store open from May through October. A bicycle shop, a mechanic, a laundromat, a diner, and a small gift shop had pretty much rounded out the place since I was a kid. Oh, and a bank.

"Well, don't blame yourself. The downtown isn't exactly where you'd think it would be. You know the second public access area to Buttercup Lake?"

"The one near the resort?"

She nodded. "Yup. That's where the new and improved village of Buttercup Lake resides. There are three restaurants, our little coffee shop, a post office, a couple of touristy stores, and a place where you can rent kayaks, paddleboards, and stuff like that. The ice cream store opened a second location there too."

"Seriously?"

She nodded. "And more is coming soon. At least, that's the hope."

"I had no idea. I just drove into town on the main road and made it to my grandma's, and that's where we've been all week, aside from one trip to the lake. We obviously went to the other public access."

"You must come to the coffee shop tomorrow and see the downtown. It's so cute. Ever since the resort expanded—"

My jaw dropped. "The resort expanded?"

"Oh, yeah. They're up to like three hundred rooms or something like that. In addition to their restaurants on site, the ones in town are thriving too." She grinned. "And there's like one of those tiny house villages being constructed for more tourists. This place is happening."

I nodded, unable to hide my smile. Maybe staying here wasn't a completely crazy idea.

"All I know is that the best Sunday Scramble is at Buttercup Café two doors down from us. You and your daughter should hit there too."

Izzy wandered up to me, and I gave her a squeeze.

"And this dip is delicious." She looked at Izzy. "You're beautiful. Oh, my word. What are you, like, sixteen?"

Izzy straightened and smiled. "Fifteen."

"The boys around here are going to go nuts."

I laughed and groaned. "I think they already have."

"Mom." Izzy elbowed me, and I chuckled.

"I was just telling your mom about downtown,"

"Downtown?" Izzy looked as surprised as I felt.

"Yup. My husband and I own a coffee shop, and there's a great breakfast spot." She glanced at me and then my daughter. "Hey, actually . . . I mean, I know it's your summer and everything, but we're looking for some part-time help with the shop."

Izzy perked right up. "Really? I'd love to earn some money."

"Yeah, really." Abby looked at me for approval.

It never occurred to me that Izzy might want a job, but I quickly nodded in agreement. "If she's up for it."

Izzy beamed. "Totally."

"Great. The schedule is totally flexible. Maybe we can

work on it together when you come by tomorrow, and I can show you around. Is that okay, Mom?" Abby teased.

"Absolutely."

"How about ten o'clock?" Abby offered.

"Perfect," Izzy answered.

And then a thought occurred to me. "Abby, do you know a woman named Tracy who might live around here?"

Abby thought about it for a second and shook her head. "No, I haven't ever met a gal named Tracy, and I think I know most everyone in town."

I nodded and quickly wanted to dismiss the topic as Izzy started asking questions about the coffee shop. But instead, my mind wandered back to Jackson.

I hadn't expected him to pop in with his blonde-turned-cousin to clear things up. Oddly, it only seemed to complicate them.

Ugh.

Merely seeing him made my insides flutter and my heart pound in my ears, and that was from all the way across the room.

But the one thing that really perplexed me was that I knew I would have seen that poster when Izzy and I entered the community center doors. I was a sucker for good signage.

Maybe the center just forgot to put it up beforehand. I bit

my lip in deep thought and yelped as Izzy turned to see me dabbing my mouth with a napkin.

Abby had wandered off, and I hadn't even noticed.

Great.

This was what Jackson did to me.

Thoughts of him baffled me, enticed me, and made me forget my surroundings.

Exactly like when I was a teenager.

I had to pull myself out of it. Whatever it was, it was done.

We'd have a nice meal tomorrow night, and I'd just make myself busy.

Grandma Millie wandered over. "Are you ready to discuss the down and dirty parts of the book?"

I laughed and glanced around the room to see most of the women finding their seats again.

"I didn't think you liked it."

She chuckled. "I've never met a book I didn't like. I just love ruffling Mandy's feathers."

"Grandma, you're impossible." Izzy shook her head and got some more food before finding her seat.

"That was nice of Jackson to clear things up," Grandma Millie offered as she filled her plate.

"What things?"

"Don't play coy with me. It was written all over your face when he showed up."

"It was not."

Grandma Millie laughed. "Why not just let go a little?"

I scowled. "Let go of what?"

"Your past. Your fears. Your worries. Enjoy everything Buttercup Lake has to offer." She smiled and gave me a quick hug. "And that includes people too."

"Speaking of, why didn't you tell me there was a downtown now?"

She shrugged and took a bite of my dip with an extra-crunchy chip. "You didn't ask."

I laughed. "Are there any other happy surprises around Buttercup Lake I should know about?"

"None come to me at the moment, but that doesn't mean anything."

"Great. You kind of failed to mention that this book club doesn't just read books."

"Well, that's what we *mostly* do," she clarified.

"Abby seems pretty happy with things."

Grandma Millie beamed. "Elijah is a great guy. I knew he'd be great for Abby the moment I met him."

"Is that so?"

Mandy tapped a metal chair next to her to get everyone's

attention.

"And is this something that the club is known for?"

"If I told you, I'd have to—"

"What? Did I just sign up for a secret mafia or something?" I whispered.

"All I know is that we've helped complete disasters find love—total wrecks, really." Grandma Millie winced and shook her head. "Total wrecks."

"Well, what would you consider me?" I asked as we found our seats again.

"Confused." She shook her head. "Very confused."

Chapter Twelve

Jackson

I stood in the line at the coffee shop, a little bewildered but waiting to place Uncle Carter's coffee order.

It was really odd, actually.

I'd been with the man for weeks, and all he ever did was complain about how overpriced these fancy coffee shops were. Then, this morning, he desperately needed a latte Americano, which I tried to explain didn't exist as a unit. There was either a latte or an Americano, but they didn't combine to make one drink. By the end of it all, he switched to a hot chocolate coffee, and I knew I'd just order him a mocha.

I thought he might want to come for the ride, but he just pushed me out the door and told me to get here by ten.

Never mind the fact that I had a tee time for ten.

Since becoming a pro golfer, I have always had control

of my schedule. I decided when and what tournaments I would play, what I would sit out, and where I would go. So it was really odd to have absolutely no control over my own life now that I'd temporarily moved in with my uncle, especially in the last week.

But he was old, and it was my job to help him get better.

Although I was pretty confident that we'd already crossed that bridge

And then there was Grace.

I didn't know what to make of anything with her. Watching her steal her own dip in the middle of a wedding reception would stay with me for a lifetime.

But there was this ache inside me that wanted a lifetime more of that.

Except I knew that when she let her guard down and brought the dip over, her resolve to stay away grew even stronger.

When it was my turn to place my order, I walked up to the counter and rattled off an Americano for me and my uncle's mocha. I added a couple of croissants and moved down the counter right when I saw Izzy bounding through the front door with her mom right behind her.

I couldn't help but smile and shake my head.

Son of a gun.

Another setup.

When my drinks were called, Grace's gaze landed on me, and she narrowed her eyes. She was dressed in a flowing dress that somehow managed to rest against every curve of her body. But unfortunately, she wasn't wearing a bra, making my imagination wilder.

I pleaded innocence with a simple shrug, two hands full of beverages, and bagged croissants tucked under my arm.

A woman's voice broke our vibe.

"Hi, Izzy. Welcome." I glanced behind me to see a redhead wander out from a door I hadn't even noticed and glide over to Grace's daughter for a hug. "I'm so happy you came. I think you're going to love it here."

I watched Grace and couldn't help but wonder if there would ever be an opportunity to kiss her again. The mere thought of my lips against hers created a desperate need that I had to dilute with a sip of my Americano.

She didn't remove her gaze from mine, and I wondered what she was thinking.

Only one way to find out.

I made my way over to Grace, which gave her enough time to fold her arms across her chest and cock her head slightly.

"Are you stalking me?" she asked with raised brows.

I glanced around the coffee shop and grinned. "Considering I got here first, I think I'm the one who should be worried."

A little hint of a smile surfaced on Grace's lips.

Man, I wanted to kiss that mouth.

"As if." She rolled her eyes, and I chuckled.

"Ah, Clueless."

"You remember?" She smiled as her eyes came back to mine.

"I don't think I have a choice in the matter. You brought the DVD with you every summer."

The happy memories came flooding back, and she glanced around the coffee shop before looking at me. I was sure I was the only teenager my age who'd had to see a ten-year-old film five times each summer.

"It wasn't like we only watched the movie while it was playing," she whispered.

Heat instantly rushed through my body as she slowly parted her mouth and licked her bottom lip.

Did she know what she was doing, or was she thirsty?

"So, you've been stalking my every move and landed here for some java," I said, grinning at Grace.

"Don't get your hopes up. Izzy has an interview of sorts, except I think she already has the job."

"That will be fun. Have you recovered from last night?"

She laughed as we made way for new customers. "You mean when we wedding crashed a poor couple's celebrations, and I ridiculously went back in to steal my food?"

"Yeah. That was pretty much what I was talking about."

"Sort of." She took a deep breath and let her arms fall to her sides. "But I can't stop thinking about something."

"My cousin?"

Grace rolled her eyes. "No, but I do appreciate your clarification."

"Why's that?"

She pursed her lips together playfully before answering. "No reason. Anyway, I swear that sign wasn't standing in the middle of the lobby when Izzy and I got there."

"Yeah?"

She nodded.

"Maybe someone at the community center forgot to put it out."

"Maybe."

"You don't think . . .?" I loved seeing the curiosity and mischief dash through her gaze as her thoughts darted through her mind.

"Well, first, we have the beach." She swayed her hips a little. "And then we have a wedding where you would be and

I happened to crash because I thought it was a really popular book club."

"I suppose."

"And then you're here at the exact moment I am, and I've never even been here before."

I smiled and nodded. "I don't think we can chalk it up to much more than coincidence."

"Is that so?"

I nodded.

"So, you come here regularly?"

"No, actually. I've only been here a couple of times. My uncle wanted a mocha, though."

"I see." She nodded slowly, determined to make her point.

And while I fully agreed we were set up, I didn't want Grace to think I was a part of it. In fact, I was pretty sure the best way to get Grace to even notice me was to play hard to get, and all of these mini setups weren't helping the cause. All I wanted was to peacefully plant little seeds in Grace's head, but it was like a tornado of chaos was threatening my plans.

"Are you still coming for dinner?" Grace asked.

"If you'll have me."

Grace laughed. "Well, now that I know Daisy is a relative, it helps."

"Yeah? That would have been an issue."

"I mean, no, because we're just friends."

"Ah, so we made it to friends?" I asked.

"That wasn't a hard one to get to."

"But after that?"

"What do you mean?" she asked, glancing at her daughter.

I shook my head. "Nothing. Listen, I'd better get Uncle Carter his mocha, or there'll be hell to pay."

She chuckled and nodded. "I can only imagine."

I grinned and started to make my way past her. "It was nice seeing you this morning."

"You too, even if it is suspicious."

I laughed, walking outside to smell the fresh air that suddenly smelled like bacon.

I glanced up the street to see the sidewalk packed with people waiting to enter a restaurant.

Boy, Buttercup Lake had changed, but it had stayed the same in so many ways.

Kind of like Grace.

She was still the fantastic and beautiful woman I'd fallen for so many years ago, but now she'd been through so much.

And I knew better than to start something up with her, yet I couldn't help myself, wanting to plant those little seeds of wonder.

But it was all for nothing because the moment my uncle said I wasn't needed, I'd probably hit the road again and head over to Scotland for one of my favorite tournaments, which was precisely why I needed to hit the course soon.

As I climbed into my truck, I wondered why the thought of getting back on the tournament roster didn't excite me like it usually did. I'd been going and going for so long that I'd actually forgotten what it was like to wake up and let the day guide me rather than the other way around.

Was it because of Buttercup Lake or Grace?

As I pulled onto the road back home, I wondered about tonight's dinner. Would it be too much if I brought flowers?

It probably wouldn't have been too much if we didn't keep magically appearing everywhere simultaneously. I shook my head and chuckled to myself, remembering how good this town was at meddling.

When I arrived home, Uncle Carter flew off his rocking chair on the porch and marched over to the truck.

He was obviously feeling better.

"What in the hell are you doing back here so soon?" he barked.

I reached for his mocha to hand to him.

"I didn't want your drink to get cold."

"My word, man." He took the drink and shook his head. "It wasn't about the drink. It was about the woman."

I laughed and shook my head as I climbed out of the truck with my own drink and the croissants.

"Has it ever occurred to you that maybe I can handle this on my own? Maybe all this interference might actually be deterring, possibly even detracting from, Grace and me?"

Uncle Carter took a sip. "Nonsense. We're just speeding it up, is all."

"Who's *we*?"

"I plead the fifth."

"That's not how it works."

"You don't know that."

I let out a deep breath. "She's been through a lot. I don't think anyone should be interfering with her grieving process or trying to set her up or any of that. Plus, she's getting wise to it."

"Oh, yeah?"

I nodded. "Yeah. Surprisingly enough, people tend to get a little suspicious when you keep showing up at the same places as them."

"Hasn't she heard of a coincidence before?"

I laughed and shook my head, noticing the plants needed watering. "I mentioned that to her."

"Well, next time, let the coffee get cold."

"Uncle, there won't be a next time. Let me handle this."

My uncle shook his head and laughed. "It's not that simple."

"But it should be."

Chapter Thirteen

Grace

Izzy had been buzzing with excitement ever since she'd gotten home. She loved her job, and I loved that her first job was somewhere so perfect. Izzy would get to chat with the tourists. She was in a safe area with someone kind of watching over her, and I could pop in whenever I felt an urge to check on her.

A win-win.

By the time Grandma Millie arrived, we'd started making two salads. Izzy wanted her favorite broccoli and bacon salad, and I felt like a peach and walnut salad. I had specific instructions not to touch the marinating chicken in the fridge until my grandma arrived.

"Things smell like they're cookin' in here." Grandma Millie grinned. She was dressed in a pair of lavender shorts and a white blouse. "Is that a peach vinaigrette I'm smelling?"

Izzy spun around and gave her great-grandma a hug before Grandma Millie planted herself at the kitchen table.

"I'm amazed you can smell the dressing," I told my grandma.

"What they say about old people not being able to taste or smell is hogwash. Maybe it happens to some, but I'm not one of them. I hate to be defined, you know. Old is a state of mind, and I still have mine."

I chuckled. "Oh, we know."

"Now, let me get the grill going," Grandma Millie muttered as she went outside.

Izzy looked impressed. "She's gonna grill?"

I smiled and shrugged. "If the woman is busy sleeping at her boyfriend's house, doing yardwork, and attending a book club, I guess it makes sense that she knows how to light the grill."

Izzy laughed. "And it's only week one."

Her words sank in. She was right. We'd been here for such a short time, and it felt so comfortable and like we'd been here forever . . . and belonged.

"Have you thought more about staying here longer than the summer?" she asked, and I cleared my throat.

"Izzy, we've barely been here a week. How about we wait at least a month to decide anything? One week is still vacation mode. One month is when the reality might start to set in."

Her shoulders slumped slightly, and I smiled.

"That wasn't a no."

"Okay, fine."

Oh, no. That was precisely how our conversations used to go.

"Hey, did you see the bicycle? I asked. "I'm almost done with it."

Izzy sighed and shrugged. "No."

"Well, it's pretty cute. I think Grandma Millie will love the basket I put on the front. My plan is to fill it with flowers and—"

"I gotta go upstairs for a minute," Izzy interrupted and walked out of the kitchen.

My heart sank.

This last week had been magical, and I ruined it by not making a promise I couldn't keep.

But the truth was that I didn't know how I'd make a living here. Sure, we had a hefty savings account and a bit of life insurance, but I'd have nothing later if I used it all up now.

I let out a harsh sigh as my grandma returned to the kitchen.

She glanced around. "Where's Izzy?"

"I don't think she was pleased with me for telling her we'd wait to see if we would be staying in Buttercup Lake past the summer."

Grandma Millie laughed. "Of course, you'll be staying."

I grinned and shook my head. "Easy for you to say."

She winked at me. "Well, I know this place you could live rent-free."

"Don't forget I have two sisters. If they find out I'm getting all the perks of being your favorite . . ."

Grandma Millie chuckled. "I don't mean to hurt your feelings, but I don't have favorites. I love you all."

I knew that to be more accurate than anything my grandma had ever said. She was always the beacon in the storm for us sisters. Pushing the thoughts away, I focused on chopping the nuts.

"Have you spoken to your mother?" my grandma asked, pulling the chicken out of the fridge.

I let out a deep breath and stared at the nuts. "Not for a while."

"How long is a while?" My grandma's voice softened.

"I'd say six months, maybe a little longer. Why?"

"What about your dad?"

My dad was Grandma Millie's son, but my grandma never played favorites. Not to her grandchildren and not to her own son and daughter-in-law. To my grandma, my mom and dad both weighed equally in her mind, both with their successes and their terribly traumatic failures.

I shrugged. "I don't know. It was around Valentine's Day. Why?"

My grandma knew I wasn't close to my parents, and I use that term loosely.

"Your mom is sick."

The words stung like I'd rolled around in a sleeping bag of nettles. Little nips and spurts of pain while my mind tried to focus on the meaning. She hadn't been a part of my life since I turned eighteen.

I cleared my throat. "When isn't she?"

Drug use tended to make most users pretty sick most of the time.

"No, this is something different."

I turned to face my grandma and let out a sigh. "Cancer?"

She nodded. "Esophageal. She's refused all treatment."

"Still using?" I asked.

With my parents, a person didn't need to be told by them to know. We just knew. It was always hard to get ahold of them. Sometimes, they weren't very coherent. Other times, they were listing off grandiose ideas of what they planned on accomplishing. Sometimes, they'd just cry. It wasn't pleasant, and I knew one or two calls a year were plenty when I had my Izzy.

I shook my head, wondering why a tidal wave of sadness wasn't pushing me over. "Using until the bitter end."

"It seems that way." Grandma Millie nodded. "They're out in Seattle now somewhere. I think living in a tent. From what I gather, the authorities chase them out of one tent city, and they all build another one under a bridge or in a park."

I nodded. "I've seen the pictures. It's pretty hard to believe that my own parents are in one of those tent cities. Did you know over the years that Tim tried several times to get treatment for them? He was willing to foot the bill, fly them to rehab, the whole thing."

Grandma Millie nodded. "I knew that. Tim was a good man. He tried. You all tried, but there comes a point when you realize that your life also matters, and their life doesn't have to become your life."

A lump in the back of my throat appeared out of nowhere.

I smiled at my grandma. "I don't know if I've said it enough, but thank you for always being there for my sisters and me."

She pulled me in for a hug. "I wouldn't want it any other way. If I'd known how bad it was for you all, I would have taken you all year. Not just the summers."

"It was our dirty little secret." I nodded and drew a breath, pushing down the knot in my throat. "They were our parents, and we grew up thinking it was our job to protect them."

Grandma Millie wiped away a tear from my cheek. "And it should have been the other way around like you've done with Izzy. I'm so proud of you as a mom."

I sniffled and smiled. "Thank you, but enough of this. I've got to get my game face on and brace myself for my daughter's guest tonight."

Grandma Millie smiled. "And here I thought it was going to be Jackson you had to brace for."

I started to move away and stopped. "I do have a question for you."

"Yeah?"

"My Jackson mentioned there was a little history between you and *your* Jackson. Any truth to that gossip?" I wiggled my brows, feeling happy just to be off the topic of my parents.

Grandma Millie smiled and nodded. "He was my first love."

My eyes widened. "What happened?"

"War. Life. Parents."

My mouth dropped open, and I smacked it shut. Just like the book we'd read?

"But enough about that. A story for another day, maybe another year. I promised Maya I wouldn't tell anyone the story without her present."

I chuckled, nodding as I tossed the nuts into the salad and put it in the fridge.

It sounded exactly like my sister not to want to miss out if she knew a love story was in the making.

"What do you think Tim would think about all this?" I asked.

"You mean coming back to Buttercup Lake, or running into Jackson?"

I leaned against the counter.

"He knew how much you loved Buttercup Lake. I think he'd be pleased that he knew you so well."

My brows furrowed. "What do you mean?"

"Oh, nothing. He just knew your heart was with the lake."

I smiled and let out a deep breath, freeing the pent-up anxiety that had suddenly built up about my parents.

My grandma continued. "And well, Jackson? They used to be best friends. And Tim stole you away from Jackson."

My foot stomped. "Not really. I mean, Jackson ditched

me and I moved on. I'm not going to put up with that kind of crap."

Grandma Millie smiled and reached for the chicken. "Our guests will be here any minute. I need to put the chicken on."

I laughed and rolled my eyes. "How very convenient. I'm going to chat with Izzy and hopefully get back to more than a one- or two-word response."

"You do that, honey."

I climbed the stairs to see Izzy on her bed with the door open.

That was a start. Back in Chicago, it was usually closed, locked, and booby-trapped.

"Hey, there." I smiled and tapped on the doorframe.

"Why are you crying? Is it about your mom?" she asked.

Izzy had never found it in her heart to call my parents Grandma or Grandpa. But she felt that was what Tim's parents were for, as well as her great-grandma.

"How do you know about her?"

"I came down the stairs and heard Grandma talking about her."

I pointed at her bed. "Do you mind?"

She smiled and shook her head as I took a seat.

"I wish I had a simple answer about my tears. Only a

couple snuck out." I pressed my lips together. "I guess I could say it's for the life my mom never created for herself. The times we missed with her growing up." I shook my head. "But I just don't know. I'm simultaneously pissed and hurt by the whole thing. I just look at you and cherish every single second we've had together, and I just can't wrap my head around my mom never making us a priority. It's something I just can't fathom. Maybe on some level, I thought she'd turn her life around and suddenly appear."

"That would make me tear up." She smiled and let out a breath. "It's weird. I don't even think about them much. Dad filled me in more than you have over the years. I think he wanted to ensure that I never tried anything I'd regret."

I nodded. "Your dad was a smart man."

"I'm sorry you have to go through this. We came here to escape it all."

"And it's pretty much working, isn't it?"

Izzy smiled. "It is."

I patted my daughter's leg, and so much love drifted through me. "I am one lucky mama."

"I'm lucky to have you, and I'm sorry."

I almost fell over.

"For what?"

"Pouting down there. It's just that I really like it here."

I nodded. "I do too, Izzy."

"Um, Mom?"

"Yeah?"

"Is that what you're wearing for Jackson?"

I glanced down at the grease-stained shorts and dirty T-shirt from working on the bicycle. My goal to ready it as a prop rather than a mode of transportation was my first big summer project.

"OMG. Thank you! I'd better change before he gets here."

She giggled. "I'm not saying, but I'm saying."

"And thank you for that," I called over my shoulder as I dashed to the bathroom for a quick shower.

I shouldn't care. It's just a group dinner at my grandma's house.

But I did.

The moment the warm water hit my hair and ran down my back, I sucked in a breath and let out the tears for the life my parents had never lived, the world they'd missed out on, and for me.

The parents I never got to have.

But one thing I knew more than anything was that Buttercup Lake was where I was meant to be.

Chapter Fourteen

Jackson

"I won't embarrass you," Uncle Carter said, giving me some side-eye as we pulled into Millie's driveway. A black mountain bike had been propped against the porch, and I heard voices in the back yard.

I laughed, grabbing the pecan pie. "You never would."

Uncle Carter let out a deep chuckle as he opened the door. "Is that a challenge?"

"God, no." I hopped out and met Uncle Carter at the hood of the truck.

"Does she know why you never showed up that night?" Uncle Carter asked.

The question itself shook me to the core. That night changed the entire trajectory of my life.

"No, and I'd appreciate it if you didn't say anything

either."

He held up his hand. "Not a word."

We marched around the side of the house, following the voices, when we saw Millie, my Uncle Jackson, Izzy, and the boy from the beach, but no Grace.

My heart sank a little.

"Hey there, strangers. Come and make yourself at home. Dinner will be ready in about five minutes."

I walked over with Uncle Carter right behind me, who barely gave his brother in the flower garden a glance, and we made our way to Millie.

"Need a hand?" I asked.

"Absolutely not. There are three skillful ladies handling tonight's feast." Grandma Millie winked. "Grace is inside."

I laughed. "Good to know."

"Don't be shy." She grinned.

"If there's one thing in this world I'm not, it's shy."

Izzy walked over and took the pie from me as Grandma Millie opened the lid on the grill to display enough chicken for an army.

But there was a teenage boy here, so that made sense.

"How's Grace handling Izzy and the boy?" I teased, and Grandma Millie glanced at the two teenagers.

"Grace hasn't seen him yet. She was in the shower when

he showed up."

At that moment, I turned to see Grace coming outside. Uncle Carter lit up, and I rolled my eyes.

Grandma Millie's boyfriend, also known as my other uncle, turned around and gave a quick wave.

He'd had silver hair since his fifties, but his eyes were so blue that the silver really looked incredible on him. He wore a pair of jeans below his waist and a red polo. The man didn't look a day over seventy, even though he was deep into his eighties.

"Hi there, Grace." Uncle Jackson walked over, and Grandma Millie introduced the two while Uncle Carter stared at them. "I don't think we've seen each other since you were dating Jackson."

Hoping Uncle Jackson would stop there, I wandered over and sat next to Uncle Carter. "What's got you in a bind?"

"He's just so damn annoying. You know, I don't think the man has had one joint replacement in all his years."

I laughed. "Now, that's a grievance I haven't heard before."

"You know how many I have?"

I had this number painfully memorized. "Six."

"Damn right. Six." He shook his head. "Two hips, two knees, and two damn partridges in a pear tree."

"I thought it was your shoulders."

"Them too."

"I'm sorry," I said, trying to appease my uncle. "It's got to be rough."

"What burns me up is that he didn't have the decency to help. You had to stop work and come stay with me for the summer."

I glanced at Grace as our eyes connected. "Well, I'm not complaining."

"I suppose not."

"You seem to be bouncing back from pneumonia pretty well," I offered.

"Enough about me. Go talk to Grace. She keeps looking over here."

He was right. I'd caught her gaze a few times, and it was like the world around me stopped every time.

Her hair was wet and dangling past her bare shoulders from a white gingham bandeau top that went well with her denim shorts. It was pretty hard not to admire how beautiful she was.

She gave a quick wave when I stood and made my way over.

"Any other coffee runs today?" she teased. "I'm still suspicious about everything."

"You probably have every right to be."

Her eyes stayed on mine. "Did you see my project?"

I shook my head. "No. What are you up to?"

The one thing I knew that Grace loved to do more than anything was to turn old things new again. Ever since I knew her, she'd get an old straw hat and add some flowers, glitter, and ribbon and make it fresh again. Or Grace would find an old watering can and paint it up and sell it for ten times what was paid for it. I didn't know if it was something she still enjoyed, but just maybe.

"I decided to retire the turquoise bike."

"Oh, yeah? No more riding that death trap?"

She cupped her hand over mine and pulled me to the opposite side of the house Uncle Carter and I had walked around just as Grandma Millie hollered that dinner was ready.

The shade of the house made it about ten degrees cooler as the wind picked up. She pointed at the frame of the turquoise bike that looked so awesome.

"The turquoise wonder." She glanced up at me. "I took off the chain and everything. Cleaned it all up. My plan is to make it a planter for my grandma. You know, add a basket with flowers or whatever, and she can prop it against her fence."

"She will love it."

Her eyes met mine again, and a sudden pull ran through me. My eyes dropped to her lips, and it took everything I had not to kiss her.

"You think?"

"I know she will. It's so cute and country. Very Buttercup Lake."

Her eyes swelled with pride, and she nodded. "I miss doing stuff like this."

"You haven't kept it up?"

She shook her head as Grandma Millie called for us again. "No. I just couldn't really do much living in the city with no yard."

"Yeah. That would make it tough."

My mind wandered to Tim. He had to have known how crafty and into antiques Grace was. So why would he move to the one place you couldn't do anything?

Not your business, Jackson.

"I mean, I've done a few things here and there. But usually, I'm on vacation and see a hot item in an antique store, buy it, and resell it."

We wandered back to meet everyone who had already taken a seat at the table.

"That's awesome."

She nodded and eyed Izzy, who appeared to be happily

chatting with the boy next to her.

"Apparently, she's not shy," I muttered, and Grace scowled at me.

"Don't make me more scared about this," she teased just as the breeze hit and the sweetness of Grace surrounded me.

She always smelled so sweet and soapy and . . .

Just like Grace.

As we made it to the table, Izzy glanced at her mom and me and then smiled. "I brought the salads out that we made."

"Thanks, sweetie," Grace said, sitting across from her daughter, and I sat next to her. "Is this Ball Boy?"

Izzy giggled, and the teenage boy grinned and straightened. He held his hand out over the table.

"Nice to meet you, Mrs. Henry. My name is Caleb. Caleb MacDonald."

Grace looked stunned at the gesture, and I nudged her knee under the table to remind her to behave like a responsible adult. She smiled and shook Caleb's hand.

"It's nice to meet you, Caleb." Grace smiled as she scooped some salad onto her plate. "How old are you?"

"Fifteen. I turn sixteen in September," he offered.

"And do you live here in Buttercup Lake?"

Caleb nodded. "My dad manages the resort."

"Nice. Well, welcome." Grace grinned and looked at her

daughter, who appeared to be pleading with her to take it easy on the guy.

I scooped some broccoli salad onto my plate, followed by some peach salad. Next, Grandma Millie put two pieces of grilled chicken on my plate, followed by corn on the cob.

"This is amazing, Millie," her boyfriend said. "Excellent stuff. Love this broccoli salad."

Grandma Millie beamed. "You can thank my great-granddaughter for that."

Uncle Jackson smiled at Izzy. "Good stuff."

Uncle Carter grumbled under his breath, and all eyes turned in his direction.

"What was that?" Uncle Jackson asked his brother.

Uncle Carter looked across the table and smiled at Uncle Jackson. "I'm fine, thanks for asking."

Uncle Jackson cocked his head. "I didn't."

"Exactly." Uncle Carter rolled his eyes.

Uncle Jackson glanced at me. "Is he always this full of sunshine?"

"We get along great. I just think you must bring something out of him."

I took a bite of chicken as Grace reached for the peach salad. Her fingers grazed my hand and left a tingle in their wake.

I glanced at Grace to see if she'd noticed anything, but all I saw was her focusing on the peach salad. The table around us was lively with conversation but simmered down between my two uncles while Grandma Millie stood and turned on some music. She started dancing back toward the table, and Grace smiled.

"I hope I'm like that," she whispered to me.

"You already are."

Her cheeks blushed, and she took a bite of chicken as Izzy winked at her mom. It was as if there were some secret code between them.

"Jackson here is a famous golfer," Grandma Millie told Caleb.

"And he should be playing this summer, but he's taking care of an old man instead because his selfish brother is banging—"

I stood up quickly, shushing Uncle Carter as Grace snickered. "Okay, so I say we play a game of Truth or Dare."

Grace pushed a piece of wet hair behind her ear and groaned. "I think that's going to go about as well as the two brothers stuck alone in a room overnight."

Izzy and Caleb laughed.

I sat down as Grandma Millie flashed me a grateful smile and said, "I'll go first."

She looked squarely at me. "Truth or Dare, Jackson?"

I glanced at Grace, who flashed a wicked grin in my direction while Uncle Carter clapped his hands and shouted. "Dare. Take the dare. Always take the dare."

I drew a breath and had a bad feeling that Millie was going to ask about that night, so I did what anyone in my position would do.

"I'll take a dare."

Unfortunately, that only made Millie light up like a Christmas tree as she rubbed her hands together."

"Kiss Grace." Grandma Millie wiggled her brows.

The table hushed, and I looked at Grace, who was glaring at her grandmother.

But I noticed a slight turn of her lips.

I looked over at Izzy, and she gave me the thumbs-up sign, which I certainly wasn't expecting as her date chuckled beside her.

"Grace, do you mind?"

She turned to look at me with the most beautiful eyes.

"No sweat," she said, offering her cheek.

I did a quick and simple peck on her cheek, which should have done absolutely nothing to me.

But that wasn't what happened.

Instead, an ache grew deep inside. My lips felt numb. I

could barely see straight.

"Okay, your turn," Izzy chirped at her mom.

Grace looked a little distracted, but she quickly nodded as I asked her the same simple question.

I smiled. "Truth or dare?"

She stared at me. "Truth."

There were so many things I wanted to know, but now wasn't the time with our families sitting around the patio table.

"Would you and Izzy enjoy a golf date with me?"

Izzy laughed. "I don't think that's how it's supposed to work."

"You've never invited me out for golf," Uncle Carter grumbled.

Grace's cheeks flushed, and she nodded. "Yes. Yes, we would."

Chapter Fifteen

Grace

Sitting next to Jackson through dinner was torture. I felt like I was suddenly in high school again, wanting to play footsy.

And the kiss.

Well, really, it was nothing more than a peck on the cheek, but it was incredible. The place his lips touched left my skin tingly for minutes.

Minutes.

And it led to a really wild night of dreams.

Just the thought of what my imagination conjured made my cheeks turn red.

But today was a new day with new resolve. I'd spent most of the morning looking up the name *Tracy* in surrounding areas on Google, and for some reason, no one with that name chose to live around here, making the task much harder than I expected.

I always felt my marriage was full of love, but this development threw a wrench in it. It made me wonder about so many things. What was he hiding? Who was Tracy? Did he have another love? Another family? He did travel a lot.

The thought tightened my chest, and I let out a deep breath as Izzy wandered into the bedroom.

A sharp pain in my butt cheek made me yelp, and Izzy's eyes widened.

"You okay?"

I waved my hands. "Sorry. Yeah. Just a rogue splinter."

"Must be quite the splinter." She grinned, and I nodded. "Is it okay if I don't go to the next book club? It's kind of early."

I nodded. "Uh, yeah. Of course."

She sat down on my bed next to my laptop.

"Cool. Is it okay if I go to the lake today with Caleb?"

My heart skipped a beat. I knew what I wanted to say.

No.

But I knew what I needed to say.

"Sure. Just make sure you take plenty of sunblock, water, and grab my debit card from my wallet."

"Mom, I'm not going to take your debit card."

"Why's that?"

"He invited me, so he can pay."

I laughed and shook my head. "Whatever you say, Izzy Henry."

She chuckled and shrugged. "I need to show him early on that I'm not a cheap date."

"Oh, your dad is probably loving this right now," I teased Izzy, making her beam.

"Do you ever think Dad is watching us?"

I nodded slowly. "I do."

"But not all the time, right?"

My eyes darted to Izzy's. "Why? What do you plan on doing that you wouldn't want your dad to see?"

She rolled her eyes. "Mom."

"It's a fair question."

"I'm fifteen."

I laughed and threw a pillow at her. "I know, and I was fifteen too. That's why I know to ask the question."

"Would you want to kiss a guy in front of your dad?" She cringed. "Okay, maybe that was a bad analogy. But a normal dad like mine."

I laughed, knowing what she meant. The truth of it was that my dad wouldn't have noticed anything I did right in front of him. A sad state of affairs, that parenting unit was.

"Well, have fun and try to be home before seven for

dinner. Grandma Millie won't be here, but I plan on making fried chicken. Sound good?"

She nodded and smiled coyly. "If things go well today, can I invite him to dinner?"

Surprise rocked me to my core. "Of course. I'll be sure to make plenty."

She gave me a quick hug and kiss. "Love ya, and see you later."

"Bye, Izzy."

I watched my teenager nearly hop out of the bedroom, and I couldn't help but be thrown into that same time.

At that age, the excitement and pure joy of discovering a boy, hanging out at the lake, and taking in the simple pleasures was all incredible.

It was a fun time.

As I clicked back on my browser to see absolutely no helpful search results, I reached for my phone and dialed Jackson's number. He answered on the first ring, which made me chuckle.

"You waiting for a call or something?"

"Yours," he said with a low laugh that made my insides ripple with excitement. "Corny, I know."

"Well, I was thinking about asking around and searching out some clues surrounding what Tim left behind, and I was wondering—"

"Absolutely," he interrupted. "You want me to pick you up?"

I couldn't help but notice that the old Jackson was like the young Jackson I'd fallen for so many years ago. He was attentive and protective, and it was like those traits only grew stronger the older he got.

"Sure. Izzy just took off for the lake to meet Caleb."

Jackson let out a low whistle. "Uh-oh."

I chuckled. "I know. I know. Don't say it."

"Buttercup Lake gets 'em every time."

I sighed. "It's such a magical place."

A few seconds of silence sat between us.

"Wanna grab some lunch too?" Jackson asked.

"Absolutely," I agreed. "I need to call my sisters for a few minutes, and then I'll be waiting on the porch."

"Great. I'll be there in about thirty."

"Perfect. I'll be in the rocking chair."

I ended the call and made my way over to the dresser mirror. I hadn't planned on seeing anyone other than my daughter today, so I woke up, showered, dabbed some lip gloss on, and called it a day. I was so lazy that the thought of having to pull up and button shorts was too much for me, so I slid a dress over my head instead.

I grabbed the envelope with the key, my phone, and my purse. I knew I needed to reach out to my sisters to find out if they'd heard about our mom.

While I was still willing to talk to my parents now and again, Maya and Nina wanted nothing to do with them ever again.

But I wanted to give them the chance to change their minds.

I let out an exhausted sigh just thinking about the conversation and trundled to the kitchen to get a glass of lemon water. The entire kitchen smelled of rosemary and mint from my grandma pruning her herbs and bringing them in from her small greenhouse.

As I began dialing Maya's number, my stomach clenched with worry. How did I bring it up? Just go right into it?

When my sister picked up and I said hello, she knew something was up.

"What's wrong? Is Izzy okay?" Maya blurted before I had a chance to answer the first question.

"Yes, Izzy is great. So great, in fact, that she's at the lake with her soon-to-be boyfriend."

"And so it begins." Maya laughed. "Then what's going on?"

"Do you mind if I pull in Nina too?"

Maya groaned. "It's about Mom and Dad, isn't it?"

I ignored Maya and patched in Nina. She picked up immediately but sounded groggy.

"Did I wake you?" I teased.

"As a matter of fact, you did." She yawned into the phone.

"I've got Maya on the phone."

"Oh, no." Nina sighed. "Are they in jail? A ditch? What are we talking about this time?"

I bit my lip and tried to come up with a compassionate tone, but I was pretty confident the words alone would be enough to do it.

"Mom has cancer."

Neither of my sisters said anything for about ten seconds, and then Maya cleared her throat.

"I'm sorry to hear that about Tamra." Maya's voice fell flat. "What a waste."

"I am too," Nina seconded. "What kind?"

"Esophageal cancer is what Grandma said."

When we hit our teenage years, my sisters refused to call my parents Mom and Dad. I understood why, but it was ingrained in me to still think of them as Mom and Dad. Not a *good* mom and dad, but they did bring me into this world.

But I also recognized that because of my parents' actions,

Jackson and Tim looked appealing. They were both my escape route to another life. College had never been an option. It was only some vague concept I'd heard about from my friends.

When Jackson told me he'd received a golf scholarship, my heart was simultaneously broken and filled with pride.

"Well, I'm not sure if I should go out to Seattle or—"

Maya popped up. "Oh, is that where they're located now?"

"From what I understand."

"How's Grandma taking it?" Nina asked softly.

Our grandma meant the world to all three of us, and we tried to make her proud, but we weren't foolish enough to think that she didn't still hold out hope for her son.

"She's good at hiding it. She told me right before Sunday dinner. I'm sure that was a strategic move so she didn't have to talk much about it."

"I can't imagine worrying that every time you get a call from or about your son, you're worried about what you're going to find out." Maya sniffled a little, and I wondered who the tears were for. "I mean, it's been either jail, or the hospital, or the police, or on and on."

"But she always picks up the calls," I added.

"I hope I can be half as amazing as she is when I'm her age," Nina said fondly.

"And did you two know that Grandma has a boyfriend? She barely sleeps here at the house." I laughed. "Actually, correction. She never sleeps here at the house. I have her bedroom, and Izzy has the guestroom."

Nina whistled. "Ooh-la-la."

"Pretty much."

The tension about my parents was already starting to dissipate.

"It's pretty cute to see."

Jackson pulled his truck down the drive, and my heart skipped a beat merely seeing him in the driver's seat. I gave a quick wave.

"Hey, so I'm headed out to lunch with a friend, but I just wanted to let you know. I'm still trying to figure out what I want to do."

"Let us know," Maya said.

"Yeah, please do," Nina seconded.

"Okay. Love ya."

We hung up, and I let out a deep breath, finally feeling like all the air had escaped from my lungs for the first time since I'd found out about my mom.

As I started to move forward, I forgot I had a water glass in between my legs, and the liquid dumped all over my lap. I looked up at Jackson, who shook his head and smiled as I rolled my eyes and pointed at him, laughing.

It was like we didn't even need to be in talking distance to know what just happened.

I slid off the seat, and the pesky splinter from days ago electrified every part of my being. I squealed, and Jackson came tearing out of his truck.

"What happened? Did the glass break? Are you bleeding?"

He rushed up the steps as I hopped up and down with my phone in one hand and my glass in the other.

I hissed, trying to shake my rear. "It's just . . . I think there's still a splinter I didn't get out. I was just hoping it would work its way out."

"Grace, it's been like a week. It could be infected." He started to bend over, and I swatted him away.

"Don't overexaggerate."

He stood back up and shrugged. "Just let me take a look."

I scowled, feeling the burn turn into a pulse. "No."

"You are so stubborn. What if your ass cheek falls off?"

"It'll just make it more difficult to find shorts. Now, let's get to lunch and put on our detective hats."

Jackson stood in front of me. "No."

I put my glass on the railing. "Seriously. Let's get going."

Jackson folded his arms across his chest, accentuating his

broad shoulders, which made me realize he'd be a tough one to push over.

"Listen, I know you've seen just about every part of me, but that doesn't mean, as a grown woman, I want to bend over and have you stare at my butt cheek. Okay?"

"It's really on your ass?" He stood there with such immediate intensity.

I pulled my hand through my loose hair and pulled it to one shoulder while noticing a twinkle in his gaze.

"Yeah. So, it's not like I really want my daughter, grandma, or old boyfriend taking a look."

"Come on, Grace. It's not like I haven't seen your rear before."

He was right, and it wasn't exactly like I wanted to recruit my daughter or grandma.

I pushed my lips into a contemplative pout as he studied me carefully.

"I will make it as professional and platonic as possible," he added. "No tomfoolery."

"What kind of shenanigans could you get into checking out a splinter?" I eyed him suspiciously.

He grinned. "Listen, I'll take a look, or I can take you into the walk-in clinic a town over. Your choice, but we are getting this splinter out of you today."

I quickly sighed and set my phone down on the rocker. "Fine. I'll go get some alcohol, cotton swabs, and tweezers."

"Wow. This must be serious."

"If you're gonna do it, you're gonna do it the right way."

He laughed. "I guess so. Should I follow you inside?"

I cocked my head in awe. "You think I'd let you do this to me on the front porch so some neighbor can start a vicious rumor about what you were doing to me?"

Bemusement darted through his gaze, and he shook his head. "Guess not."

I walked into the house, and Jackson was right behind me.

"Okay. Feel free to get yourself a refreshment. I'm just gonna grab the stuff from upstairs."

Jackson's brilliant blue eyes stayed on me as I ran up the stairs, which gave me a little lift that it shouldn't have.

I had to keep reminding myself that I wasn't looking to date.

I had no time to date.

I had a daughter who needed to be raised.

I had enormous life decisions to make.

I didn't have time to get lost in some soap opera orchestrated by the people of Buttercup Lake.

As I quickly rifled around in my grandma's first aid

basket, I found exactly what I needed and went back downstairs, where Jackson was getting himself a glass of water at the kitchen sink.

"Okay. I'm ready."

He took a couple of swallows, washed his hands, and spun around.

"Where to, patient?"

"Here's fine. Maybe by the window for better light."

"Whatever you say."

I handed him the alcohol and drew a long breath. "No peeking, Jackson."

"What in God's name is there to peek at?"

I bent over and flipped my dress over my rear before propping my elbows on the kitchen table. I was in a lace thong because the splinter had given me so much trouble.

"Jesus, Grace." He let out a deep sigh. "This is really bad."

My heart stopped. "Seriously? Like how bad?"

I looked over my shoulder and saw him grinning, making me stomp my foot on top of his, naturally.

"Ouch. What are you going and doing that for?"

"You're getting far too much of a kick out of this."

"Sorry. It's just . . . fine." He bent over and squirted the rubbing alcohol on top of the splinter. My eyes squinted.

I heard him mutter a few curses before placing his hand on the cheek in question.

"Is everything okay?" I asked as his fingers dug deep into my flesh.

Keep it cool, Grace. It's just a splinter. He's merely performing a medical procedure.

But the butterflies performing some sort of spastic dance in my stomach didn't seem to agree.

"It's deep, Grace. I'm not sure you shouldn't still go to the doctor."

"Just get it out," I pleaded.

"Okay. Just take a few deep breaths. It's all red and raised around the splinter, but I think . . . I think I can do this. On the count of three, I'm pulling it out."

I glanced over my shoulder, but I couldn't see his head any longer. "Fine."

"One . . . two . . . three."

The wiggle of the splinter sent an electric current down my leg like a pinched sciatica, and I let out a yelp.

"Got it. Wanna see the bugger?" Jackson asked, bringing it to me.

"That's pretty impressive."

He tossed it in the trash. "I'm going to squirt some more alcohol on it, but I think we should put some antibiotic ointment on it too and some sort of covering."

I laughed. "You mean like a Band-Aid?"

Jackson's grin soothed me, and I couldn't help but wonder what he thought about being back there.

"Yeah. One of those."

"There's a basket on my grandma's bathroom counter. Just grab what you need." I clasped my hands together, still bent over. "I'm just going to stay like this."

Jackson laughed and walked out of the kitchen. "Sounds like a great plan."

Chapter Sixteen

Jackson

Having Grace Henry bent over the kitchen table with her dress flipped up to expose a lacy thong wasn't exactly how I thought today was going to go, but there was absolutely nothing predictable about this woman.

It had always been like that.

I shook my head and thumbed through the basket to only find a box of Minnie Mouse Band-Aids and some antibiotic ointment.

Was Millie eight or eighty?

Chuckling to myself, I grabbed the items and headed downstairs to see Grace in the exact position I'd left her.

"Good thing your daughter's at the beach. This would be a tough one to explain."

Grace smiled at me, and I held up Minnie Mouse.

"This is all I could find."

She squinted at it. "Why's it look like that?"

"It's Minnie Mouse."

Grace laughed, which sounded like heaven on earth. "Sounds about right."

I tore open the Band-Aid and squirted the ointment on the pad before carefully, and I mean ever so carefully, applying the Band-Aid just right.

"It's an art, really."

"What is?" Grace asked, glancing over her shoulder.

"Placement." I smiled, securing the adhesive.

"Jackson Locke, you put that on this second."

I smiled and walked around to the other side of the table. "I already did."

She laughed and stood up. "You're something else, and you can't tell me for a second that you haven't made the best use of your status as golfer extraordinaire."

"You're kinda right, Grace." I grinned, noticing her still at the confirmation. "Just like this weekend when a woman came up to me at the wedding. I could see it in her eyes. I knew what the night held."

She eyed me. "Yeah, and what was that?"

"The woman wanted me to autograph the bride and groom's cocktail napkin for her husband."

Grace giggled, and I shook my head. "When I'm focused,

I'm focused. You may not believe me, but women haven't been part of that."

"Whatever you say. But it's really none of my business." She slid her hands over the skirt of her dress and looked at me. "What happens in Grandma Millie's kitchen stays in Grandma Millie's kitchen."

I grinned. "Fine by me."

"But thank you for doing that. I know it was kind of weird." Grace suddenly looked sheepish. "It's just one of the many things I'm still kind of adjusting to."

I nodded, knowing what she was trying to say without having to say it.

She sighed and stopped next to me. "Husbands can be handy."

"My sister doesn't seem to agree."

Grace laughed and shrugged. "Well, I thank you for doing that. It's not like I really know anyone here who I want to look at my fanny."

"It was a great view," I added.

"You're such a man." Her hand raised to my cheek, and her fingers danced across my jaw.

Something caught her eye, and I froze. Her gaze was focused on my arm.

"What's that?" she asked.

Her fingers moved to my arm, and I felt myself pulling back.

"Nothing."

She grinned. "I can see something right there, so it's obviously not nothing."

Her eyes connected with mine.

"Just a tattoo I got when I was a kid."

"A kid?"

"Fine. You know what I mean. It was after we dated."

"Obviously." She winked at me. "I would have remembered if my boyfriend had a tattoo."

She stepped a little closer, but there was something different in her gaze.

Curiosity?

Confusion?

I didn't know, but I felt her breathing change as she closed the gap a little more.

I could feel the heat rolling off her, and I studied her as she kept her fingers on my arm.

The truth was that I wanted nothing more than to undress her right in this kitchen and taste every square inch of her.

"You should probably quit touching me like that and keep your gaze averted."

That made Grace smile wider and bring in a deeper

breath, but her fingers stayed on my bare skin.

"Why's that?" She kept her gaze focused on me, and I could see the heat dancing behind her gaze.

"Because the way you're looking at me makes me want to kiss you." My gaze dropped to her lips before meeting her eyes. "And the way your fingers are running across my arm makes me remember a simpler time."

"Is that bad?" she asked breathily.

"I don't know, Grace." I let out a deep breath as longing pulsed through me. "You've been through a lot."

The words somehow wounded her. I could see it in her eyes.

"Don't . . ." She stopped herself from saying anything else and looked away.

"I won't." I completely closed the gap between Grace and me.

Tipping her chin up slightly with my finger, her breath hitched as I traced her lips with my thumb.

"I've wanted to kiss you since I pulled you out of the mulch pile."

She laughed. "Then why didn't you?"

"You didn't seem very happy to see me."

Grace nodded as her gaze dropped to my mouth, and every internal warning bell went off as the pull to kiss her grew.

As her eyes stayed on my mouth, she bit her bottom lip, and I knew that we were headed into shaky territory with so many unknowns for the future and so much heaviness from the past.

But the heat only intensified as I watched her longing grow.

I shoved the guilt away. We couldn't help this physical need erupting between us.

Before I couldn't handle it anymore, I slowly circled my arms around Grace's waist and pulled her into me. When she didn't resist, my chest tightened with the realization of what I was about to do.

There was no turning back.

Grace seemed to think I was taking too long because before I knew it, she'd smashed her breasts against my chest as she leaned in deeper and closed her eyes with a little groan. Unable to resist, I pressed my lips to hers, tasting sweetness and everything Grace. She slowly parted her lips, and my tongue slid across the softness, beckoning a deeper kiss. She welcomed me with a slow curl of her tongue as her breathing turned ragged.

My lips crushed against hers as our need grew, and I pulled her closer as her hips pressed into me. She looped her arms around my neck as my tongue pushed quicker, deeper to match her need. She let out a little moan as she tightened her arms around my neck.

I smiled as her little hips stayed pressed against my hardness. I knew she felt the same need as I did with every little wiggle of her waist and stroke of her tongue against mine.

She wrapped one of her legs around mine, and I picked her up, putting her on the table as her arms loosened slightly, but our mouths eagerly inhaled each kiss. I propped my arms on each side of her, caging her in as I slowly broke my lips away from hers. She opened her eyes slowly like she'd been drugged. Her completely tousled hair framed her face like I'd always remembered. Full of hope and mischief.

I smiled and ran my thumb slowly on her bottom lip before bringing my mouth just behind her ear. I felt her body shiver with anticipation as I ran my tongue slowly along her skin.

"Jackson," she whispered, wrapping her hand along the back of my neck as if guiding me to her secret places that were never a secret to me.

Grace wiggled her waist closer to me and wrapped her legs around me as I straightened slowly and brought my mouth back down to hers. My fingers slid up her thigh to her lace thong, and I felt her body tremble as I slid underneath.

She let out a hiss and pulled away from me. I released my hands and opened my eyes to see her grimacing, and my heart dropped. We'd rushed things. I'd pushed it too far.

"I'm—"

She shook her head and slid off the table. "I sat on my butt wrong."

"Seriously?"

Relief spilled through me. It was just the splinter.

"Let me get you some ice," I offered, heading to the fridge. "To hell with it. I need to get myself some ice."

She laughed and came up behind me as I pushed the lever on the ice-maker and handed her a cube.

"That's one lucky ice cube," I joked, and she playfully pretended to bat at me with her free hand.

"This feels so much better."

"I don't know. I was thinking what was going on was pretty incredible."

Grace's gaze dropped to the floor.

Shit. I definitely pushed too hard for that kiss. She was probably riddled with guilt and used her butt cheek to stop it.

When her eyes met mine again, a smile covered those gorgeous lips I'd kissed moments before.

"That kiss wasn't incredible, Jackson. It was out of this

world." She quit circling the ice on her butt cheek and tossed it into the sink.

"Maybe next time, we might even pick up where we left off."

Grace grinned and shrugged. "Why ruin a good thing? I don't think anything you could do to me would be better than that kiss."

"I'm a professional athlete, Grace."

She looked at me wryly. "I didn't think you paid attention to anything but your sport?"

I laughed and shook my head. "What do you think I'm dreaming about when I'm on the course?"

Grace's brow rose. "I don't know. Maybe, how to get a hole in one." Her hands flew to her mouth. "I don't mean like my hole. I meant like the golf course hole."

I laughed and wrapped my arms around Grace and pulled her into me, kissing the top of her head. "You just make me smile."

Her arms wrapped around me, and I let out a deep breath, rustling the hairs on top of her head. "This feels nice."

"It does."

"But I'm complicated. It's complicated." She sighed, pressing her head against my chest. "I didn't come here to find a relationship."

"I know," I said softly.

Her embrace loosened, and she took a step back. "And with what I found after Tim passed, I'm not really sure I'm ready to place my trust in anything other than Izzy and myself."

Pain darted through Grace's eyes, and it made me wonder what she'd found, what she needed help with.

I nodded, touching her cheek. "I want to help you any way I can. I don't know what you found or what you're searching for, but I'll do my best to assist you." I drew a breath, wishing I didn't have to say the next part. "And this doesn't have to happen again. I understand."

I bit my lip and shook my head. "No. That's a lie. I don't understand. I can't even fathom what you've been through this last year and a half, but I'm here to listen and to understand."

Grace's eyes slowly moved to meet mine, and I saw tears resting on the brim of her lids.

Damn. I hated to see her cry, and I did that to her.

"That has to be the nicest thing anyone has said to me since it all happened."

"It's the truth, Grace. Now, let's get some lunch and get our day started."

She nodded and reached for my hand as we started out of the house. She grabbed some stuff off the porch, and we made our way to the truck.

The ride to the new downtown wasn't long, but it was silent.

Not an awkward silence, just the type that lets two people have their own thoughts without any distraction.

I spotted the café that Uncle Carter said he liked and parallel parked in front.

"I'm impressed," she said, glancing in my direction.

The pain in her eyes from earlier had diminished, but her lips were still full and pink from the earlier mistake.

And I knew it was a mistake. It couldn't happen again. I wouldn't let it. She was the vulnerable one, and it was my job to protect her.

By the time we to got our table, I was focused on one thing.

Choosing lunch.

Tension filled my jaw and neck as I vowed not to be swayed.

"What's wrong?" she whispered, leaning into the table and setting her menu aside.

I shook my head and scanned the menu. "Nothing. Just hungry."

"Hungry or hangry?" she teased, and I lifted my gaze to meet hers.

Ugh. Why'd she have to be so damn cute and sexy all the time?

It didn't help that I was uncomfortably hard from earlier with no end in sight.

"What are you having?" I asked, glancing at the menu.

Ah, my luck was turning around. They had an old favorite of mine for lunch.

"French dip," she answered.

The female server came over and took our food and drink orders, and I brought my attention back to Grace.

"So, what did you find of Tim's that is so concerning?"

Chapter Seventeen

Grace

My lips still felt numb from kissing Jackson. No, kissing wouldn't be an accurate description. It was more like inhaling him like he was a meatball sub. Everything about the experience was completely unlike what I'd ever experienced before with either my husband . . . or Jackson, for that matter.

Guilt pummeled through me. I knew I shouldn't compare. Being married to Tim was incredible. I had a great life with him, and we shared so much love and Izzy. Oh, Izzy.

I smiled and let out a deep sigh.

No, I couldn't compare. Life was different then. Life was different now.

Especially, having my first love sitting across from me in a diner in Buttercup Lake.

What were the odds, really?

Jackson's words ripped me out of my state of confusion,

and I nodded. "Right. I don't know what to make of it. My mind has created all of these scenarios, and truthfully, most involve secret wives and families, and . . ."

Jackson looked horrified.

I dug in my purse and grabbed the envelope, shaking the contents onto the table.

"First, it starts with the name Tracy." I licked my lips, noticing they were a little tender.

I liked it.

"Then the location is Buttercup Lake." I shook my head. "Finally, there's this key."

"I've been asking around town for a Tracy. Not even the busybodies of the Sunshine Breakfast Club knew a woman named Tracy."

Jackson's gaze fell to the small key. "A safety deposit box."

"You think?" I asked.

"Pretty sure. It looks similar to mine."

My eyes shot up in surprise. "You have one? Is this like guy code I'm not familiar with?"

Jackson let out a low chuckle and shook his head as he reached for the key and flipped it over.

"Yup. This series of numbers is the routing number. It should tell us the bank when we Google it."

Relief flooded through me.

Answers. I might be getting close to answers.

"You don't remember Tim ever mentioning a woman named Tracy?" he asked, his eyes filling with something I couldn't quite decipher.

Pity?

Acceptance?

I shook my head. "No. I'd remember." I pulled out my phone and typed in the routing numbers.

"Any luck?"

My heart fell. "The bank isn't local to here."

"Where's it at?"

"Back in Illinois."

"That's not far."

"No, but I'm really enjoying not being there." I pressed my lips together. "Equal parts laziness and fear of what I'll find."

"It's odd that Buttercup Lake is mentioned, yet the bank is back in Illinois."

I nodded, reading about the bank's criteria for opening the safety deposit boxes.

"It looks like if I'm not listed on it, and this Tracy person is, I won't be getting in it anytime soon." I frowned.

Jackson straightened in his seat as the server brought our

meals over. "I'm sure he put you on there."

I smiled. "Thank you for that. I'm not so sure about it, but I appreciate the confidence."

Jackson chuckled and shook his head. "What about the difficulty if it's only in his name?"

"Well, since I have all the legal papers pertaining to his death, I should be able to get inside, according to the website." I felt . . . glum. Glum was the perfect word.

"First problem is solved," Jackson said, smiling. "Figuring out what the key went to. The second issue will just be getting into it. I'm available tomorrow."

I laughed and glanced at my sandwich, which looked delicious. "I'm sure this sounds cowardly, but I'm not ready yet. Apparently, I want to wallow in this stage of self-pity and uncertainty."

Jackson nodded and put his hands up. "Take your time. Just know, I'd be more than happy to be your chauffeur."

I smiled at the man sitting across from me. "I think I might take you up on that."

"I'm counting on it."

He bit into his sandwich with a manly passion that I hadn't seen before when it came to food.

I grinned at him. "Enjoying the Monte Cristo?"

"Do you know how hard it is to find this sandwich?" He

dipped it into the raspberry jam and took another manly bite.

And a little bit of the glumness dissipated.

"I do." I dipped my fry into some ranch and took a bite.

"So, tell me what you have been up to all these years." Jackson looked at me with familiar intensity, and my entire body lit up.

Jackson's complete focus was on me. He wasn't bothered with the sports on TV hanging near the food counter or with checking his phone. He wanted to hear from me. It was nice.

"Once I had Izzy, my life truly started," I told him. "I'm sure that would make some women roll their eyes, but it is true. At least for me, being a mom has been everything. Getting to watch her grow and develop into such an amazing young woman pretty much sums up my happiness."

I also didn't want to say aloud that I still clung to those dreams I'd always had. It was easier to discuss priorities changing than allowing myself to dream a dream that was nearly impossible, financially and just about any other constraint.

Jackson was quiet for a few seconds and nodded. "Things worked out how they were supposed to."

I knew what that statement really meant. "They did, but it's like I can't regret any of my life choices leading up to Izzy because if I changed anything, she wouldn't be here, and that thought is soul-crushing."

Jackson dabbed his mouth with a paper napkin. "Agree completely. She is an incredible young lady."

"We really lucked out. She was an easy baby, an even easier toddler, and except for a few hiccups once she hit tenth grade, I'd say it doesn't get any easier than Izzy."

His ears seemed to perk up. "What kind of trouble?"

"Just kind of ridiculous stuff, really. She got around some bad kids, and she was their meal ticket and scapegoat."

"That's unfortunate."

I nodded, feeling the twisted torment that I'd managed to shelve since I had my deep conversation with the squirrel back in Chicago.

"If it's making you uncomfortable, we don't have to go down that path."

Another couple came wandering into the café as I took a bite of my sandwich.

"This is delicious, by the way. And no. I don't mind talking about it. They would do things like toilet paper a row of lockers, and Izzy would show up with the last roll for them and get caught, or she'd go off property while they all tried to sneak smoke breaks. Izzy didn't smoke, but she skipped classes to go hang out." As I said it out loud, my heart sank. "And there were the after-school shenanigans like not coming home when she said or borrowing money that she'd give to her friends to get cigarettes for themselves. But the thing is that I know Izzy didn't even smoke. She just wanted to be accepted so badly that she let herself be used."

"I wouldn't want to be fifteen again for all the world." Jackson shook his head and pretended to shiver as he crumpled his napkin. "She seems to be so happy here. I don't even get a hint of that side."

"It's true. You're right. She rarely spoke to me and never really asked for permission to do anything. She just did it. Here, she's asking if she can meet a boy or inviting me, her own mom, to the lake. It's like night and day." I took a few bites of a fry. "Izzy wants to stay here."

"Because of Caleb?"

I grinned, thinking back to that age. Had Jackson not left in the summer too, I was sure I'd be begging and pleading to stay in Buttercup Lake.

"I'm sure that will make her pleas more intense, but she had suggested it pretty much the moment we arrived."

"And what was your answer?"

"I told her we'd wait and see. That we are still in vacation mode. We can't decide something like that after only being here a week and a half." I cringed, feeling like I should have just told her okay.

"How'd she take it?"

"Okay, but I promised we would revisit the idea in a month or so."

His eyes lit up. "Interesting."

"What?"

"I just never in a million years thought that I'd run into Grace Henry again, and in of all places, Buttercup Lake."

I chuckled, resting my gaze on his. "It hasn't been all bad, has it?"

He smiled. "There hasn't been one bad part of it at all. Even that splinter of yours rewarded me."

"It must be nice to live such a privileged life."

Jackson's deep laughter wrapped around me, and I never wanted it to stop. "Grace, it's been really nice seeing you again."

His gaze stayed on mine, tickling my stomach with thoughts of earlier.

The kiss.

The need.

I *needed* to change the subject.

"You know, I think that book club is up to something more than books."

His brows arched. "You don't say."

I laughed. "I do. In fact, I think your cousin might be the

next target. You might want to warn her."

Jackson chuckled and shook his head. "I don't know that she'd mind, to be honest. She's had a disastrous run when it comes to relationships." He tapped his fingers together and scowled. "And I'm not sure bartending at the resort is exactly going to help the situation."

I smiled. "I'm sure she'll be a very popular bartender."

Jackson grinned. "Yeah. She did great back in Washington. I was shocked she left the Silver Ridge Resort, but she said she needed a change."

"I know how that feels sometimes."

He finished off his sandwich with one more dip in the jam. "Me too."

Surprise flitted through me. "Really? It seems like you've got it made. You're living out your dreams. I'm sure you've made more than enough to retire when you want someday. What could you possibly want to change about your life?"

Jackson looked perplexed. "Sometimes, dreams change and shift over time. I can't expect that what I wanted at twenty-five is still as satisfying at thirty-six."

"What dreams have shifted?"

He bit his lip and slowly slid his tongue along the bottom, and all I could think about was kissing him again.

My brain filled with all kinds of conflicting wants. I wanted to be kissed by him again, but I didn't want to have to think about a future. Most likely, Izzy and I would head back to Illinois, and he'd head back to wherever the tournaments took him.

"I've been thinking how nice it is to lead a slower life these last few weeks since I've been helping my uncle. It's nice not to be running from airport to airport, to wake up and not have to worry about winning all the time."

"I can pretend like I know what you're talking about, but it sounds kind of exciting."

He laughed and nodded. "I think, like with everything in life, moderation is key."

"Do you like being single?" I asked.

"I didn't mind it."

"Until?"

"Until recently." His mouth slightly twitched.

"I see."

A rambunctious cohort of butterflies danced in my stomach as his eyes stayed on mine.

But my mind was a real mess. I was stuck in two worlds—a grieving wife and mother and a single woman with desires. And it wasn't like I was necessarily the driving force behind his shift in dreams. Then, I had the news about my mom, and I didn't know what would be needed from me with them, if anything.

"I know this might be a touchy subject." He drew a deep breath, and his expression turned serious. "How are your parents? Did they get better?"

My stomach knotted, and I let out a groan mixed with a sigh.

"Oh, that good, huh?" He frowned.

"Tim actually tried to help them both over the years, but it was like when one was ready, the other wasn't, and they just fed into one another. They're out west living under a bridge."

Shock rippled through Jackson. "Under a bridge?"

"Yup. They won't take any offers of housing because most come with a stipulation of not using drugs or alcohol, so . . ."

"Oh, Grace. I'm so sorry. You don't need that on your plate with everything else."

I'd already demonstrated what a mess things were for me, so I might as well go all in.

"And I just found out from my grandma that my mother has esophageal cancer. Lots on my plate."

He opened his mouth to say something but snapped it shut.

"It's okay. There's not much to say. She's refusing

treatment." I shrugged. "And I just spoke to my sisters this morning, but they don't have much of a relationship with our parents."

"Do you?"

I shook my head. "No, but I at least take a call from them every few months or so, sometimes longer. My sisters refused to take their calls or call them, and I get it. They set up very strict boundaries, and they needed to."

"What about you?"

I shook my head and sighed. "I always hold out a little bit of hope, I suppose."

"Yeah. That strikes me as you."

"But I know better than to ever send money or let them near Izzy. I just can't go there."

"Nor should you. They are deep into their addiction, and offering much other than treatment is enabling."

"That's what we've been told." I nodded "So, now I just have to convince myself to visit her before it's too late."

"If you ever need an ear, Grace . . ." Jackson's gaze stayed on mine, and it felt as if the weight of the world had been slightly shifted to more than just my shoulders.

"Thanks. The offer means a lot." Not wanting to carry on such a heavy conversation, I twisted my lips into a grin. "Back to the Sunshine Breakfast Club, I'm pretty sure that they've been behind some of our chance encounters."

His brows lifted. "You don't say." The sarcastic tone made me chuckle.

"Okay, so I might be a little slow on the uptake sometimes."

"It worked, though, didn't it? We went out to lunch together of our own free will."

I chuckled. "So, you're on their side?"

He laughed, those eyes of his unable to hide a thing. "Well, I didn't mind playing doctor earlier, if that's what you mean."

"You are such a guy."

"Right. I'm the only one of us thinking about that kiss."

My cheeks heated up instantly, and I laughed. "Whatever. You started it."

He shook his head and smirked. "No, I didn't start anything. You were the one who woke up this morning and decided to put on that sexy dress and even sexier underwear."

I giggled, reveling in being called sexy. I think the last time I heard that was three years ago.

"Haven't you heard of briefs or boyfriend shorts?" His smile melted me.

"For your information, today's selection was a fluke. It just so happened that my ass hurt so bad, I had to wear the one and only pair of sexy underwear I had to avoid chafing."

He grinned. "Oh, boy. My knees just knock when you start talking dirty to me."

I'd told myself that I'd probably never feel comfortable again with the opposite sex since Tim passed away.

But I was wrong.

Sitting here with Jackson made me feel like there was hope again.

That it was okay to laugh.

Chapter Eighteen

Jackson

Beneath the surface, I could see something igniting in Grace as we joked around. It was nice to see her letting go a little.

I wasn't sure what all she needed to free herself from, but I saw bits of it beginning to happen.

Her phone buzzed, and she looked down as the server took our plates away.

"Oh, shoot." She grimaced. "I forgot I was making dinner for Izzy and Caleb. They're thinking about leaving the lake soon."

"No problem. I can get you home."

"Actually, can you take me to the market? I still need to grab a few snacks since it sounds like they're going to show up hungry."

"I'd love to."

Right when we stepped outside, Abby from the book club and coffee shop greeted us with two iced coffees.

"I heard you two were grabbing lunch together here, and I thought you both might enjoy a pick-me-up for the afternoon. I'm assuming you'll be spending it together." She winked at Grace, who looked horrified.

The door closed behind us as the warm breeze swept down the street, and I eyed Grace.

"Thank you. This is really sweet of you," Grace said, glancing at me as I took mine as well.

"It's also a thank you for raising such a wonderful daughter. She just brings such cheer to the coffee shop. I can't wait for her to show up again tomorrow."

Pride warmed Grace up, and she beamed. "She loves working with you. Thanks for giving her the job."

Abby grinned. "It's a perfect fit. Enjoy!"

We watched Abby nearly skip down the sidewalk before Grace turned to me.

"This town is full of spies." She wagged her finger and chuckled. "Spies, I tell you."

I opened the door to the passenger side of the truck and helped Grace climb in with her coffee.

"I don't disagree."

She laughed, buckling up. "But if it gets me free coffee

now and again, I'm fine with it."

As I climbed into the driver's seat, I looked around town, noticing the ease and tranquility that rippled through the town. Families wandered toward the beach access with lattes and ice creams in hand. Couples strolled down the sidewalks hand in hand. Bicyclists pedaled down the road without worry that a car would hit them.

It was like stepping back in time but with all the modern conveniences.

"You know, I could get used to resort life," I told Grace, pulling onto the street to the market.

"Is that what this is called?" she asked, letting her head loll onto the headrest.

"Works for me."

Pulling into the parking lot for the grocery store, I found a place close to the door and parked.

"Want company or . . .?" I asked Grace.

"Sure. You can remind me what a teenage boy wants to eat." She grinned. "Besides, if I said to stay in the truck, would you?"

I laughed and shook my head.

The inside of the market was like walking into an icebox compared to the warm, moist air from Buttercup Lake.

Grace pulled a shopping cart free, and I followed behind

her.

"What do you think about chips? Potato chips or tortilla chips?" she asked.

Before I had a chance to answer, she grabbed both. "Let's get some dip too. Do you think he'd eat guacamole or just salsa?"

"Let's live a little and do both." I came up next to her.

She nodded in agreement as we strolled the aisles, grabbing pretty much anything that looked like it crunched or could be chewed. "I'm gonna get some fruit and veggies, and we should be set."

By the time we checked out and drove back to Millie's, Izzy and Caleb were slowly walking along the street.

Their hands were interlocked into a tight bond of teenage lust.

"Looks like things are progressing," I teased Grace, who gave me the death glare. "Want me to help bring the groceries in?"

Nodding, Grace looked relieved as Izzy came up with Caleb.

Caleb let go of Izzy's hand and glanced at me. "Need some help?"

"Absolutely." I glanced at Grace, who looked like she was about to fall over as Izzy blushed with delight.

Uh-oh. This was happening fast between these two kids.

Kind of like Grace and me.

And look at how that turned out.

Caleb and I managed to get all the groceries into the kitchen in one trip.

I helped Grace put away the groceries as Izzy and Caleb wandered out back to the table. I could tell Grace wanted to hear what they were talking about, but by the way that Izzy was giggling and blushing, I was pretty certain it was better if Grace didn't know.

Grace reached for two large yellow bowls and poured potato chips into one and tortilla chips into the other. I took that as my cue to dump some salsa into a small bowl and scoop some guacamole into another.

I glanced at Grace, who looked like something had taken over her thoughts. She was staring at the kitchen table, still holding the bowls to take out to Izzy and her guest.

"You okay, Grace?"

She brought her gaze to me and smiled, but I saw a hint of sadness behind her gaze.

"It's odd. Whenever Tim would visit Grandma Millie's with me, I always felt on edge." She started toward the door to out back and stopped. "But with you, things feel easy."

I didn't know what to say, so I stood there holding the

condiments as she opened the door and turned to me and said one last thing.

"Too easy."

She wandered outside as I tried to over-analyze exactly what she meant.

Too easy.

Too easy?

She wanted a challenge?

She was suspicious because we were so in synch?

I shook my head.

Too easy?

Nothing about my life was easy. I prided myself on being complicated and unavailable. It was how I'd stayed single for so long.

Grace popped her head back inside. "You coming with the dips?"

"On it." I made my way out to the patio and set the bowls down in front of the lovebirds.

"I should get going," I explained. "I'm sure Uncle Carter is getting hungry."

Grace's face fell, but she picked it right up. "Are you sure? You're more than welcome to stay for dinner. You could take some home to your uncle."

So maybe too easy wasn't necessarily a bad thing?

"Yeah. Stay for dinner," Izzy suggested. "My mom makes the absolute best fried chicken."

Izzy reached for her phone and typed a quick message before waiting for my reply, so I didn't necessarily believe she was all that invested in my response either way.

I smiled at Grace. "I'll take a rain check. Duty calls."

She nodded, trying to hide her disappointment right when my phone buzzed in my back pocket.

I slipped it out to see a text from my uncle.

"Huh. That's weird," I muttered.

Grace's brows rose. "What's that?"

"I just got a text from my uncle telling me he had a late lunch with his neighbor and didn't want dinner."

Grace folded her arms over her chest. "Huh. What are the odds?"

I looked at her and smiled. "Yeah. What are the odds?"

As Izzy innocently dipped a chip into some guacamole and Caleb stayed uncomfortably quiet, I realized that there were truly Sunshine Breakfast Club spies everywhere, and Grace happened to be living with one.

I rubbed my hands together. "Okay. Fried chicken it is. How can I help?"

"You two okay?" Grace glanced at the teenagers and smiled, returning her gaze to me.

"Yeah. This is great. Thanks," Caleb said as Izzy stood up.

Grace motioned for me to follow her back inside, and she closed the door behind us.

"I hate to be the bearer of bad news, but I think you have a spy on your hands."

Grace chuckled. "You were thinking the same thing?"

I nodded, laughing.

"What I don't understand is how they can be tied in so quickly. One text from a teenager, and your uncle gets it in his head to message you?"

"Maybe they're on a group chat."

She looked fascinated. "Who's *they*?"

I scratched my chin, thinking back to the twinkle in Millie's eyes whenever I'd show up, even before Grace came to town.

"I think it's safe to say Millie is in on it."

Grace grinned. "For sure, and I'm guessing Abby at the coffee shop is too. Her mother-in-law might be involved. She's part of the book club. In fact, Abby herself was set up with Mandy's son all because of the Sunshine Breakfast Club running interference."

"Is it really a book club or is it a matchmaking service?"

Grace chuckled and shrugged, reaching into the fridge.

"Only time will tell."

If I were decent, I would have turned away, but I couldn't help but take in Grace's heavenly curves as she bent over and grabbed the chicken. She turned around quicker than I realized, kicked the door shut with her heel, and caught my gaze at butt level.

Amusement ran through her eyes as she set the packages of chicken on the stove.

"Can you get me two cups of flour?" She pointed at the door to the pantry. "Flour is on the top shelf, and a bowl is by the fridge."

"Sure thing."

Grace started mixing herbs and spices to add to the flour I'd poured into the bowl. She took the bowl from me and dumped in some cornmeal. "That gives it just the right crunch."

I grinned, watching her move through the kitchen with such finesse. Whenever I cooked, the place looked like a bomb went off, but I noticed every time she used a dish or utensil, she did a quick rinse under the faucet and placed it in the sink.

Interesting.

"Tell me what it's like being on a course, knowing there is so much money at stake, and it's your job to win as much of it as you can." Grace started the oil in a couple of cast-iron skillets and then looked at me before she started breading the chicken.

I smiled, realizing no one had really asked me that before. "It's pretty intense. In the beginning, winning was how I ate, and then it became how I paid for my place to live, and then when that wasn't a worry any longer, the intensity changed. Golfing wasn't for survival but to win for personal satisfaction."

"You've always been driven." She threw a smile in my direction. "I have not."

"Don't say that, Grace. You're super driven. You've worked at a great company, kept a family together, and raised an amazing girl. That takes drive."

A wistful sigh left her lips as she dropped the first piece of chicken in the oil with a sizzle.

"I suppose. I just . . ." Her voice trailed off as she continued adding more chicken to the skillets.

"Tell me," I prompted. "What would make you happy?"

Grace turned on the faucet and washed her hands after all the chicken had been dipped. She turned around and leaned against the counter.

"To show my daughter that there are things out there in the world that can make a person happy." Her head cocked slightly. "She knew my passion wasn't about frozen vegetables, but running reports paid the bills."

"What is your passion, Grace? Is it the same? Do you have the same dream you did when you were young?"

She let out a deep sigh and brought her gaze to mine. "I do, but I know it's out of reach. It's just not feasible."

It looked like the words she said stung her a bit.

"Never say never."

She shrugged. "I won't say never, but I know how much money it would take and how impossible it would be to find a place to buy or lease. Running an antique shop isn't cheap."

I nodded in agreement.

"Not to mention finding the inventory to fill it and praying that you chose the right things to entice people."

"Even when you're talking about the cons, you light up about it."

"Maybe so, but I'm realistic enough to know that sometimes dreams aren't the ticket to happiness."

"That I believe." I nodded, wanting to pull her into my arms.

I wanted her to have that magic again, that belief and hope that anything she wanted to do was possible."

"Anywho," she said, propping herself against the counter, "let's get the potatoes going."

A splash of water hit the glass door, and laughter erupted from outside, where I saw Izzy spraying an unsuspecting Caleb. Izzy looked truly in her element and filled with joy.

"Remember those times?" I asked Grace, who craned her neck to see what was going on.

"Oh, yeah. And I always won with the hose."

My brows arched. "Do you think that was by design, perchance?"

Grace threw her head back, laughing. "Don't even give me that. You know I could tag you then, and I could tag you now."

"You wanna bet?"

Chapter Nineteen

Grace

I was dripping wet, but it didn't matter. I wasn't going to lose to Jackson and Caleb. Not with my daughter watching.

The chicken had been taken out of the skillets long ago, but we were in the middle of the match. The boys had a hose from the side of the house, and we had the hose from the back.

"Hide around the corner," I whispered to Izzy. "I'll make it look like the hose is going in the opposite direction."

Jackson shouted the countdown, and my pulse pounded with adrenaline.

"The score is tied, Mom. We have to get them first."

I nodded and looked under the porch. God only knew what kind of animals were under there, but it was the only way to ensure a proper attack. If I had to hide out with a den of skittish foxes or a stinky skunk, I would.

Jackson wasn't the only winner in the group.

I darted to the deck and rolled under it with the nozzle of the hose.

"Mom, don't do it." Izzy's eyes were wide as I snaked closer to victory, feeling twigs poke me in all the wrong places and leaves crunching underneath my body. I scanned for small animals and thankfully didn't spot any as I positioned myself to squirt Caleb and Jackson the moment they got to the end.

As I tried to adjust, I heard a croak and glanced over to see the largest toad known to man. My eyes widened as it looked at me with its gullet expanding and another croak echoing from under the deck.

I put my finger to my lips to quiet the frog, but it ignored me and croaked again just as Jackson hollered zero.

"Come and get it," I whispered, and the toad immediately stopped croaking as two pairs of sneakers rounded the corner.

Panic flooded through me, but I found the trigger and pulled it as the water absolutely pummeled them, drenching the boys while Izzy started squealing in delight.

"We won. We won."

Jackson laughed as I snaked my way out from under the deck. "What the—"

"I committed to winning," I said, trying to dust myself off from all the dried leaves, cobwebs, and twigs.

"I'm impressed," Caleb said as Izzy came bounding in our direction.

"We won fair and square." Izzy beamed, her hair still dripping from the guys' earlier assault.

"There is a really fat toad under the deck, by the way. He's kinda cute, actually."

Jackson grinned. "Do I have competition?"

I glanced at Izzy, who seemed oblivious in Caleb's presence as he rustled his wet hair with his fingers. Such a teenage boy.

"You're sure you're in the running?" I teased, making Jackson pretend to clutch his chest and take a few steps back.

"Okay, I'll go get some towels, and then we can eat."

"Hey, Mom?" Izzy asked before I went inside.

"Yeah?" I turned around to face her.

"Can I go to the movies?"

I scowled. "Where? We don't have one in town."

Caleb smiled. "Actually, there's an old barn they turned into a place they show really old movies, like from the 90s and early 2000s. You know, turn of the century type stuff."

I bit my bottom lip, trying not to say something that would make me feel even older than I already felt after that statement.

Jackson chuckled. "Man, those are some oldies."

"I don't know that I feel comfortable with you guys walking to wherever it is. I can drive you."

Izzy's eyes widened. "It's a yes?"

Caleb smiled. "Actually, my mom can come by and pick us up. She wanted to meet you."

Relief spread through me. "Sounds perfect."

I'd been dying to meet his parents from the moment he asked Izzy out, but I knew it was a balancing act this soon into their friendship.

"Okay. I'll be right back with some towels," I promised, dashing inside.

When I'd made it to the linen closet at the top of the stairs, Jackson came up behind me, and my heart fluttered unexpectedly as I grabbed a few towels.

"Thought I could be of some help," he said as I spun around with a pile of ivory towels.

He was only a few inches away, and I suddenly lost my wits, dropping the towels between us and glancing at his lips.

"Grace, I just wanted to help with the towels." He drew a deep breath, and I wondered if that was true. Did all of me freak him out? The unplanned future? My parents? My world?

I placed my hands on his damp shirt and smiled. "Yeah? Just the towels?"

He smiled and nodded, picking up the towels that I'd

dropped. "Just the towels, Grace."

I playfully kicked a towel away from him, which made him grumble under his breath.

But not before he kicked the rest of them away and thumped me against the closet door in the sexiest act ever.

"I thought—"

His eyes blazed with desire as his mouth crashed to mine. I felt every guided stroke of his tongue thrusting against mine as he groaned and pressed the hardness behind his wet jeans against my belly. My hands curled through his hair as my heart raced with need, and his scorching touch melted the chill away from the cold water dripping from my clothes.

As quickly as the kiss happened, it ended, and Jackson stepped away. "The kids will wonder where the towels are."

I nodded frantically, realizing I'd lost my mind. "You're right."

Picking up the towels, I slammed them into his chest. "You take them out. I need to collect myself."

Jackson grinned and looked surprised. "Collect yourself?"

"You heard me."

"Baby, if you need to get your bearings after a simple kiss, just wait until I strip the clothes off you and make you mine."

I opened my mouth and shut it fast.

There wasn't a thing I could say to undo that imagery.

Jackson's smile only widened as he wandered away with the stack of towels, and I finally let out the breath I'd inhaled moments before.

It wasn't like I didn't know what to expect with that kiss. We'd just shared one earlier, and it nearly ruined me for the afternoon.

And I was the one who totally initiated it.

And then he rejected me.

Until he didn't.

How was this just as confusing as when I was a teenager?

I let out a happy groan as I stared at the ceiling while reveling in all of these emotions.

But I had to get a grip. I toweled myself off and dashed to the bedroom where I put new clothes on, shorts and a shirt.

I straightened up, cleared my throat, and marched down the stairs where everyone was in the kitchen with towels wrapped around themselves.

"Not fair," Jackson said as Caleb shivered.

I laughed, noticing how infatuated Izzy was with Caleb's every move.

"I actually have some men's clothes upstairs from my grandpa. Want me to bring some down?"

Caleb shook his head. "Nah. I'll dry out when we eat outside."

I nodded. "Okay then. I'll take the chicken outside. Jackson, you grab the potatoes and gravy. Caleb, you get the corn on the cob. Izzy, if you could bring some lemonade, we should be set."

Everyone followed the orders, and the moment the food went onto the table, we all went silent and started manhandling the chicken.

"I had no idea how starving I was after winning so hard," I joked, and Izzy chuckled.

"Girl power."

Caleb smiled and nodded. "I say we do a rematch."

"I second that." Jackson nodded while taking another bite of chicken.

"Hey, Mom, Caleb was telling me he's going to be a camp counselor this summer for two weeks. I guess they're looking for more volunteers."

"Yeah?" I smiled, glancing at Jackson.

Some of my best camp memories were from the moment I graduated to being a camp counselor.

"When's that again? July?"

Caleb nodded. "It's the last two weeks in July."

"Do you think Abby will mind? Two weeks is a long

time."

"I actually already texted her about it at the lake."

I couldn't hide my surprise. "You did?"

Izzy nodded. "She said it would be fine. They're hiring two other part-time baristas and a counter person for the busy season."

"If everything is going well by then, I don't see why not." I took a bite of mashed potatoes and held in the sigh I felt coming on.

Izzy was growing up right before my eyes.

"Are the first three days of the session still all training?" I asked Caleb.

"Yeah. That's what my brother said. It's my first year as a counselor."

"Ah, that's right. The infamous graduation."

Jackson grinned. "I remember what camp is all about."

"Yeah?" Caleb looked amused

"Good times."

"Did you both go?" Caleb asked.

We both nodded.

"I loved coming to Buttercup Lake every summer, but the camp was always the highlight."

Jackson pretended to be wounded. "I thought I was the highlight."

"In your dreams."

Jackson played coy. "Apparently."

Ignoring him, I smiled at Izzy. "It sounds like a blast. I know you will have fun."

"And if I don't, I can just walk home," she added.

I chuckled, knowing she was right.

Caleb went in for a second piece of chicken and more mashed potatoes while Jackson worked steadily on a piece of corn.

Things felt right.

New.

Different.

I knew none of it would probably last. Jackson would go on his way to putt-putt land, and I'd probably go back to working in analytics in the city.

Glancing at Izzy and seeing the happiness radiate off her made my chest tighten. Could I really pull the rug out from under her again?

The answer seemed obvious if I didn't have to worry about the rest of our lives for us both.

But I did.

I snuck a glance at Jackson, who appeared to be lost in his own thoughts, and I wondered how life had gotten so complicated when I meant for it to become simple.

Caleb's phone buzzed. "Ope. My mom's out front."

I nearly toppled over myself as I got up from the table.

"Need a hand?" Jackson smiled, trying to steady me.

Izzy took her last bite of corn on the cob and dabbed her mouth with a napkin as Caleb waited for her.

"I'll just stay here," Jackson said. "You know, to keep an eye on the chicken."

I chuckled as I followed the two teenagers out front, where a black SUV was parked.

A woman with sunglasses on jumped out of the car and propped her glasses on top of her brown hair.

She waved her hands in the air. "So good to meet you. I'm Bonnie, Caleb's mom. He's just so happy to have found a friend in Izzy."

I'll bet.

I smiled as she came in for a hug and introduced myself in a muffled explanation. "I'm Grace Henry."

Bonnie let go and took a step back. "I'm sorry I missed you at the book club. I was down in Madison with my in-laws."

"You go?"

She nodded. "Yeah. The morning get-togethers work better for me."

"It seems like it would be a great way to start the

morning," I agreed.

"And when Mandy makes her morning buns . . . ah, heaven." She scrunched her nose, noticing her son still had patches of water on his shorts.

"We had a water fight in the back yard," I explained. "I offered him a change of clothes, but—"

She laughed. "But he's a teenage boy."

I grinned, immediately liking Bonnie.

"What time should I have Izzy home by?" Bonnie asked.

Izzy glanced at Caleb, and I smiled.

"After the movie, I suppose? Whenever that is?" I suggested.

"Well, mom . . . Caleb mentioned there's fresh-made ice cream sold at the barn."

Bonnie smiled. "It's kind of become the hangout for teens."

"Okay, then." I glanced at Bonnie. "There's no real time. After the movie and ice cream. Just try not to be later than midnight so I can go to sleep."

Izzy's eyes lit up.

And I knew full-well she'd be home by ten, maybe eleven, tops. There was only so much ice cream to be eaten, and Bonnie looked like she was on top of it.

"I should probably mention that it's my dad who runs the

theater." She put her hands in quote form. "Just *old* movies, really."

"Ah, even better."

Izzy gave me a quick kiss. "Thanks, Mom."

"Have fun." I almost added the phrase *don't do anything I wouldn't do*, but under the circumstances, I wasn't sure that was raising the bar any.

As I watched them all pile into the SUV, my heart tugged a little.

Someday, Izzy would be doing that for real. She'd be piling in a car to head off to college or to ride with a boyfriend on some road trip.

And that time was coming sooner than I realized.

Sooner than I was ready for.

I waved as they pulled out of the driveway and started toward their destination when I heard the storm door shut behind me with a whack.

I turned to see Jackson strolling over.

Dang. He looked sexy. His dark hair was still damp, and his blue eyes sparkled when his gaze met mine.

"I put all the food away," he said.

"Seriously? That was nice of you."

"I figured it was the least I could do."

"I could get used to that."

He didn't say anything, but I sensed a restlessness about him.

"How do you feel with Izzy headed off to the movies with Caleb?"

"I feel a lot better knowing that his grandfather runs it."

He chuckled. "Isn't this place something?"

"It is," I agreed. "Sometimes, everything about it feels too good to be true."

"Yeah. Well, I should get going," he suggested.

Disappointment filled me right up, but I nodded. "Okay. I understand. It's getting late."

"Thanks for all the good food and the fun."

"You're pretty competitive out there with the hose," I teased.

"We let you win."

"Sure, you did, buddy. Just keep telling yourself that to get through the night."

His smile widened. "Whenever you need a ride to the bank, just let me know."

I nodded. "Thanks for the offer. It means a lot."

"I stand by it. The trip down south would be fun."

"It would."

But it felt like his words were tidying up everything we'd experienced today. He looked more reserved, and I wouldn't think of trying to kiss him now like I did earlier.

Maybe when he had a few minutes to himself, he realized exactly what the package of me was.

"Okay, well . . ." I sucked on my bottom lip and glanced toward his truck. "I'll see you around."

"Damn it, Grace."

Chapter Twenty

Jackson

Seeing Grace shift her weight from one foot to the other while she looked around her front yard killed me. I knew what she was waiting for, and I was afraid to give it to her. We'd shared two mind-blowing kisses today, and I didn't think I'd be able to stop if I tried it again.

And she had a lot on her plate. She'd made mention of that more than once.

I didn't want to add confusion to her life because the whole thought confused the hell out of me.

But seeing the hopeful look in her eyes created an ache I couldn't shake.

I took a step forward and pulled her into my arms.

Grace's eyes connected with mine as she smiled.

"This is more like it," she murmured.

"Yeah?" I said gruffly, trailing my thumb along her

bottom lip.

The charge running between us reminded me of why I'd fallen for her so hard the first time.

Grace's hands moved just under my damp shirt as she ran her nails along my back.

I knew I wanted her now more than ever, and it would take everything I had to stay away.

To give her space.

"Kiss me." Her eyes looked dreamy with want. "Please."

"Grace, I don't want to hurt you."

"You won't," she whispered, skating her fingers along my back. "Just a kiss."

Just a kiss.

That was impossible with Grace Henry.

She pursed her lips into a perfect little pout, and I couldn't handle it any longer.

My mouth found hers as she let out a little moan of pleasure, her tongue pleading with mine to go deeper. I ran my hands tenderly along her jaw until they cradled her head, and the longing thrummed through me in an unstoppable way.

I felt her lips turn into a smile as our tongues swirled into a closeness that had been years in the making. Her breasts heaved gently into my body as her hands traced around my sides.

The thought of her hands on every part of me made me harden even more.

"Mm," she murmured, and I fluttered my eyes open as our kisses slowed. "That ought to hold me."

"Until when?"

She looked at me with dopy eyes fueled with the same desire I had racing through me.

"I don't know, Mr. Locke. But I needed that."

"I need more than that."

Her cheeks flushed, and she smiled. "Maybe, one day."

I nodded and smiled. "Right. Maybe, one day."

The heat running through me made it nearly impossible to focus. If she hadn't broken our kiss, I would have swung her over my shoulders and brought her back inside.

So, it was better this way.

She knew her limits.

She had her boundaries.

"What about a round of golf with me?" I asked, knowing she used to trudge along the courses with me when we were teens.

Grace nodded and hugged herself, but it wasn't because it was cold outside.

The temperature was warm and balmy, not even a breeze to inch across us.

"That would be nice."

"Izzy, too," I offered.

She smiled. "Thank you."

"For including her?" I frowned and shook my head. "Why wouldn't I? She's you, and you are her."

Grace laughed. "I never really thought of it that way."

I nodded and looked toward Millie's house. "Thanks again for dinner."

"My pleasure."

"And for letting me get that splinter out earlier. It's led to some really good things."

She grinned and nodded, glancing toward the house. "It has."

I gave a nod toward my truck. "I'll text you some tee times and see when you're free."

Grace nodded and started toward the house, and I wondered what made her interrupt the kiss. I could feel the need running through her, the heat rolling off her skin.

Was this all too fast? Too familiar?

I ran my palm over my face and let out a silent sigh before heading to my truck. Right when I climbed in and shut the door, Grace spun around and waved at me.

It was so confusing. Things felt effortless, and the attraction was there, but then there was something that would stop us. Stop us both.

I shook my head and pulled slowly out of the driveway as I watched Grace walk up the porch and into her grandma's house. I was too worked up to head home. Uncle Carter would be waiting to pounce and would probably flip me some shit for even being back at home before the sun went down.

But it was better this way. Grace and I both had a lot to figure out. I didn't even know when I was leaving town. My uncle appeared to be doing great, and I was pretty sure I was only around as an extra convenience for him at this point.

Instead of pulling into my drive, I kept on driving until I hit a little tavern advertising the best cheese curds in Buttercup Lake. Sounded like an investigation was in order.

I found an empty stall next to the front door and heard lively music the moment I hopped out of the truck.

A door swung open with a couple of ladies wandering outside for some fresh air.

"Oh, if it isn't the Jackson Locke," the short one said. "My boyfriend is a huge fan."

I gave a quick nod as she pulled down her tank, exposing most of her breast.

I glanced around the lot and shook my head. "I'm not—"

"Will you sign this? He cheated on me last night."

"Um. I'm not sure how that would make it better."

"I'll get your autograph tattooed."

I grimaced. "Still not sure how that would help the situation. Plus, I don't have a Sharpie. Sorry."

Grace would be getting such a kick out of this.

Or she'd be pissed.

I smiled and shook my head. Either way, all I could think about was Grace.

"How about if we see each other around town again and you're in a better place mentally, I'll think about it?"

She made a clicking sound with her tongue and put her tank back up. "Good deal." The other two females propped her up as she wobbled toward a bench and smiled at me. "Smoke Break."

The cheese curds sounded less appealing after this run-in, but I forged ahead and went inside the little tavern. Beer signs lit up the bar counter, and a game of pool was being played in the far corner. Most of the booths and tables had been taken up, so I wandered over to the bar and took a seat at the counter.

"What can I get ya?" the bartender asked, sliding a coaster in my direction.

"Coke and some cheese curds."

"Ranch?" the guy asked.

I nodded, knowing that must be a given. "This place is hopping."

"Best curds in town."

I grinned, knowing that was what most bars and restaurants said about themselves in Wisconsin.

The bartender set the Coke down. "And we have the best Fish-Fry Friday."

"I'll have to remember that."

"Do." He leaned onto the counter. "Hey, man. I'm really sorry to ask, but you are by far my favorite golfer. You even won me three grand a couple of years back."

I laughed.

"Could I get an autograph?" He slid blank receipt paper to me, and I quickly signed it for him.

"Thanks. I'll let you get back to your drink in peace." He waved the paper. "Means a lot."

"No problem."

"Curds are on us." The bartender placed my order with the cook, and I glanced around. Everyone seemed so content. Well, everyone except shorty outside, but she had some genuine grievances.

I shook my head and thought back to Grace and everything she must be going through.

It certainly didn't help that she had someone named

Tracy, to whom Tim was connected, who also seemed relevant in terms of a safety deposit box. I was hoping for the best, but I was bracing for the worst.

I couldn't imagine not telling my wife about something like that. Why keep things hidden?

Unless, of course, Tim was hiding something on purpose, which I knew was exactly what Grace feared the most.

The bartender slid the basket of cheese curds in front of me when the group of women from earlier stormed into the bar.

"Oh, great," the bartender muttered.

"You know them?"

"The short, feisty one is my girlfriend."

"Uh-oh."

"What?" The bartender glanced at me.

"I just happened to bump into them outside, and it sounded like you might be in the doghouse."

The guy rolled his eyes and laughed. "Let me guess. She told you I was cheating on her?"

I pressed my lips into a thin line and nodded.

"Yeah. She accuses me of that every other week or so." He shrugged. "It's probably not the best profession to be in."

The short female shot the bartender a look of daggers before turning all smiles to me.

"So did you?"

"God, no. I can't even imagine what she'd do to me if I actually did. But women slide me numbers all the time. I always try to shove them in the trash before leaving, but I must have kept one in my pocket on accident."

"Ouch."

"Yeah." He nodded. "But I get paid in tips. It wouldn't be great for business if I tossed the numbers out in front of the customers."

"Good point." I smiled, thinking about the bartender getting numbers shoved in his direction, and apart from shorty out front, how very little interest came my way from females.

I thought back to Grace, feeling even more connected to her. I couldn't fathom our ever being in a fallout like this in public. She was so put together and kind and . . .

Everything.

Which was why women after her always fell short.

But there was something stopping her. I could feel it.

And I didn't blame her. She had more thrown at her than most women her age ever did.

I bit into a cheese curd and had to agree. They were damn good.

"What did I tell you?" the bartender asked.

I nodded in agreement and tossed in another one as his

girlfriend marched up to the counter.

Bracing myself for a blowout, I kept my gaze on the curds.

"Do you want to know what a decent human being looks like?" The woman smacked her palm on the counter.

"What?" the bartender asked, confused.

"A decent human being? A perfect male specimen?" She waved her hands around in frustration. "This man right here."

Oh. Dear. God. Why did I ever leave Grace's house?

I almost choked on my cheese curd as the woman wrapped her arm around my neck. "I offered him my boob to sign, and he told me to sit and wait on the idea." She shook her head and sighed. "If a woman came in here and asked you to sign her boob, I bet you would immediately."

I let out a sigh as she unlooped her arm from my neck.

"That would never happen. I serve drinks, not slices." The bartender sounded tired.

"Whatever. I just think I need to hold out for someone like this guy right here."

The thought terrified me.

"Just let the poor man eat his curds. Quit bothering Jackson Locke."

She started massaging my shoulders, and I closed my eyes as I shook my head, trying not to laugh. I had a feeling that would only exasperate the situation.

"Is she bothering you? I know she's mine, but I can call Nate if you want."

I opened my eyes and shook my head. "No, don't call the police. I'm fine. I just might get a to-go box."

"Absolutely." The bartender looked mortified as he dumped my curds into the cardboard box. His girlfriend was oblivious.

I whispered a quick *good luck* to the bartender and went on my way.

And all I could think about was Grace Henry and how to convince her to give me a shot.

Chapter Twenty-One

Grace

It had been four days since I last saw Jackson. We'd texted a few times, but there were no accidental run-ins, which made me suspicious, and we'd even picked a date to join him at the country club.

Having bumped into him so many times over the last two weeks left me kind of bummed when he stopped appearing everywhere I went. At the grocery store, I was almost certain my cart would crash into his, or at the lake, I'd roll over on my towel just to see Jackson and his uncle waterskiing or something.

But nothing.

I had gotten used to his company.

And maybe his kisses.

I let out a sigh and rocked slowly on the porch.

The time had given me lots of space to think about things. Since we'd arrived at Buttercup Lake, it was this calm tranquility driven by nonstop action. Whether it was Izzy finding a boy, or hearing that my mom was sick, or wondering about a stranger named Tracy, or bumping into Jackson time and again, my mind hadn't stayed still much.

And I needed stillness.

Because those kisses from Jackson spun me into another orbit where I suddenly thought I could conquer the world and didn't need to worry about jobs or money, and I could reach for the stars and my dreams while Izzy's perfection dazzled us all.

But I knew I needed to come back to earth and look reality squarely in the eye.

I was a single mom who needed to figure out the next stage of our lives.

Plus, I needed to get some reading in. The selection this time was from Grandma Millie, and I knew I'd better be prepared.

"Mom, I'm headed to work soon." Izzy opened the storm door and poked her head outside.

"Okay. I'll drive you."

She shook her head. "No need. Abby is swinging by. I guess she was in the neighborhood."

"Oh. Wow. Okay."

It looked like something was on Izzy's mind.

She twisted her lips and then blurted, "You doing okay?"

I nodded and waved her outside.

She took a seat in the rocker next to me and let out a deep breath.

"Everything okay with you and Caleb?" I asked.

Izzy smiled and nodded. "Yeah, but I was thinking."

Please, not about sex.

I turned to face her. "What about?"

"I think you should go see your mom."

It was like the wind was knocked out of me. Izzy and I hadn't discussed anything much to do about my mom, other than the diagnosis. It was something I'd been debating since I found out, but it was privately. I didn't even discuss it with my grandma.

"What makes you think that?" I asked.

Izzy shrugged. "I know they haven't been real parents to you or Aunt Maya or Aunt Nina, but I know how I'd feel as a daughter not saying goodbye. You can know that you did everything in your power to be at peace if you visit."

Her words were so profound that I just sat in awe.

The complex world I grew up in, where I'd get forgotten at friends' homes, or our birthdays would be missed, or weekends were spent in tears because we didn't know where our parents had gone, all got wrapped into a tidy package.

How would I feel if I didn't say goodbye?

My daughter knew me well.

I would always wonder if I should have visited my mom. I also knew neither of my sisters would ever wonder that, and it didn't make them bad people. In fact, it made them the opposite. They knew what was the healthiest for them and for my mom.

I rested my head against the rocker and nodded. "I think you're right. I probably should."

"And I think you should take Jackson."

I sat straight up in the rocking chair.

It was one thing to recruit him for the mystery of my late husband's possible mistress, but roping him into visiting my dying, addict mother was quite another.

"I think it might be a solo trip."

"Either you take Jackson, or you take me."

"Izzy Henry, since when did you give your mom ultimatums?"

She chuckled. "Have you met Grandma Millie? It runs deep in our family."

I smiled and let out a deep breath. "I'll think about it."

"Don't think too long. We don't know how much time

she has."

"Izzy, I love you so much."

She beamed. "I love you too."

"I feel like you're angling something with Jackson and me."

A look of surprise dashed through her gaze. "Really? Why?"

"For starters, you're telling me he needs to go on a trip with me." I eyed her. "And I don't believe that day you had us spontaneously go to the lake was all that spontaneous after all."

"Would you like me to buy that tinfoil hat now?" she teased.

"Seriously, Izzy." I scooted so I could see her better. "I don't know if you're ready for any of that."

"Any of what?" She cocked her head.

"Me dating," I confessed. "I don't want to put that pressure on you. What if you don't like who I'm with or you think I'm taking too much time away from you?"

She shook her head. "I wouldn't."

"You don't know that. We don't know that."

She scowled. "Well, I do know that I like Jackson. He's funny and nice."

I nodded in agreement.

"And he worships the ground you walk on," she offered.

I shook my head. "I don't know about that. Besides, it probably wouldn't be Jackson who I wound up with. He's not planning on sticking around Buttercup Lake, and who knows what we plan to do?"

I caught my thoughts for a second.

"And I don't think I want to date until you're out of high school. It just would make things easier."

Izzy's scowl deepened. "For whom?"

I chuckled. "Are you just trying to get me to have a hobby now that you're into Caleb?"

Izzy smiled. "No, but I know that you loved Dad with all your heart. And I also know Dad stole you away from your first love."

"Not what happened at all. I got stood up by Jackson, and your father swooped in."

She shrugged. "Whatever the case, don't shut yourself off."

I wasn't sure how much I should really be talking with Izzy, but she was all I had.

So, I nodded. "You're right. But I think Jackson figured out that I'm too complicated. He's kind of taken a step back."

"We're still going golfing with him," she offered.

"True."

"Mom, don't be dramatic. The man has the hots for you, and he should. You're incredible."

Abby's car pulled into the driveway, and Izzy hopped out of the rocker. "My ride is here."

She gave me a quick hug, and I waved at Abby, who gave a little honk of the horn in return. I watched Izzy bound off toward the car and climb in, happily chuckling the entire time.

And I realized that my daughter was no ordinary fifteen-year-old. She had an old soul, and she was right.

My sisters' truth might not include seeing our mom one last time, but I needed to see her and be at peace. And maybe instead of getting scared every time I thought about kissing Jackson, I should just take it one step at a time.

Exactly. Maybe Jackson would fall so hard that he'd follow Izzy and me all over the place while we got settled.

Or what if that place was Buttercup Lake?

I rolled my eyes and laughed, realizing what I was doing was equivalent to writing *Mrs. Locke* all over my notebook in eleventh grade.

Without thinking twice, I texted Jackson a quick note.

I've been thinking about going to Seattle to see my mom.

Never mind the fact that I'd probably have to track her down first.

Within seconds, I got a reply.

A reply that I almost expected.

Need company?

I nodded to myself and let out a deep breath before typing back.

I think I might.

After I hit *Send*, Grandma Millie and Jackson Senior pulled into the driveway, and I waved.

Grandma Millie slid out of the truck with lime-green shorts and a flower top on her petite frame as Jackson Senior wandered to her side and reached for her hand.

It was cute to see Grandma Millie so happy. Grandpa Renny and her were inseparable, but to see that she had enough room in her heart to try something new made me fill with a little hope for myself.

There were moments when guilt washed over me when I noticed the male species—most notably, Jackson—and I wasn't sure when or if I'd ever shrug that off.

Kissing Jackson was out of this world, but I didn't know what to do next. After the kissing, would emotion be dragged in? Would feelings get hurt? Lives screwed up?

"What in the heck is that look for?" Grandma Millie scowled at me. "Turn that frown upside down."

I chuckled and shook my head. "I didn't even know I was frowning."

Millie's boyfriend wandered over to the hose and turned it on before dragging it over to a flower bed that looked a little dehydrated, which I hadn't even noticed. And that wasn't a complete surprise considering I could kill a houseplant by giving it the side-eye.

"What's on your mind?"

I laughed and stretched. "It would probably be easier to explain what's not on my mind."

She tapped my knee and took a seat in the rocker next to mine.

"Is it Izzy?" she asked.

"No. She's doing amazingly well. So much so that I think it would be a crime to leave Buttercup Lake in the fall."

"Is it Tim? I know there are some days I just can't believe my Renny is gone."

I turned to look at my grandma. "Even with your boyfriend?"

"He's not a replacement for Renny. I can miss the man I'd spent decades with while still learning to kick up my heels a little."

I nodded slowly.

"Ah-ha." Grandma Millie nodded. "That's what the frown is for. You're conflicted."

"I was born conflicted." I grinned. "I don't know whether to stay or leave after the summer. I don't know whether to visit my mom or not. I don't know whether I should cut things off with Jackson. I don't even know if there are things to cut off with Jackson. I don't know if the life I had with Tim was built on honesty. I just don't know squat."

Grandma Millie reached for my hands and gripped them between hers as she leaned over.

"You know more than you're letting on, or you wouldn't be conflicted in the first place."

"I don't know about that."

"I spoke with Nina and Maya, and neither of them were moved to see your mom. They're not conflicted. You know in your heart what you need to be at peace with her."

I nodded. "Izzy said the same thing to me today."

"Smart girl."

"She really is."

"And as far as dating. If not now, when?" My grandma

let go of my hands. "No one is promised tomorrow. There will never be a perfect moment for you to decide when to be vulnerable."

I shook my head. "It's not about being vulnerable."

"Oh, isn't it?"

"No. I just don't want anything to interfere with Izzy."

Grandma Millie looked around the porch. "Who is where?"

I chuckled. "Good point. I know. She's growing up."

"And what is this about not knowing about your marriage being built on honesty?"

Grandma Millie's boyfriend trundled toward us just as my phone rang. "Long story."

"Well, I hope you'll indulge me soon."

"I will," I vowed.

But not until I knew what was going on first.

I picked up my phone, and it was Bonnie, Caleb's mom.

"Hey, Grace. I know this is kind of last-minute, but Caleb wanted to pick out some flowers for Izzy, and I thought you might know her favorites."

I touched my chest and couldn't help but squeeze a little at the gesture.

"That is so sweet. Sure thing."

"Okay, great. There's this nursery about ten minutes out

of town that also has a great floral selection. I'll pick you up in ten, okay?"

"Oh, sure. Yeah. That would be great."

Grandma Millie watched me. "You seem to be making friends here."

I smiled. "It's Caleb's mom. I guess he wants to get some flowers for Izzy."

"Young love." She touched her chest. "Well, I just came over to pick up some jewelry for dinner tonight. My Jackson is taking me over to the supper club at the end of the lake."

"That will be fun."

"They have the best salad bar." She stood. "Have you read my book selection for the book club yet?"

"I'm on it."

"It's better than last week's. I'm telling ya." She winked at me, and I chuckled, watching her trundle into her house.

Maybe she was right. There would never be the perfect time to decide to start dating.

And Jackson was nearly impossible to get out of my head. Plus, he was familiar, and I knew what to expect. There was a high chance that I'd get stood up again.

I frowned at the thought as Bonnie pulled into the drive. I waved and stood, grabbing my wallet next to my feet.

By the time I got into her car, she was all smiles and

waved at Grandma Millie and her man as they stood on the porch.

"Your grandma is so dang cute."

"Yes, and she's getting far more action than I ever could."

Bonnie laughed. "Me too."

"Aren't you married?" I joked.

"Exactly." She chuckled and turned the vents blasting cold air at her.

"You're so lying."

"Yeah. I'm actually dealing with the opposite problem. It's like once my husband saw forty coming, he wanted to prove to himself, to me and to the world, that he still has it. But I know he still has it. He's amazing."

I chuckled, and she glanced at me, her expression falling.

"I'm so sorry."

My brows furrowed. "For what?"

"You know, because of your loss, and I'm just such an idiot. I really apologize."

My stomach knotted, and I shook my head frantically. "You have nothing to apologize for. I can totally relate, and I'd rather have someone talk to me honestly than to have them feel like they have to walk on eggshells."

Bonnie let out a deep breath. "I just wasn't thinking."

"Seriously. I promise. It made me feel normal again. For so long, people have been tiptoeing around any topic that has to do with relationships, and it makes me feel really awkward. Worse, actually, than talking about normal things."

Bonnie nodded and smiled at me. "I can see how that would work. Then fine. The truth of it is my husband has been exhausting, but I will weather it."

"It's nice to feel wanted, though."

Bonnie nodded. "So true." She glanced at me. "I can't believe this was our first actual discussion. My sex life?"

I laughed, knowing Bonnie and I would get along just fine.

"I'd rather it be your sex life than our kids'."

Her eyes widened. "Oh, my word. I know exactly what you mean. I'm terrified of that, but I didn't want to bring it up."

"Maybe subconsciously, you put yourself out there so we'd circle back to the teenagers."

Bonnie nodded. "Could be. I thought I had at least another year before that worry came into my head, but I don't know."

I nodded, thinking back to Jackson and me. The age of fifteen had led to a lot of firsts.

"The best plan for us is to be open and honest with each

other. If we see anything or think anything, we will just talk it out."

"Deal."

As we pulled into the parking lot, I spotted Jackson's truck and quickly glanced at Bonnie, who seemed oblivious.

"You said you're a regular at the Sunshine Breakfast Club, huh?"

She nodded, not meeting my gaze. "Yeah. Just the morning sessions."

I smiled. "Interesting."

Chapter Twenty-Two

Jackson

I was pushing around a garden cart with Uncle Carter pointing at various shrubs I was sure I'd have the honor of digging holes for when something caught my eye in the floral shop. For a split second, it was like I'd caught a glimpse of Grace.

But I knew that was impossible.

Crazy.

I was turning crazy.

Delusions had to be a sign of something. I just wasn't sure what.

"This Hosta. Right here." Uncle Carter pointed at a nearly all-white plant.

"Okay." I hoisted it onto the cart next to a hydrangea and a viburnum.

When I straightened, I noticed another glimpse of Grace, but as soon as I saw her, she vanished.

"What's got your tail in a knot?" Uncle Carter asked, staring into the same floral section.

"Nothing. Just seeing things."

"If that ain't something." He scratched his jaw and looked guilty of something.

I just wasn't sure what.

"I think I need to get back to the house," Uncle Carter announced.

I scowled. "We only have three plants. Earlier, you made it sound as if we were planting an entire garden bed on the side of your house. This wouldn't even cover a fraction of it."

"I'm old. I'm tired. Now, let's get inside and pay."

"Whatever you say." I pushed the cart toward the automatic doors, and Uncle Carter lollygagged behind me as they opened.

And there, right before my eyes, was Grace Henry, bending over and looking into a cooler full of fresh-cut flowers.

She looked even more incredible than the last time I saw her, and I knew my memory was purposefully detracting from her so I wouldn't be a wreck in between sightings.

I grimaced to myself. Sightings? What was she, a giraffe

on my dream Safari?

Uncle Carter came up beside me and elbowed me in the rib cage.

"Ouch. What did you do that for?"

"Look who's here." He wiggled his brows up and down and pointed directly at Grace.

"It's rude to point."

"It's even ruder to pretend you don't see her."

I glared at my elderly uncle and nodded. "I know, and I do see her, but she's busy."

Uncle Carter rolled his eyes. "What, are you shy now?"

I bit my tongue and let go of the cart. "Fine. You watch the plants."

"My pleasure."

But I knew very well that once again, we'd been set up, and Grace and I were the feature film.

A woman next to her nodded as Grace pulled out a bouquet of peonies and roses. "I think Izzy will love this."

"It's gorgeous and smells delightful." The woman glanced at me and smiled as Grace's eyes connected with mine.

"Fancy meeting you here, Jackson."

I laughed and nodded, noticing all the tchotchkes, decorative yard signs, and candles surrounding us.

Grace smirked and turned to Bonnie. "Bonnie, this is Jackson. Jackson, this is Bonnie, Caleb's mom."

I grinned. "Nice to meet you."

"You too." She couldn't stop her smile from getting wider and wider.

"Do you, by any chance, happen to belong to the book club too?" I asked, rocking back on my heels.

"Oh, yeah. I didn't go to the last meeting, but I go when I can."

"I see."

She smiled and glanced at my uncle. "Well, I should pay for these and get home to Caleb."

Grace turned and nodded. "Izzy is going to be in heaven. There will be no prying her away from Buttercup Lake now."

Bonnie chuckled. "You are staying, right?"

She shook her head. "I don't know yet."

"Oh, dear. I'd better not tell Caleb. He would be devastated."

Seeing that the two women were busy and my hunch about Grace since the kiss the other night was correct, I bowed out gracefully.

"I'll see you and Izzy on our golf trip. Have a great afternoon."

Grace's expression fell slightly, but she recovered

quickly and gave me a quick wave. I knew she regretted that kiss the other night. The texts had slowed. The messages had become shorter. I'd rushed things between us. She needed a friend, and I was pushing too hard for something more.

It didn't matter if she was the one sending signals that lit up the sky. I had to be the responsible one. She needed to be able to count on me.

Uncle Carter smacked the back of my head, and I cringed. It didn't seem to matter to him that I towered about a foot or so above him.

"What the heck did you do that for?" I rubbed my head.

"The woman was asking you a question."

I looked at Grace, who was snickering, and Bonnie folded her arms over her chest with an amused expression.

Grace attempted to compose herself as Bonnie tried again.

"I asked if it would be okay if you took Grace home while I took your uncle home and had my son dig the holes for Carter's plants? He's grabbing a burger at the stand just down the road and needs to earn money to pay for the flowers." Bonnie stared at me, waiting for my answer, while I glanced at Grace, who was trying to put the pieces together.

"Yeah. That would be fine and would save my back." I nodded, noticing a smile curl onto Grace's lips. "I don't think my manager would be thrilled if I returned to my profession with a bum back from gardening."

Grace's smile slipped away, and I wondered what I'd said.

Uncle Carter nodded and smiled at Bonnie before turning to me. "No need to worry about my dinner. I'll grab a burger when we pick up the kid."

"Of course, you will," I said wryly as Grace hid a smile.

It wasn't until we'd left the two masterminds in the floral shop that Grace turned to me. "Can you believe they're this brazen?"

"No." I opened the truck door for Grace, and she climbed in. "I honestly thought they'd given up. It has been quiet for the last several days."

"Hasn't it? They must have just been scheming."

I wandered around the hood of the truck and got into the driver's seat.

"So, where are we supposed to go with this arranged date?"

She smiled, and I couldn't help but notice the rosy glow of her cheeks. "Had I known I was getting set up again, I would have at least put on some mascara."

I started the truck and shook my head. "You're beautiful. You don't need any of that junk."

She chuckled and rolled down the window. "You used to tell me that all the time."

"And it's still true. You're gorgeous, Grace. Always were. Always will be."

"You always did make me feel like I was beautiful."

Didn't Tim? I wanted to ask, but I knew it didn't matter. But didn't he?

"I had a brief chat with my grandma about visiting my mom." She rolled up the window to only a crack. "I think I wouldn't be able to live with myself if I didn't at least see her."

"I don't think you should go alone."

She nodded and let out a heavy sigh. I wanted to take away all the pain and heartache that Grace kept getting dealt. No woman should have to lose her husband. No child should have parents who choose their addictions over their responsibilities. But we didn't live in a perfect world.

Not knowing where I was driving to, I just kept going.

"It's a lot to ask of you."

I could feel her gaze on me. "Uncle Carter hasn't needed my help for the last week, easily. Probably longer. I'm not ready to get back on the circuit." He shrugged. "I can't think of anything I'd rather do than support you."

"Why?" she asked, surprising me.

"Because you've been through a lot."

"Ah, so the pity card."

I pulled the truck off the road and put the hazard lights on.

"Where in the hell did that come from?" I asked, turning in my seat.

"Sorry. It snuck out. I just feel like ever since I got labeled as a widow, everyone wants to treat me like I'm fragile, but no one wants to actually help me pick up the pieces."

I nodded, hearing the pain in her voice, but I didn't have any words.

"After the funeral, everyone basically split from our lives. His coworkers stopped calling to check on us. Our married friends seemed to have forgotten our number. And surprisingly, his own parents, Izzy's grandparents, have barely remembered they have a granddaughter. They were great while Tim was alive, and now, I'm left covering for them and pretending they've been as supportive as they should be for Izzy. But then I remembered it was their son, and I tried not to be a horrible person. Their grief is something unfathomable. Basically, I'm a hot mess of emotions."

I tipped her chin up for our eyes to meet. "I would never pity you. There's nothing to pity."

"What do you mean?"

"You've had the shit end of the deal, but I see you with your daughter. I see the light that you bring everywhere you go. Just being around you makes me happy."

"That's because I'm like the Ringling Bros Circus trying to make it through life." She shrugged and dropped her gaze. "I'm a wreck inside. I want you to kiss me. I want to kiss you. I don't want to kiss you. I don't want to be kissed. I want more than to be kissed. I want a fling. I want a future. I don't want to be scared. Feel free to let me hitchhike home."

Seeing the pain and devastation churn through Grace made it impossible to breathe, but I needed her to see that she wasn't a wreck. She wasn't damaged. She was perfection.

I slowly cupped her face in my hands and brought her chin up slowly.

"Grace Henry, you're the strongest woman I know, and I would be glad to buy a ticket to your circus any day."

She giggled, but before I could think about what I was doing, I brought my lips to hers. My mouth covered her perfectly pouty lips as she let out a little whimper. Her eyes fluttered closed as she parted her lips, inviting me in.

It was a familiar dance, but this time the need was so much greater. With every thrust of her tongue, I hardened to a painful degree. A couple of cars passed by, and I didn't even care.

Grace's soft lips nipped my bottom lip, and I let out a low growl as her hands slid along my thigh.

I had no idea where we were, other than some country road that led out of town, but all I could think of was taking her, making her mine.

The chirp of a siren behind the truck broke us free as Grace's gaze widened, and she put her hand up to her mouth in horror.

"Oh, no," she whispered, squeezing her eyes shut. "I can't go to jail. What would Izzy think?"

I chuckled. "You're not going to jail, Grace."

Looking in the rearview mirror, I couldn't help but shake my head and laugh.

"Just great."

As Nate, the friendly police officer, rolled up to the side of my truck, he couldn't keep the smirk off his face.

"Driver's license, please," he said, peeking his gaze into the cab and smiling at Grace. "Good to see you, Grace. Seems like you're getting along just fine here in town."

I glanced at Grace, who looked like she wanted to tear Nate a new one, but instead, she stared straight ahead.

Handing my license to Nate, I glanced at him. "So, when is it illegal to make out with a beautiful woman, Officer?"

Nate smiled. "Well, it looked a little hot and heavy, and a passerby called it in."

I laughed. "You're so lying."

"No. It's a serious thing. Public indecency isn't a thing to be trifled with." He started to turn toward his patrol car with my license.

Grace snorted, which made Nate stop in his tracks and turn slowly. "Nate, when did you turn so uptight?"

Uh-oh.

"I remember when you glued all the toilet lids down at the camp." She cocked her head and flashed a wicked smile. "And I remember when you broke into the kitchen and put hot sauce in all of the ketchup containers. I could go on if you want."

Nate's smile widened, and he nodded. "I see how you're playing this, and I'd be lying if I were surprised."

"Oh, yeah?" Grace chuckled. "It's nice to see you again, Nate. I just never expected you to be on this side of the law."

Nate handed me my license back and grinned. "People can change." He winked at us. "Don't you forget that. And please keep it PG for the kids around here."

Grace stuck her tongue out at me the moment Nate disappeared, and without warning, I pulled her into my arms again.

Chapter Twenty-Three

Grace

"Mom, it's all over town."

I looked up from the book club book and stared at my daughter, who was holding the beautiful bouquet of flowers. "What's all over town?"

I was sitting on the sun porch, my lips still numb and throbbing from Jackson Locke, and Izzy stood in front of me with the bouquet of flowers Caleb must have just given her.

"That you were doing it with Jackson on the side of the road."

Shock pulsed through me.

I smacked my book down. "Doing it? What in heaven's name are you talking about?"

Izzy's eyes widened. "You almost got arrested."

"Where did you hear this?" I shook my head, feeling the blush creep up my face.

"Mom, you're turning red. It's true." Izzy's eyes looked like they were going to pop out of her head.

"Izzy Henry, it's not true. I was at a plant store, for crying out loud, and Jackson drove me home."

She put up fingers in the air. "Drove you home."

"Izzy, I'm smart enough to know what not to do in a town as small as this one."

Her brows rose. "Is that so?"

My eyes widened. What did she have on me?

"And those are beautiful flowers." I tried to distract her.

She smiled and let out a happy sigh. "Caleb got them for me. They're my favorites. He even knows my favorite flowers."

"Indeed, he does." I cocked my head slightly and watched my daughter sniff in the heavenly smell.

"Who in the world is saying this stuff about your mom?" I asked as she put the flowers on the coffee table.

"A policeman came in to get his coffee and croissant . . ."

My brows rose. "A policeman?"

I shook my head slowly, unable to hide my smile. "And does he happen to have red hair and a red mustache?"

She nodded. "How would you know that unless he caught you?"

"Did he actually say we were doing it?" I used quotes

like my daughter.

She nodded. "Something like that. He said he rolled up behind a couple who got reported by some farmers for doing it."

I groaned and laughed. "He plays dirty."

"Mom. He's a cop. He wouldn't play dirty."

"Sweetie, that man's name is Nate, and while I'm sure he's an amazing police officer, I have some stories from when he was a teenager that would make even you blush. When Jackson and I were camp counselors, the things we'd find him doing were *really* over the top."

She looked mortified.

"No pun intended, but I will cop to my part in the rumor mill. I was feeling a bit sorry for myself when Jackson was driving me home, and he happened to pull the truck over to the side of the road, and I might have kissed him."

"Mom, I haven't even kissed Caleb."

My right brow jetted up. "Yeah, right."

Izzy grinned and shrugged. "Thought I'd try to make you feel better."

I laughed. "Lies never make a mom feel better."

"How did you know I was lying?"

"Because you get all flustered when I bring up Caleb. These flowers will probably mean more to you than your actual wedding flowers. And because you're willing to spend every waking moment with the boy. Do I think you've kissed? Yeah."

She crashed on the couch and smiled. "Fine. We've kissed."

"And?"

She smiled and let out another happy sigh. "It was the best kiss I've ever had."

I sat up. "How many kisses have you had?"

She chuckled. "Just his, but he doesn't know that."

"Aw. You should tell him. I bet it would make him happy."

"I can't show all my cards, Mom."

"Since when did you become such an expert in the dating world?"

She thought about it for a second and shook her head. "I don't know."

Izzy leaned over and smelled her flowers again. "Do you think Jackson is going to stick around past summer?"

I puckered my lips as I contemplated her question. "My gut says no."

"But with Jackson, your gut has been wrong before."

"How so?"

"I'm sure your gut didn't tell you he was going to stand

you up."

"*Oomph*. A sucker punch right to the belly."

She laughed and shrugged. "You know what I mean."

"Okay. So maybe the man keeps me on my toes. I don't know what the future holds. It might not even hold a future with him beyond August. We could go our way. He could go his."

Izzy rolled her eyes. "Yadda, yadda."

"Whatever. Now, I'm just going to have to figure out how to set the town straight on what actually happened today. It was an innocent kiss."

"I was only teasing, Mom. The policeman only came in and told Abby."

"Curious."

She shrugged. "But I still love it here."

"And it's not only about the boy?" I asked.

"Not about the boy at all."

I grinned at Izzy and nodded. "Of course not."

She watched me for a few seconds, and I suddenly wondered if I had lipstick on my chin or something. "Not to switch the subject, but have you thought more about what we talked about with your parents?"

"You mean visiting my mom?"

Izzy nodded.

"I have, and I think you're right. I was going to talk to Grandma to see if maybe she'd be into watching you in between your camp counselor adventure."

"I can keep after myself, and I'm sure I'll be plenty busy at Camp Buttercup."

I grinned. She sounded just like me when I was her age. The only difference was that I actually had to look after myself unless I was at Grandma Millie's house in the summer. Then I could pretend that my life was completely normal.

"Well, regardless. That's when I think I'll go visit Seattle. It will probably take me that long to track them down. They seem to move every week or so."

"With their tent?" Izzy asked.

I nodded. "It's a sad life, and I don't want to make it sadder."

"Agree." She scrunched her face into an odd shape and blew air out of her mouth. "Did you know that he contacted Dad for money a few times?"

My heart fell out of my chest. "What?"

Tim had never mentioned it at all. They had asked me for money, but when I said no, I'd assumed that was that. If he hadn't been my husband of so many years, I would have been mortified.

"That sounds just like your dad not wanting to worry me.

Did he tell you?"

She shook her head. "Yes and no. Your mom called one time when I was in the car. I asked what she wanted, and he said money for drugs."

My eyes widened. "Just like that?"

Izzy nodded. "He didn't want to sugarcoat it with me."

"Apparently."

"He'd mentioned it wasn't the first time."

"Wow."

"I hope that doesn't change your mind about seeing them," she added.

"No, it just reminds me why it's been so long."

"You're not going alone, are you? Remember my rule?"

I smiled and glanced around the sunroom. "No. I'm not going alone. Jackson agreed to come along."

"That's nice of him."

"More than any one of us realizes, I have a feeling." I brought in a deep breath. "And I do need to run down to Chicago in the next week or so. Are you sure you don't want to come with me?"

She tightened her ponytail and glanced at me. "If you're going by yourself, I'll come, but I don't want to. I'd rather hang out at the lake all day or go to work."

"Jackson said he'd come," I offered.

Relief flooded through her.

"So, with all this working, what are you planning on doing with the money?"

"I've got some ideas. But they're a surprise."

"Oh, dear."

"Mom, it's nothing bad. I promise." She reached for her Kindle and turned it on.

"I believe you." I pulled out my phone and started looking at real estate around Buttercup Lake on the off chance that we decided to stay in town longer than the summer.

"It's nice spending time with you," she said, looking up from her device.

The words spun into a blissful reality. "You don't know how much I've wanted to hear that, Izzy Busy."

She rolled her eyes and smiled. "I'm sorry for giving you so much grief this last year. I just didn't fit in there. And when I got here, I realized that it's not my job to fit in. The right people will find me."

"You are wise beyond your years, Izzy." I flipped my phone around so she could see it. "I've been looking at places to rent or buy once we sell our place in Chicago."

At the moment, it was just sitting empty with only our belongings. If I'd been more business-minded, I would have rented it out for the summer, but that seemed like a pain.

"Are you serious?" She squealed and bolted off the couch to hug me. "We really might stay?"

I nodded, smiling. "Maybe."

Izzy released me and couldn't wipe the smile from her lips. "What about staying here?"

"It's Grandma's house, and if she and her boyfriend don't work out, it would be tight."

"There's a basement underneath."

I grinned. "Yeah, that has stone walls. I can't even imagine what would be needed to make it livable. The last time I was in it was when there was a tornado warning years ago."

"It has a lot of space."

"You went down there?"

She nodded. "Grandma wanted help finding a photo album."

"Well, it would take a lot to make it livable, and I don't think even that would be enough space for two adults and a teenager. Grandma Millie is particular."

"She's always seemed cool to me."

"She is, but living with her would be entirely different."

I flipped the phone around to look at the listings. "What about this one? It's right on the lake. It has three bedrooms and two baths."

She sat next to me and nodded. "It's cute."

The doorbell rang, and Izzy sprang from the couch. "I'll get it."

I wasn't expecting anyone, so I started to follow Izzy. She turned around and put her hand up.

"It's a surprise."

I grinned, not sure I could take many more surprises for the day.

Hearing the low murmur of voices, I strained to hear, and then Izzy shut the door.

She walked in with a pizza box. "Surprise. Dinner."

"Izzy, you didn't have to do this. I could have ordered it."

It probably took an entire afternoon's wages to get this pizza.

"I just wanted to say thank you. I even put extra pepperoni on it for you." She set it on the counter as I came in to give my daughter a big hug and kiss. "You're the most thoughtful girl. Thank you."

She spun slowly and pressed her lips together. "And there's something else."

I laughed and groaned, looking at the ceiling. "Give it to me."

"Caleb's family is going camping next weekend for the

Fourth of July, and Bonnie invited me. I'd have my own tent. They even invited you."

"Me?"

She nodded. "I don't know, Izzy. Going camping with a boy is a big deal."

"But it would just be like two families getting together on a camping trip." She contorted her lips into a pretend pout. "Bonnie even said Jackson could come."

Horror splashed through me. "How did that come up?"

"I asked."

I groaned in between laughing. "I was just with Bonnie this morning. When did this all come up?"

"At the coffee shop. She and Caleb dropped the flowers off for me there."

I smiled and let out a chuckle. "So, the one afternoon I drive myself out to the country to go antiquing and thrifting, and this is what happens?"

Izzy grinned. "What can I say? I have an active social life in the middle of nowhere."

I smiled and nodded, looking at Izzy. The truth was that we both knew this place wasn't in the middle of nowhere. It was very much somewhere and filled with exactly what we needed.

"Give me a day to think about it." I shook my head. "I'll

decide after our round of golf with Jackson. Deal?"

She nodded, smiling. "Deal."

Chapter Twenty-Four

Jackson

I'd picked up Izzy and Grace, and now we were staring at two sets of loaner clubs that I'd just anchored onto the golf cart. It was important to get back on the course, especially with the news I got from my manager. A really lucrative deal was in the works for me, which was going to shorten my time at Buttercup Lake.

"Can I drive?" Izzy asked.

"Of course." I glanced at her mom. "As long as your mom says it's okay."

"Totally fine as long as I can leave the course living and uninjured."

"Mom, I'm a good driver." She rolled her eyes.

"And since when have you been driving?"

She glanced at me. "Dad let me drive when I was seven."

Grace cocked her head and grinned. "He let you steer.

There's a bit of a difference."

I laughed and handed them each a golf glove. "This will help with blisters."

Izzy snickered. "Blisters? It can't be that strenuous."

Grace flashed her a warning look, which made her laugh more.

I liked Izzy's sense of humor. "You'd be surprised. The friction the club causes against the skin can really hurt."

Grace glanced toward the brilliant blue sky and held in a laugh. I had no idea what struck her as funny, but I liked it. I wanted to see more of it.

"Have you been golfing before, Izzy?" I asked.

"Yeah. I'm not awful."

"Tim took her to the driving range several times and on a few courses," Grace added.

"Good to hear it." I glanced at Grace. "I don't know what to say about your mom, though. She wasn't exactly great at it."

"I had more important things to worry about," she informed me.

"Yeah? Like what?"

Her cheeks blushed, and I remembered some of the things that happened between us on the course when no one was around.

"Oh, wait. I have this for you." Grace reached into a fanny pack that I hadn't even noticed because I was too busy taking in her gorgeous legs. "Close your eyes and open your hands."

"Okay."

I felt a golf ball drop into my palm. "Can I open now?"

"Yup."

I blinked my eyes open and glanced down at the ball. My jaw dropped open.

"Grace, this is . . . this is too much."

She shrugged. "You know how I love vintage everything. It just so happened that I found this in an antique store. I don't think they really paid attention. It was in a jar full of old golf balls."

"Wow. Well, thank you, but you really didn't have to do this."

A ball with Arnold Palmer's autograph was worth hundreds of dollars.

She shrugged and chuckled. "It only cost me fifty cents, so don't get too warm and fuzzy over it."

"Thanks, Grace. This is really special."

"Anyway, let's get going," she said, sliding next to her daughter, who was happily sitting in the driver's seat.

I took a seat in the back, and Izzy started toward the signs for hole number one. The ride was a little jerky, and Grace couldn't help but give her nonstop directions, but Izzy seemed pretty happy about the entire thing.

When I'd picked up Grace this morning, she was wearing the shortest tennis skirt I'd ever seen and a tight-fitting polo, all pink. She'd spun around to model it, and I almost swept in to kiss her, but Izzy sprang out the door.

The cart jerked to a stop, and Grace laughed as she nearly crashed her head into her daughter's.

"Okay, so let's do this." I hopped off the cart and went to the back to pick out the driver to use.

"Which club should we use?" Izzy asked, staring at her clubs.

"It's a Par 5, so let's try out the number one driver."

"It's pretty with all the swirly wood," Izzy said, pulling it out.

Grace came back to meet us. "Looks like a number one to start, heh?"

I narrowed my eyes at her and laughed, knowing she'd overheard my discussion with Izzy.

"You up first, Izzy?" I asked.

She grabbed a hot pink golf ball out of the new box I'd bought and picked out a yellow tee before nodding at me.

This girl meant business.

Grace and I followed her to the knoll as she scanned in front of her. She put the tee into the ground, balanced her ball on top, and readied her stance. Her grip was exactly how it should have been, and her stance was easy and ready to swing.

Tim had definitely worked with her.

I shook my head and smiled. We'd always played golf together when we were kids.

"Nice job, Izzy," I hollered.

"Thanks."

She brought her arms back with a near-perfect swoop and whacked the ball with a flawless swing.

My mouth dropped open as I watched the ball glide through the air and drop with a thud in the middle of the fairway.

"Wow." I looked at Grace, sliding my hands on her shoulders. "Did you know she was that good?"

Grace shook her head. "No. I did not."

"Geez. Well, you're up, Grace." I pulled my hands away, and she glanced at me.

"I was kind of hoping Izzy and I would suck together so we could cheat when you weren't looking."

"Ah, that's the spirit." I winked at her as she grabbed her ball and tee before marching to the knoll.

I had no idea what was in store for us, but she looked

incredible.

Grace looked at Izzy and then at me and smiled. "Be prepared to be blown away. Soon, you'll see where my daughter gets her raw talent from."

Grace stood next to the ball, and it became apparent really quickly. She bounced her knees up and down, drew the club back, and swung with all her might, missing the ball completely. She swirled around like a ballerina.

"You were certainly right about that. It's really apparent who the talent came from, and it wasn't a she."

Izzy chuckled as Grace threw me a look of annoyance. But she walked right back up to the ball and swung again. This time, the wind from the club whooshing by made the ball fall off the tee, but that was about all the action it had.

"Mom sucks at this," Izzy whispered, and I tried not to laugh.

"Nothing a few lessons won't help," I assured her.

"If you say so." Izzy eyed me with a grimace.

Just as we turned back to see Grace, we watched her toss the ball down the green.

"Mom, you can't do that."

Grace ignored her daughter and jumped up and put her hand up to block the sun. "Did you see that?"

"Yeah, we saw it. You threw the ball. You didn't hit it

with your club."

"Not that." Grace shook her head and turned to face us. "The little fox or something prancing across the fairway."

"Grace, are you just making stuff up to divert from the fact that you just cheated?"

Grace chuckled. "Is it really cheating if I'm going to lose anyway?"

I smiled as Izzy glanced at me. "I apologize for my mom's behavior. She doesn't get out much." Something caught Izzy's eye. "Oh, wait. My mom's not kidding. Look at that thing."

I focused on the grass in front of us, flanked by woods and thickets on each side, when I finally found what they were talking about. It was slowly approaching Grace's ball.

"Is that a fox or a baby wolf or?" Grace shook her head. "I can't see."

"It could be anything in Wisconsin." I scratched my chin. "Let's check it out."

We quickly put our clubs away and hopped in the golf cart. Izzy drove cautiously toward the small animal. As it came into view, I realized it wasn't a fox or a baby wolf.

It was a puppy.

"Is that a dog?" Izzy asked, coming to a complete stop.

"Looks like it." Grace looked focused. "Or an alien of

some type. Did it run into a tree or something?"

Izzy frowned. "Mom, you can't say that."

"Its face is completely flat. It's not an insult. It's just unique and very, very flat," Grace defended herself.

I chuckled and shook my head.

"We need to get it so it doesn't get a concussion from one of these balls flying at it," Grace said, sounding worried.

"Or hit by a golf cart," Izzy added.

"I don't see a collar," I said, climbing off the golf cart. "I'll go slow, and you two get ready in case it runs in your direction."

"Got it," Grace said, silently clapping her hands as if she were a catcher in a baseball game, squatting and focused.

Izzy looked at her mom like she had four heads and rolled her eyes as she readied to catch the puppy in case it darted away from me.

As I approached the furball, it started lowering in a play bow and barking at the ball, but the moment it saw me, it dashed toward Izzy.

"I got it," she hollered as the long-haired, floppy-eared, pancake-faced pooch reeled the corner and slipped out of Izzy's reach, heading right toward Grace.

Grace's eyes turned wide as the puppy raced forward with all its heart, barreling toward her with tiny legs and more conviction than anything to escape capture. Grace held her arms out, waving them at the puppy as the puppy ran between Grace's legs and circled back toward me. I knelt down, ushering the puppy toward me, hoping that I could coax it in with the ball I'd confiscated.

By now, the puppy's tongue was hanging out of its mouth, and it was slowing down. The moment it saw the ball in my hand, the puppy sauntered over, slowly sniffing at the ball as I grabbed it with my free hand.

Grace and Izzy flanked us immediately.

"Aww," Grace cooed. "She's so tiny."

Izzy looked underneath the puppy. "It's a girl."

"I think she's only a couple of months old, but I think she's been lost for a while. She feels a little too slender." Grace looked truly concerned, and I suddenly wanted to go to veterinary school.

Izzy let the puppy sniff her hand and then patted its head. "It's hard to tell with all that fur."

"What do you think it is?" Grace asked.

"You mean apart from a canine?" I teased, and Grace pretended to stomp on my foot.

I glanced toward the knoll and saw a group of golfers waiting to tee off. I gave a quick wave.

"We might want to call it a day and get this little one

some help."

Izzy nodded in agreement and ran over to the golf cart and drove it over. Grace took over the puppy, and I sat in the back as Izzy drove us back to the clubhouse.

"Her fur is all dirty," Grace said, sounding sad. "I wonder what happened to her?"

"Do you think she's lost?" Izzy asked. "Or do you think someone dumped her off?"

"I hate when people do that," I said, shaking my head.

"Well, we picked you up," Grace said in a baby voice, rubbing her nose against the puppy's face. "You're safe now."

I smiled and shook my head, seeing how happy Grace was with this puppy.

Izzy parked the golf cart and climbed out. "Do you think someone is looking for it?"

"I'll place an ad in the paper, and a note here at the club, and put up some posters, and reach out to the vets around here," Grace said. "But I don't have a good feeling."

She nuzzled the puppy again and glanced at me. "Isn't she cute?"

"I thought you said she looked like an alien?" I teased, and she pretended to cover the pup's ears.

"If anything, she looks like a pancake," she informed me.

"That would be a cute name," Izzy said, grabbing her

water bottle from the golf cart.

She poured a little liquid into the tiny cap and held it under the puppy's nose. Surprisingly, she took a few laps as I went in to return the rental clubs and cart.

By the time I came back outside, I could tell that it was over. Grace was in love with the scruffy mess.

And I had to admit that I was too.

But it was probably better if Grace and Izzy got attached since my schedule was always so all over the place when I was working.

"Well, should I get you three ladies home?" I asked since Izzy had already started toward my truck.

The puppy looked up at me and batted her eyelashes under all the hair, and I shook my head.

"Why don't you look at me like that, Grace?" I teased.

Grace glanced over her shoulder and shrugged. "Stick around, and maybe I will someday."

As we slowed toward the truck, Izzy climbed into the cab and slid into the middle seat, buckling up.

"Hey, I was wondering if you might be able to clear your schedule for a trip down to Chicago soon?" Grace asked.

The thought of getting to spend the day in the car with Grace was appealing, really appealing.

Especially with how great it turned out the other day.

"Absolutely. When are you thinking? I'm free all next week."

"How about Monday?"

I nodded as Grace handed the puppy over to Izzy. She walked over to the passenger side and climbed in, and I wondered when I should tell Grace the bad news.

Chapter Twenty-Five

Grace

Sitting at the community center at seven o'clock in the morning reminded me of how much fun I'd been having not going to work at the same time back in Chicago. The exhaustion was especially emphasized with a puppy at home who had to go potty . . .

Every.

Single.

Hour.

We hadn't had any luck finding its owner, and I was pretty certain the lost puppy might become our puppy.

Since we'd arrived in Buttercup Lake, the sun usually trickled in through the window shades and gently woke me up around eight, when I'd leisurely wander down to the kitchen, make coffee, and daydream about what I would do for a living the rest of my life. This puppy reminded me that a world was still spinning around me, just like this book club.

The problem was that I'd spent weeks daydreaming about what that should be and still didn't have a clue. Sure, I loved going antiquing. I always had. Ever since I was a little girl, I loved finding something old and turning it new again, making it mine.

Part of that was out of necessity when a child grew up like I did, but it was something that stuck. Even doing something as simple as giving my grandma the refurbished bicycle and Jackson the golf ball made me happy.

I glanced down at the book my grandma chose for the book club and couldn't help but wonder if she chose this to get my mind working. It was a mystery where the sleuth was an antique dealer.

After the last several weeks of mysterious Jackson sightings, nothing would surprise me. She liked to think she was subtle about introducing ideas.

I glanced around the room full of ladies. Apparently, they all felt they had that skill.

But I did feel sorry for Daisy, Jackson's cousin. I gave a quick wave in her direction, and she smiled. She had no idea what she was in for. I bet by this time next year, the book club would be throwing a shower for her.

Bonnie walked into the room, holding a plate of

something that she set down next to a platter of cinnamon rolls and a quiche, and waved at me. She pointed at the empty seat, and I nodded.

"Good morning." She grinned. "What did you think about the story? Wouldn't it be fascinating to own an antique store?" Her eyes lit up.

No, not subtle at all.

"Yeah, I've always dreamed of having one."

Bonnie's brows rose. "You should do it."

I smiled and chuckled. "Well, there's this little issue of inventory and rent."

"True, but things tend to fall into place if it's meant to be. We don't have one here at the lake. I bet the tourists would gobble it up."

"Maybe so." I nodded, smiling.

Yup, not subtle at all.

Abby wandered in with a container of coffee while chatting with her mother-in-law, Mandy, and Grandma Millie came in with a sheet of paper and her book.

She wandered over and sat next to me.

"I loved this book," Bonnie told my grandma. "Can you imagine how great it would be to own an antique store?"

Grandma Millie smiled and nodded. "It would be amazing, wouldn't it? Just imagine being this woman for a second. Right, Grace?"

I chuckled and shook my head. "Yes, it would, minus the murder."

As the women settled around the room and found their spots, I noticed how much I liked this club. Granted, it was only my second time, but now that the pressure was off to bring a dish, I could really settle in.

"Oh, did Izzy ask about camping with us next weekend?"

Grandma Millie clapped her hands, scaring the crud out of me. "That sounds fun. Doesn't it, Grace?"

I eyed my grandma and chuckled. Yeah. It sounds fun."

"So that's a yes, then?" Bonnie smiled.

"I think so."

"You can go ahead and invite Jackson if you'd like," Bonnie offered.

I shook my head and glanced at my grandma. "Oh, we're not . . . I mean, it's not . . . I'm not in a relationship with him."

My grandma frowned as Bonnie looked between the two of us.

"Oh, I thought you two were an item. I mean, Nate . . ." She stopped herself, and I laughed.

"Yes, what exactly did Nate say?"

Bonnie's smile widened. "Pretty much that you two were sucking face like teenagers, and if he hadn't rolled up, who knows where it would have gone."

I rolled my eyes. "Oh. My. Gosh. So not what happened."

Grandma Millie didn't look amused. "Really, then. Do tell."

"Grandma, seriously?"

She looked miffed. "Yes, seriously. You're gallivanting around here like you've got all the time in the world." My grandma shook her head. "Let me tell ya something. Time here on earth is short and gets shorter with every decade. I was hoping you'd learn a little something with this protagonist."

My grandma looked genuinely annoyed.

I turned to face Bonnie. "Well, I will see if Jackson is free."

"I'm sure he is," Bonnie assured me. "His uncle says he's running out of things for Jackson to work on."

"That's my girl." Grandma Millie tapped my knee before gathering the troops about our latest read.

After hearing the tenth person talk about how fascinating it would be to own an antique store, I was thrilled to break for food. I'd managed to create a mini mountain of breakfast delicacies on my plate while balancing it on my knee.

"I love these cinnamon rolls. Best in the world," Abby said, smiling with her eyes shut.

She'd wandered over with her plate and sat down in the

seat my grandma had evacuated.

"Izzy is doing so well at the shop," she informed me. "She's my best employee."

"Really?"

"For sure."

I took a bite of the cinnamon roll and realized Abby was right. The icing melted in my mouth.

"Are you planning to stay beyond summer? I'd love to work with her school schedule come fall."

I grinned, realizing that Izzy was as skilled as her great-grandmother when it came to subliminal messaging.

"I've been thinking about it. I'm definitely leaning in that direction."

Bonnie let out a sigh of relief. "Thank goodness. Caleb has been praying that would happen."

I smiled and nodded, thinking back to Jackson. Had he lived in Buttercup Lake instead of just visiting it in the summers like I used to, I was sure I would have wanted to stay too.

"I know it's none of my business," Abby said out of the blue, "but what happened between you and Jackson all those years ago?"

And it became even more clear just how embedded this book club was in Buttercup Lake.

I took another bite of cinnamon roll. "Well, my version is that he stood me up. His version is that I stood him up."

"How's that possible?" Bonnie asked.

"I don't know, but I was very definitely standing there for hours, looking like an idiot with all my friends."

"And it wasn't in the day of cell phones."

I nodded. "True."

"He seems like a really nice guy," Bonnie added.

"He is, and he was." I grinned, thinking back to Jackson. "But I wouldn't trade how any of it happened for the world. I have my Izzy, and that's all that matters." A few seconds of silence went by. "And I had an incredible marriage."

Bonnie and Abby nodded. "Does that make you fearful for the next relationship with whoever that might be?"

I never really thought about it before, but I nodded slowly. "Yeah. I suppose it does. I've heard of so many horror stories. I certainly don't want to stumble into one of those, especially with Izzy."

Abby nodded.

My mind drifted to Jackson. There was so much I could tell him, and yet there was so much more inside of me, and it was like each kiss opened me up a little more. Something I certainly wasn't going to reveal to these ladies.

"Well, no pressure, but I think Jackson isn't what horror

stories are made of." Abby grinned. "And Nate said you two have definitely made out, so we know you're compatible."

My mouth fell open. "So, it was true what Izzy told me."

Abby grinned. "What did Izzy tell you?"

"That a police officer came into the coffee shop and said he caught us doing something."

Abby chuckled. "Is it true? Did he catch you? One never knows with Nate."

My cheeks burned. "Yes, he came up behind us when we were on the side of the road. We might have kissed, but we were just hanging out. Nothing serious. It's not like he's ready to help raise a teenager and stay in Buttercup Lake."

Saying the words aloud pained me. Was that what I really felt?

She eyed me. "You've asked?"

I frowned. "I don't have to ask to know."

"I'd give Jackson the benefit of making that decision."

I shook my head. "We aren't even to that point. Right now, we're just having fun with a kiss here or there." I shrugged. "Followed by immense guilt pummeling through me, which I then shake off and start all over again."

Abby's expression softened. "I won't pretend to know the emotions you're going through, but I feel in my gut that Jackson is the real deal."

He was way back when . . . until he wasn't.

And I don't want to run into that side of him again.

I laughed and shook my head. "We shall see come Monday."

"What's happening on Monday?"

"He's driving me down to Chicago to take care of some stuff."

"Wow. That's a long drive. Are you spending the night?"

My eyes widened as I shook my head. "Oh, no. Not at all. It just might be a late night coming back."

Bonnie whistled with a grimace. "If you say so."

"Izzy is scheduled to work on Monday. Do you want me to pick her up and just have her stay with us until you come back?"

"You wouldn't mind? I was going to have my grandma watch over her, but then she'd probably feel like I was saying she needs a babysitter, which obviously at fifteen, she doesn't." I glanced at Bonnie. "But now there's Caleb and an entire world of sneaking out."

Bonnie chuckled. "Great minds think alike."

"I'll make it sound impromptu and like a girls' night," Abby promised.

"Thank you. That's so nice of you." I bit my bottom lip for a split second. "But there's a bit of an issue. We have a new puppy."

Abby winked at me. "Then it will be a girls' night at your place. Problem solved. Now, you can just drive at a leisurely pace and not worry about when you roll in the door."

I nodded, smiling, and an excitement came out of nowhere about Monday's trip.

Chapter Twenty-Six

Jackson

"What if you get to the bank, open up the box, and it's empty?" I said, glancing at Grace as we followed the directions to the bank.

It wasn't in the city proper, but she didn't seem to be familiar with it from when they lived in the suburbs or the city, which was odd.

Grace reached for my hand and squeezed it. "That would be my luck."

Feeling her grip on mine made my mind race. Since the kissing incident on the side of the road, it had been nearly impossible to quit imagining something more with Grace. Even something as simple as this touch made my mind delve into the future, and that wasn't fair to her.

"It's funny," I started. "I usually hate car rides, but this has been a lot of fun."

"You're only saying that because you're exhausted from your uncle's endless to-do list."

I smiled and nodded. "Maybe, but I think it might have to do with who I'm in the car with."

She looked over at me and smiled, letting out a soft sigh. "Okay, so I've been waiting until the right time to ask, but I can now say that there is no right time."

"Uh-oh. This doesn't sound good."

She laughed and watched me as I merged onto the roadway leading to the bank. "Well, it's about this weekend."

"What about this weekend?"

Grace let out a slow sigh. "I don't want you to take this the wrong way."

"Oh, God. Just spit it out."

"Okay, fine. Caleb's parents invited us to go camping next weekend."

I turned into the parking lot of the bank and parked. "Okay. Sounds fun. I'm sure you and Izzy will enjoy it. Did you need to borrow some camping equipment or the truck or . . ."

She bit her bottom lip and blushed. "No, like us. You, too."

Far more surprise registered on my face than I expected.

Grace's shoulders slumped. "I knew it was a bad idea."

"No. It's an awesome idea. Amazing. I just . . . I wasn't expecting that."

Her eyes brightened slightly. "So, you'd consider it?"

"Consider it? Count me in."

"Really?"

I nodded, seeing the relief flood through her. "Awesome. Because I could really stand to have someone else watch the dog besides me."

Chuckling, I kept her hand in mine. "Ah, you just want me as a pet-sitter. I see how it is."

Grace giggled, and I wished I could bottle the sound. It wasn't like when I left Buttercup Lake I could take her and Izzy with me.

"Then it's decided." She grinned. "You, me, Izzy, and Pancake."

"Pancake?"

She nodded happily. "That's our puppy's name. Officially."

"Well, it's a lot more considerate than Alien."

Grace nodded and glanced around the parking lot. "Now that I'm here, I'm freaking out inside. I don't know that I want to find out what he was keeping from me."

The apprehension came in waves behind her gaze. Every

emotion Grace felt was plastered all over her face.

"Do you want me to stay out here or go in with you?"

She sucked in a deep breath and closed her eyes. "I think I need moral support in case I see a picture of his other wife, Tracy." Grace opened her eyes and looked at me.

"So, it sounds like you're doing well with this whole thing."

She chuckled. "I knew who Tim was. He was a great husband." Grace stopped herself and looked sheepish. "I probably shouldn't be talking to you about that."

"If not me, then who? Pancake?"

Grace smiled. "Well, I did try to recruit a squirrel as a therapist before we moved out to Buttercup Lake."

I reached for Grace's hand and squeezed it gently. "It's going to be okay, no matter what you do or don't find in that box. Just focus on the fact that you have a wonderful support system, an amazing daughter, and a great place to hang out for the rest of the summer."

She nodded, clutching my hand. "But summer is zipping by."

I nodded in agreement.

"Before I know it, Izzy will do her training as a camp counselor, and it will be the end of July."

"One thing at a time, Grace. It's the easiest way to get

through life."

She chuckled and drew another deep breath and let out the air in a gust before letting go of my hand. "Right. Onward."

"Exactly." I gave a quick nod as we hopped out of the truck and hoped I could be just as nonjudgmental once we got inside.

Aside from Tim stealing away the only girl I'd ever truly cared about, I didn't think he'd be the kind to have a second family or hide some dark secret.

But with each step closer toward the bank, I grew unsure.

When Grace clutched my hand as I opened the door, I swore I could feel her pulse in her fingertips.

A lady from behind the counter greeted us, and we walked over to her. Grace explained the situation as the woman started to look things up.

Grace's body tensed as she waited for the woman to rebuke her efforts.

Instead, the woman smiled and nodded. "You're listed on the box as well."

"I am?" It looked like Grace wanted to climb over the counter and hug the woman.

We were both thinking the same thing. If Tim wanted to hide another family in the wings, he wouldn't have listed

Grace as someone who could have access. That would just be cruel.

"I have a question," Grace asked.

The woman nodded. "Of course."

"Is there anyone else listed beside myself and my late husband?"

"Nope. Just you two." She smiled. "Shall we?"

Grace nodded and let go of my hand as we followed the woman to a large vault. It didn't take very long for the banker to open the door and motion for us to follow her inside. She found Grace's box, stuck her key in it, and waited for Grace to do the same before sliding it out of the drawer.

The banker set it on a table in the middle of the vault. "I'll be out front when you're done."

"Thank you." Grace smiled and nodded, but I could tell her mind wasn't on what the woman said. She just wanted in that box, and I didn't blame her.

"You still want me with you?" I asked, coming up behind her.

"Yeah, if you don't mind."

"Not at all."

I rested my hand on her shoulder as she used the key once more, this time to open the box that was inside the drawer.

She drew a deep breath and opened the lid.

A thick envelope had been curled up inside. She glanced at me and pulled out a stack of papers.

"Here goes nothing." Grace scanned the first page. "This doesn't make sense. It's talking about Buttercup Lake."

I looked over her shoulder at the pages stapled together. She flipped the page.

"I don't believe this," she muttered.

"What?"

"It looks like Tim bought some sort of building for cash near Buttercup Lake." She shook her head. "Where would he get a chunk of money like that? Why would he keep a secret like this from me?"

"In all fairness to Tim, I don't think the property is that expensive in Buttercup Lake. At least compared to Chicago."

She pretended to scowl at me, but I saw through it.

"Do you see anyone listed named Tracy?" I asked. "Is there an address?"

She shook her head. "A-ha."

"You found something?"

Grace nodded. "There is a Tracy Long listed with an address two towns over from Buttercup Lake. She's on the deed."

"Maybe she's the real estate agent or something?"

She shrugged. "I don't know, but none of this makes

sense. From the looks of it, he owned something in Buttercup Lake. Maybe *they* own something in Buttercup Lake. I have no idea what is going on. Why wouldn't he tell me?"

"When we get back to the truck, we can type in the address and try to find out if it's a house or property or . . ." The moment I saw the look in Grace's eyes, my heart fell. Hurt pummeled through her gaze, and all the teasing we'd done about another woman didn't seem so far-fetched. It was as if I could see her building her walls back up brick by brick.

Grace nodded. "I also want to contact this Tracy woman. I can't tell if she's a real estate agent or an attorney or what."

Or what . . .

Grace wandered out of the vault, looking somewhat pained but still in a daze as the banker came over to us. Grace thanked the woman and let her know she wouldn't need the box any longer. It was near closing time at the bank and in the middle of rush hour, so I was kind of hoping Grace might want to grab a bite to eat, want to talk a little.

By the time we got back to the truck, Grace was massaging her temples. "I can't even begin to tell you how happy I am to know that Tim wasn't who he appeared to be."

"I'm still holding out hope. Maybe he bought a dairy farm for when he retired, and this Tracy person is running it until then." As the words tumbled out, I rolled my eyes at my own explanation.

"Very funny." She opened the documents to the address, and I typed it in. The satellite image was of absolutely no use.

"Well, we can drive by tonight when we get back, but it will probably be pretty hard to see."

Grace laughed. "I've been in the dark so long that I think I can wait until morning to see what in the world is waiting for me in Buttercup Lake. I'm just going to give a quick call to Tracy. Maybe she will be able to fill us in, and this will all be straightened out."

I nodded as she dialed and didn't say anything for a minute or so. She whispered *voicemail* to me and then left a message.

"What pisses me off the most is that he put me on the box inside. It's like he wanted me to find out." She groaned and shook her head. "I thought we had a good marriage, a solid marriage. Sure, he traveled a lot for work, but I never thought it wasn't true." Grace let out a hefty sigh and glanced at me. "This makes me feel like I've been living a lie."

"We don't know what this property is or who Tracy is. Let's just take it one step at a time."

"No. You're right." She nodded and studied me. "You're completely right. I'm sure there is a completely logical explanation for a woman I don't know to own a piece of property with my deceased husband in the town where Tim and I met."

Grace smiled wryly, and all I could do was nod.

"When you put it that way . . ."

"Okay. Let's get going. It's a long drive back."

I could tell she was trying to put it behind her until she got to Buttercup Lake. Her mind was compartmentalizing. Her hands were fidgeting. It just sucked. The whole thing sucked. From what I could tell, Tim put this property in a trust for someone named Tracy, but I was no lawyer and certainly didn't want to tell Grace that if I were wrong. She already looked like her head was about to explode.

"Do you want to grab some food for the ride back or . . .?"

Grace looked at me and let out a deep breath. "Sure. That sounds good."

"And I want to prove to you that not all men are dogs."

"Umm." A little smile crept onto her lips. "You do remember that you stood me up, right? Like, I'm not sure you're the shining example."

"I didn't stand you up." I went to start the truck, and it wouldn't turn over.

She glanced at me. "You know, I did kind of wonder if we should actually be taking this truck on such a long drive."

"Hey, now. This baby is just fine. It'll start." I caressed the dash and tried again.

Nothing.

I scratched my chin. "This isn't right."

Grace laughed. "No, it isn't right at all. It doesn't sound promising."

I hopped out of the truck, lifted the hood, and searched for a brief second, unable to believe what I saw.

Cursing under my breath, I shook my head and shut the hood before climbing back into the cab.

"You're not going to believe this."

Her brows rose. "Indulge me."

"My spark plugs are missing."

She frowned and cocked her head. "How is that possible?"

"I don't know." I shook my head.

"Did you have them in Buttercup Lake?"

I smiled. "We wouldn't have gotten out of there if I didn't."

"Oh, no." She shook her head as I pulled out my phone and scanned for the closest auto parts store.

"I'll just see if this place has any, and I should be able to put them in if I can buy them."

She nodded, looking somewhat impressed as the banker

came outside.

"Do you mind telling her what happened in case we have to leave the truck in the parking lot for a little while?"

"Sure." Grace hopped out of the truck as I talked to the guy at the auto parts store.

She returned smiling as I hung up the phone.

"They don't have it in stock, and neither do the other stores around, but the good news is that they ordered it from their warehouse and will have it first thing in the morning."

Her eyes widened. "How's that a good thing? I'm in Chicago, and Izzy is in Buttercup Lake."

I grimaced. "There is that issue."

She sat silently and stared out the windshield. After a few minutes of silence, she turned to me. "I think this was sabotage."

I laughed until I realized she was serious. "By whom? Tracy? Tim's ghost?"

"I know this is going to sound absolutely crazy." She sat on her hands and rocked for a second. "But hear me out."

"Okay."

"The Sunshine Breakfast Club."

The moment she said it, I scanned all the adjoining parking lots for predators.

"That would be crossing some serious lines."

"It blows crossing boundaries right out the water," she agreed.

I shut the truck door and glanced at her. "You don't really think they'd do that?"

"I kind of do."

"Wow." I shook my head. "Someone from the book club would have needed to tail us all the way down here to steal my spark plugs . . . for what?"

She looked out the side window. "I don't know."

"I think you do," I prompted, and she blushed. "And I wouldn't mind if they went over the line if it meant I got to spend a night with you."

Grace's eyes widened, and I saw a flicker of longing behind her gaze. The familiar ache deepened in my stomach. We'd come close so many times, but I could feel Grace pull away like she was now.

"You wouldn't mind if they stranded us in an entirely different state?" She straightened and snuck a look at me.

"No, not entirely. I won't deny that I'm shocked if that's what actually happened, but it wouldn't be the worst thing."

You and me. Come on, Grace. Give us a chance.

"I did get the feeling that the ladies at the book club thought I was vacillating too much."

"About what?"

"They want there to be a you and me, and I explained that we aren't to that point yet. Plus, you're a single guy who doesn't need to sign up to be a parent of someone else's kid. And while I thought I was healing over Tim, finding out the latest hasn't exactly warmed me up to the idea of another relationship."

Her words gutted me. Was that how she saw me, this thing between us?

Grace watched me for my reaction, but I didn't even know where to start.

"Your silence says it all. My hunch is right. This thing between us is just light and fun." She forced a smile. "But I do appreciate your help with driving me down here. I'm just sorry that—"

Interrupting her, I instantly cradled her chin in my hands and kissed her hard.

Chapter Twenty-Seven

Grace

I glanced at Jackson as he checked us into a hotel down the street from the bank. I was so confused about what I found, but I needed an escape. I wanted to forget my baggage instead of constantly unpacking it.

Jackson took the card keys from the woman behind the counter and reached for my hand. The moment his fingers tangled with mine, a crazy excitement ran through me.

We stepped into the elevator and the doors slid shut. It was like all of the oxygen had been sucked out of the tiny space, and my head started spinning. I leaned against Jackson and my knees wobbled as it came to a stop.

He looked down, his eyes connecting with mine as the doors slowly opened. "You okay?"

I nodded slowly. "Mm-hm."

Jackson's arm slid around my shoulders as every part of

me vibrated with an excitement that I'd only felt once before—the night I lost my virginity to him. With every step closer to our hotel room, my heart pounded with a thud so strong I was surprised he didn't feel it.

When we reached the room, he slid the card into the reader, and the door unlocked.

His hand paused on the handle, and Jackson looked at me as my body heated with desire.

"I don't want to push you, Grace."

I bit my lip and pushed the door open, pulling him inside with me. It was such a charge that ran through me, but I needed him.

Jackson smiled as I dropped my hand from his in front of the bed.

"I'd be lying if I didn't tell you that I'd thought about what this moment would be like with you."

I smiled, feeling like I was the luckiest woman alive. The little smirk that surfaced made him even cuter, and I couldn't wait to get him undressed.

I'd seen him enough without his shirt to know that my wildest fantasies were about to come true.

"Jackson, shut up and kiss me," I said, smiling.

He traced his bottom lip with his tongue as heat flitted through his gaze. Jackson took two steps forward and buried his head in the crook of my neck, slowly kissing the bare skin of my shoulders. His hands slowly moved my shirt over my head as he tossed the fabric to the floor.

Jackson smiled, taking a step back. "You're more gorgeous than ever, Grace."

My body responded so strongly with the way he looked at me that I trembled in front of him as I took off my bra and dropped it to the floor.

His gaze ate me up as he let out a low growl and wrapped his arms around me, kissing every square inch of me, cupping my breasts in his large palms, and sucking and teasing until they stood at full attention.

I let out a little moan as his teeth grazed a nipple and his hands slid along my belly until he reached my jeans and then brought his mouth to mine.

The heat of his kiss made me insane with desire to have him inside me. I pulled off his shirt and slid my hands over his gorgeous chest as we traded kisses, inhaling one another and exploring.

Jackson lifted me up, and I wrapped my legs around his waist as he smiled. His hands held my butt tightly as he carried me over to the bed. He laid me down and smiled as his eyes roamed my breasts and belly.

"I can't wait to be inside you," he said as his gaze

darkened with intensity.

"What's taking you so long?" I said, writhing underneath him.

Jackson only flashed a smile in my direction.

He brought his mouth to my stomach and started licking slowly, moving lower until he slid my pants off and buried his head between my legs. I wasn't expecting his mouth to be so warm or generous as his tongue circled and probed in a way that should be illegal. I ran my fingers through his hair as the flicks of his tongue quickened, and my body couldn't take it any longer with every nerve in my body exploding with ecstasy. He kissed me slowly back to earth, but I needed more.

I fumbled with the buttons on his pants as he moved his lips to mine, kicking off his pants in between. My hands slid down his stomach as I felt him between my fingers, so hard and ready.

Jackson kissed along my ear, and my heart sped up with longing. I wanted him so badly. I ached with longing.

He knelt over me, and I was able to see him entirely. His body was so beautiful, it almost hurt to look, and yet it was mine. I ran my fingers over every inch of him, and he smiled at me. "I like this view."

I laughed. "So do I, but I can't wait any longer."

He let out a low growl and smiled. "You sure?"

"But Jackson, I have to warn you," I said breathlessly, feeling the throbbing between my legs starting again.

"Warn me of what, baby?" He brushed my hair away from my cheek.

"I'm a mess."

He kissed behind my ear as his hands slid along my stomach. "You're my kind of mess."

Jackson slid inside me and let out a groan against my breasts as he thrust harder, and I gasped in appreciation. He was so big, and I wanted more and more. Jackson was like my own addiction.

I pumped my hips against him as he pushed into me deeper and deeper, our rhythm building as his lips devoured mine and his hands slid along my breasts.

Opening wider, I felt his body shudder as his tongue circled mine, and my entire body went wild as his beautiful blue eyes stayed on mine. He brought me to the edge once more.

"Jackson, I can't hold on," I whispered as his gaze stayed on mine.

He cupped my hands in his and slid them above my head, caging me in the perfect position as our bodies exploded into uncontrolled passion, and I knew I'd fallen hard for Jackson Locke.

Again.

Chapter Twenty-Eight

Jackson

Last night was the best night of my life. Sex with Grace made winning the Masters Tournament seem like nothing at all. Grace was an achievement, one I wish I could hold onto, but I could tell that she still wouldn't let her heart be mine.

The way her eyes stayed on mine when I felt her clench around me and the tender touch of her fingers trailing along my body as we fell asleep together . . . it was all a dream.

And yet I felt like at any moment, it could all slip away.

Because it could. I could see it in her eyes.

I'd dropped Grace off at Millie's house before heading back to my uncle's. He was rocking back and forth on the porch, looking like he wanted to pounce on me.

"Quite a day trip, huh?" My uncle grinned a little too wide.

"I didn't expect our spark plugs to get stolen, if that's

what you mean."

"So curious." Uncle Carter rocked in his chair, and I scowled.

"How deep is this network?" I asked my uncle.

He moved his gaze to his yard and laughed. "I haven't the faintest idea what you're talking about."

"Of course, you don't." I smiled to myself and walked into Uncle Carter's home.

Just when I managed to step into the shower, I heard my phone buzzing. I stuck my head out from behind the shower curtain and saw that Grace's number was popping up on my screen.

I turned off the shower and hopped out, almost catching her call. Frantically pushing the button to call back, Grace appeared on my screen.

"Well, hello, Jackson." Grace's eyes were wide. "Nice to see all of you again."

I glanced down at my dripping body and back up at the phone when I realized I'd FaceTimed her instead of calling her.

"I was in the shower."

"Clearly." She grinned, seeming so much lighter than yesterday. "I got a call back from Tracy."

"Yeah?"

She nodded.

"And?" I prompted.

"You free this evening?"

I grinned, nodding. "Absolutely. Anything for you."

"Pancake, no." She tossed the phone, and all I could see was Grace running with the puppy to the door before a pillow fell on the screen. "Izzy, get some towels."

I chuckled and shook my head, wishing I were there with them.

Did I just think that?

I let out a deep sigh and thought about the contracts I'd just signed. I had to leave the first week of August.

Damn it.

The phone turned to darkness, so I finished drying off.

I had to tell Grace about what was coming up. I would still be able to go out to Seattle with her to see her parents. But after that, we'd have to say our goodbyes, promise to keep in touch, and hope for the best.

One thing at a time. I had to shake myself out of the dread building deep inside. I never should have slept with her.

My first goal was to support her, and right now, she needed someone to go with her to visit Tracy. I needed to get her out of my head.

I did take consolation in the fact that she seemed a little

lighter during the phone call than before, but what was I expecting? Grace lost her husband, and I couldn't be trusted to take care of her without thinking about consuming her again.

I shook my head and pulled on some clothes. Things had to change. I needed to do a better job of protecting her, shielding her from what she was so worried about.

Betrayal.

Sleeping together definitely complicated things, but I could get my head out of the sand.

The thought of being stood up all those years ago snuck into my mind. She had such a different take on what happened that night. It didn't make sense.

But neither did bringing it up again.

I was about to go on tour.

My job with her was clear—make sure before I leave Buttercup Lake that Izzy and her mom were completely settled into this town and whatever was lingering out there from Tim was solved.

Because the truth of it was that there was no better place for those two than this town. Even if there was a meddling book club. Maybe they'd play Cupid for her again.

The thought put a sharp pain in my chest.

Grace called again, and I picked up immediately. "Okay,

looks like Tracy is going to be able to meet me early. Do you mind picking me up now?"

"Not at all. I'll be there in ten."

"Thanks, Jackson. I just . . ." She paused for a minute. "I just don't think I could face this alone."

"Anything for you, Grace."

She ended the call, and I grabbed my wallet and keys before heading back to the truck.

"Busy day, huh?" Uncle Carter was in the same place I'd left him last.

"Need anything while I'm out? I probably won't be back until later."

My uncle shook his head. "Nah. I got what I need."

I gave a quick wave and climbed into my truck that started right up with a new pair of spark plugs.

By the time I arrived at Millie's house, Grace was already on the porch. She was dressed in a pair of capri pants and a red striped top. Her wet hair was spun into a bun.

She walked to the truck and climbed in.

"You look fabulous," I told her.

Her smile widened, but I saw a glint of sadness behind her gaze. Maybe I was wrong about her sounding marginally lighter on the phone earlier.

"So do you, but I'm sure I don't have to tell you that."

I chuckled and shook my head. "No, actually, it's kind of nice to hear it."

She buckled her seat belt, and I watched her. "You doing okay?"

"Not sure. Tracy wouldn't tell me anything over the phone."

"Are we meeting at that property?"

Grace nodded and tensed. "Yup, that was the plan."

"Did you get any clues about what's going on?"

"No." She looked out the window after handing me the paperwork with the address on it. I plugged it into the map on my phone.

"Off we go," I said, pulling out of the driveway.

"I don't have a good feeling about this." She turned to glance at me. "Right when I got off the phone with Tracy, I started to feel a little more settled, but I realized that was only because I'd finally talked to the person named Tracy."

I nodded, taking a left away from town. After seeing a few smaller farms, the phone indicated that the destination was ahead.

"It's an empty field." I glanced at Grace, who was completely expressionless. "With someone's pickup truck parked in the middle."

I pulled onto the side of the road and turned off the truck.

"Tracy was going to meet us?"

Grace nodded, resting her hand on the door handle.

The passenger door to the pickup pushed open, and a young man slid out and started making his way toward us.

"Should I be worried?" I asked.

Grace shook her head. "That's Tracy."

"Tracy is a man?" I tried to hide my shock.

"More like a teenage boy," she said, turning to look at me.

I shook my head, not following.

"Do you want me to stay in the car while you talk to him, or . . .?"

"No. I'd like you with me."

I gave a quick nod as Grace opened her door and got out of the truck just as Tracy walked up to her. She shielded her eyes from the sun as I made my way around the hood to them both.

"Tracy, this is Jackson."

Tracy smiled and nodded. "Jackson Locke. I know who you are."

"Nice to meet you," I told the young man.

There was something eerily familiar about him. I shooed the thought away as he grinned.

It was awkward between us, but I didn't think it was the

best idea to start trying to break the ice since I was completely in the dark.

Grace smiled and reached behind her to the seat of the truck, grabbing the papers she'd received from the bank.

"So, I'm really sorry about calling out of the blue," Grace said softly. "But I'm really at a loss. My husband passed away about a year and a half ago, and when I was going through his things, I found an envelope with a key, the name Tracy, and *Buttercup Lake* scrawled on it. I was able to figure out that the key belonged to a safety deposit box down in Chicago, and it had this in it."

Tracy's eyes slid over the documents, but he didn't bother looking. "Yeah."

"So, you know about this?" Grace shifted her weight from one foot to the other. "Or maybe you can explain."

The longer I stared at Tracy, the more I realized this kid couldn't be over sixteen.

And he did look familiar.

Too familiar.

"Tim Henry." The boy's gaze darkened before he glanced away. "My sperm donor."

Grace reached for me. It was as if the air surrounding us had ignited. She wheezed and dropped her gaze to the soil.

Her hand was trembling in mine, and I knew I needed to

step in.

"Sperm donor, as in your mom used a sperm bank?" I tried.

Tracy smirked and shook his head. "If that's what you think Camp Buttercup is."

"But . . ." I shook my head, trying to put the pieces together. "How old are you?"

"Nearly seventeen," he answered. "Tim knocked up my mom on his last summer of camp. He told her they were meant to be together, the works, and here I am."

And a year later, he knocked up Grace and they got married. Never a word.

Grace looked like she was about to pass out.

"Did he know that your mom was pregnant?" Grace managed to ask.

"Yeah. He knew. Didn't care," he said, trying to shrug off the sadness that I detected threading through his gaze. "Anyway, my mom told me a few years ago that the sperm donor bought me some property and put it in a trust for me. It infuriated my stepdad. Some city dude, trying to buy forgiveness."

I nodded. "I can understand that."

"The whole thing was posturing more than anything." He shrugged. "Maybe he felt guilty or something. I heard he had a wife, and I guess I heard right."

Grace shook her head with her lips parting, but she couldn't say anything.

"I don't want it." Tracy looked at Grace. "I don't want anything to do with it. I don't want to keep it. I don't want to sell it. I just don't want anything to do with it."

Grace handed him the papers, but I think we could all safely assume he already had them.

"It's yours. It's rightfully yours," Grace said softly. "Maybe get something out of Tim."

I knew she meant it. As the world she knew crumbled around her, she still wanted to make things right.

Tracy's jaw clenched briefly. "My mom was ruined for years by him. She had a string of horrible relationships until she finally met my stepdad. The man who is really my dad."

The hurt in this kid's voice was palpable.

"And then my mom goes and dies." The teenager's gaze lifted to mine. "So, I really mean it when I say that I don't want anything to do with it."

Grace nodded. "I'm just so sorry. I had no idea."

The kid nodded. "That doesn't surprise me. From what my mom told me, the dude was a master manipulator."

All Grace could do was nod while tears edged her eyes. She turned around and reached into her purse and scribbled something down on a piece of scrap paper.

"If there's ever anything you need, please call me. I know you don't know me, and you probably hate anything to do with us."

"Us?" Tracy's brows rose.

Grace nodded. "I have a daughter."

"I have a half-sister?" The look in Tracy's eyes was nothing short of fury. "I specifically asked Tim if he had any children when he dropped this crap off." He waved the papers.

Grace looked like she was going to be sick.

"I'm so sorry," she muttered.

Tracy shook his head. "It was nice of you to track me down all the way from Chicago."

Grace pointed in the direction of the lake. "I'm staying here for the summer. I'm just so sorry this didn't turn out how I'd hoped."

I knew she meant that on many levels.

Tracy nodded. "I suppose I ought to donate the land or something."

"In honor of your mother," Grace said softly. "That might wipe away everything else."

Tracy smiled, and his eyes stayed on Grace. "Yeah. Maybe that's what I will do."

Grace nodded and looked like she was ready to go. "One

more thing, if you don't mind."

"Sure." He eyed her.

"Why a piece of land, do you think?" she asked.

"That's easy. He knew I wanted to be a farmer like my real dad, so he must have thought this was the way to do it." Tracy shook his head. "But I'll be working the land that's been on my dad's side for generations." He pointed behind him. "This isn't even good farming land. We're surrounded by it, but this isn't it."

"So, how did Tim know that? Were you in contact?"

He shook his head. "No, but I think my grandparents tried to keep in touch."

"It was nice meeting you, Tracy. And I'm so sorry to hear about your mom and to dig this all up again. I just had no idea."

"Not a problem." He held up the piece of paper. "And thanks for your number. I'm an only child, so . . ."

Grace nodded and climbed into the truck as the teenager walked back to his truck parked in the middle of the field.

When I closed the door on my side of the truck, Grace let out a muffled hiccup.

"I don't know what's worse. That I let my mind believe that maybe Tim had bought something for our retirement or maybe even a place where I could live out my dream, or that my husband completely ignored the fact that he was a father to a boy barely older than Grace." She glanced at me, dabbing the tears from her cheeks. "Or the lies? What am I supposed to be angrier with?"

"I'm as stunned as you are, Grace." I turned on the truck and pulled away as the kid leaned against his truck and looked toward the sky. Apart from the anger, the kid seemed to really have a good feel for the situation. It was hard not to see Tim through his eyes.

What I couldn't fathom was this version of Tim. Back in the day, he'd never seemed to be into girls and always ribbed me for being so head over heels for Grace, which meant he had to have been sneaking around with Tracy's mom in secret. But why? We were a bunch of boys. That's what we did. I glanced at Grace. It didn't matter. None of it mattered.

She'd been lied to by a man she was supposed to trust.

"He must have been embarrassed about what he did back at camp. I'm sure this doesn't mean he was unfaithful during your marriage. This all happened before you got together."

"You don't have to stick up for him." Her tone flattened. "He's dead, and he didn't do you any favors."

"No, he didn't."

"What am I supposed to tell Izzy? She needs to know she has a half-brother." She held her head and closed her eyes.

"What else was a lie?"

I looked over at Grace and could feel the pain rolling off her, and I knew there was nothing I could say to make the situation better.

Chapter Twenty-Nine

Grace

Jackson had texted a few times, dropped off a couple of dinners for Izzy and me, and drove by super slow when I happened to be on the porch. It was nice to be thought of, but I was also thrilled to have our new addition, Pancake, join the family. She kept me just occupied enough to not wallow all the time.

I just didn't feel like talking much. I didn't know what to say. I felt like a fool. I felt dirty and like I was part of something I could have prevented. I wouldn't have allowed Tim to do what he did.

The man should have been part of his kid's life, and I didn't mean just a baseball game here or there or a weekend in the city now and again, but truly be there for Tracy like he had been for Izzy.

Show some sort of interest.

It made me completely suspicious of all his other actions. Was he only nice to Izzy because she was right in front of him? The thought pained me. I couldn't go there. Izzy deserved better, and so did Tracy.

The knot in my stomach tightened as the same thoughts spun through me on repeat.

I hadn't mentioned anything to Izzy yet, and the camping trip was coming up this weekend. We were headed out tomorrow.

I'd probably wait until after the Fourth of July. She'd be gearing up for camp counselor training, and hopefully, her focus would be all about CPR and Caleb. Maybe it would roll right off her.

Even when I sat in the dead-as-a-doornail truck in the middle of the bank's parking lot, I stupidly held out hope that I'd roll up to the property and it was some warehouse ready for my dream of an antique store and that the person named Tracy was just the executor or trustee.

Delusions were tricky. They could save a person's sanity until they ruined it.

I glanced around Millie's garden and sprinkled some of the plants with the hose. I vowed to get the hang of it before Millie and her boyfriend popped over to see the leaves wilted.

It was nice out here. I could see why people spent time staring at plants. They didn't do much, and it forced a person to think about things.

Except I didn't like what I kept thinking about.

Betrayal. I felt so betrayed.

How could we have been married for so long, and never once was he compelled to tell me the truth?

It made the idea of trusting someone near impossible. What was I going to have to do? Run a background check? Hire a PI before the first date? That was what was nice about Jackson. He was an open book. He always had been.

I didn't feel like I had to worry with Jackson. If something came up, he'd tell me. He wasn't busy leading a million lives and balancing different realities. There was one reality, and right now, that focused on his uncle.

Without warning, the images of Jackson holding himself over my body as he kissed parts of me that I forgot about crashed into me. Finding out what I did about Tim certainly made me feel less guilty.

No, that wasn't true. I was still a mess inside.

But when I was in Jackson's arms, I felt like less of a mess. It didn't suddenly feel like the eye of the storm was threatening my sanity. I could trust him to tell me everything.

He was my safe place, and there was a secret part of me

that prayed he'd decide to stay in town beyond the summer. But we didn't talk much about the future.

I knew he was trying to balance my feelings with his and our past and on and on. But now, with everything I know about my marriage, I didn't even understand what I could give Jackson.

Trust was going to be tough, and he was on the road all the time.

I let out a groan. I was definitely getting ahead of myself.

I still needed to deal with the recent revelations about Tim.

And by the way, if he was busy having sex with someone at the camp, why did he take a sudden interest in me?

None of it made sense.

The sound of a waterfall caught my attention when I realized I'd been spraying the same raised bed for minutes, and the water was now overflowing. I grimaced and shook my head, hoping it would dry out before the plants all died. But maybe too much water wasn't so bad in the plant world.

I heard the crunch of tires on the gravel behind me when I turned around to see Grandma Millie pull into the driveway. She gave a quick wave and hopped out of her car like she was fifty. It only took her a millisecond to realize I'd flooded her garden before she dashed over to the faucet and turned it off.

"I think the plants have enough water, dear." She shook her head and made her way over to me as I was closing the gate to keep the deer out of her garden.

I smiled, but she saw through it.

"Oh, the news has you down about Jackson?" She squeezed my arm and looped hers through mine, and I froze.

"News about Jackson? Is he okay?" I reached for my phone out of my back pocket to see when the last text came in from him.

She looked at me oddly. "Of course, he's okay."

"Then what are you talking about? What news?"

My grandma unlooped her arm from mine and shook her head. "Oh, nothing. I'm sure I don't know what I'm talking about."

"Grandma Millie, if there's one thing that's always true, it's that you know what you're talking about."

My grandma looked truly guilty. "It's not my place to say anything. I assumed since you two had gotten so close that he would have told you."

"I've been through a lot the last couple of days. Would you just tell me?"

Grandma Millie frowned. "Back up. What are you talking about?"

I'd been dreading this moment, but I didn't expect it to

occur when I was still waiting to hear news about Jackson. Suddenly, whatever I wanted to tell her about Tim didn't matter. She knew I was headed to Chicago to take care of personal stuff, but I hadn't given her a hint about any of it.

"This sounds like a conversation for the porch." She smiled at me and rubbed my back. "Come on."

With every step toward the porch, anxiety raced through me. What would my grandma think about me? About my marriage? How could I have not known?

I took a seat on the rocking chair and was grateful that Izzy was at the lake with Bonnie and Caleb.

"You know how I went to Chicago?"

Grandma Millie lit up. "I do."

That reaction would be a conversation for another moment.

"I went there because I had found an envelope with just a first name, this town, and a key inside."

"Okay."

"It was in Tim's drawer, shoved in the back. I brought it with me thinking that it was a key to something here in Buttercup Lake. The ridiculous part of me thought that maybe he even found a place where I could—"

"Open your antique store," she finished.

I nodded, feeling even more ridiculous for confirming it.

"But I didn't understand who Tracy was. I'd even asked around town, and that's the one name we don't seem to have here."

Grandma Millie nodded, looking concerned.

"And I'd let my mind conjure up all kinds of scenarios for who Tracy is, and then Jackson would talk me off the ledge."

My grandma moved a damp piece of hair from my cheek. "And is it as bad as you thought?"

Grandma Millie's voice was so tender, and it threw me right back to when I was a teenager and she would comfort me over a big bowl of ice cream. It didn't matter if it was drama regarding my parents or some silly fight I'd had with Jackson, she'd always listened.

The tears came rushing from nowhere as I nodded and sniffled and turned into a complete mess. I went to speak, but I snorted instead, and Grandma Millie brought me into her slight frame as our rockers turned to face one another.

She didn't press me.

She didn't rush me.

She waited.

When I could finally breathe again without hiccups and snot, I straightened and rubbed my face with my shirt.

"Tim fathered a son when he was a teenager, the same

summer he asked me out." I shook my head. "And then the year after, he got me pregnant, and we got married, and never a mention of the other girl or his son."

Not much stunned Grandma Millie.

But this did.

She opened and shut her mouth several times before landing on a few choice words.

"That's how I've felt." My breath caught in my throat. "Along with betrayal and hurt and anger. I don't know how I'm ever supposed to trust a man again. You don't just hide a child from someone. How could he turn his back on his own son?" All the questions I'd been running over and over again came rushing out.

"Have you told Izzy?"

I shook my head. "I was going to wait until after the holiday."

"Why?"

I shook my head. "I don't know. Maybe for selfish reasons or because I don't want to ruin this weekend for her? All excuses."

My grandma took my hands in hers and held them tightly. "You deserve the truth. You deserve to be happy."

I nodded.

"But you can't keep this stuff inside, Grace. It's not

healthy. I can't believe you didn't tell me." She shook her head. "I never would have sent Mandy down to Chicago had I known."

My gaze flashed to my grandma's. "You're kidding."

Grandma Millie pushed her lips into a fine line. "Sometimes, I get carried away and forget that life isn't all fun and games even if I want it to be."

"Well, I don't hate the fact that I had to stay overnight with Jackson."

Grandma's brows rose. "Oh, yeah. Why's that?"

I chuckled and shook my head. "Ever since I've known you, you've seemed so carefree and without a worry. Were you just born like that?"

Grandma Millie laughed. "Oh, heavens no. It took time to master, and there are many moments in a day when I remember that I've failed heavily."

Her words rocked me to my core. "Failed?"

"My son," she said softly.

"Grandma, that's not your fault."

She nodded slowly. "But I spent a solid twenty years thinking it wasn't my right to be happy. That if I dared to smile in a town this small, people would wonder why I had a heart of stone when my own son couldn't even walk a straight line."

I was quickly trying to do the math in my head, and it all

led back to my dad being a teenager when the problems started, the addiction.

"My dad had problems when he was a teen?"

Grandma Millie nodded. "He did. When he replaced the contents of our old liquor bottles with colored water, we realized there was an issue. We didn't drink, so we didn't think much about having the old collector's bottles around."

"I had no idea."

"He was fourteen." The pain in her eyes made my stomach churn. "We got rid of all the liquor immediately. At least, what was left, but he'd already been caught for stealing it from the store."

"He was so young."

"He was." She shook her head. "And by the time he was sixteen, booze wasn't enough. We'd tried getting him into treatment, which isn't easy with someone under eighteen, and the moment he came home, he'd start again."

I listened to the ache in my Grandma's voice, and this time, I held her hands.

She let out a deep breath. "Until he just stopped coming home."

I shook my head, realizing how little I knew about my dad's history.

"We scooped him up from the streets of Milwaukee a few

times, but he got better at hiding once he turned eighteen." She smiled. "When he met your mother, I thought things were headed in the right direction. She wasn't a user. Not at first."

I tried to imagine my parents as teens, but it didn't work.

"But eventually, she succumbed to his lifestyle." She shook her head. "Until she got pregnant with your sister Nina. Then they tried to shake the hard stuff."

I nodded, knowing what she meant. By the time I was born, they basically kept a steady liquid diet up with the occasional slip-up. It was something I wouldn't wish on my worst enemy.

"I know you want to visit your mom, and I have their contact information and where they're located now. It's a tent city operated by a church, so as long as you go in the next month or so, it sounded like they'd both be there."

I didn't know what to say. Talking about seeing my mom in a vague and abstract form was one thing. Actually getting the nerve to go do it was quite another.

"So, you ask if I was born this happy?" She smiled. "I was born this happy, but I had to fight like hell to stay this happy." She smiled and glanced toward the driveway as Bonnie dropped Izzy off. "And I suggest you do the same."

Izzy marched to the porch and looked horrified. "My gosh, are you this upset over the thing with Jackson?"

I tore my gaze from my grandma's and shook my head. "Would someone please tell me what's going on with Jackson?"

Chapter Thirty

Jackson

I was pretty confident all caps on a text message didn't lead to good things. I'd loaded up the truck with camping gear for tomorrow when the first round of texts from Grace landed on my phone.

Dang it!

I messed up. My eyes scanned the first text.

WERE YOU PLANNING ON TELLING ME?

And then the next.

DID YOU KNOW BEFORE WE SLEPT TOGETHER?

And then the next.

YOU DON'T HAVE TO BOTHER COMING ON THE CAMPING TRIP WITH US.

The last one stung. I leaned against the truck and chewed on my bottom lip while trying to figure out what to write.

I'm sorry?

"No," I muttered, realizing the damage I'd done. "Won't cut it."

"What won't cut it?" Uncle Carter wandered to the truck and looked in the bed, "Looks like you're all set to me."

"I'm not going." I glanced at my uncle. "I've been uninvited."

He scowled. "What did you do this time?"

"What do you mean *this time*?" My brow arched.

Uncle Carter waited for my reply.

"I signed that deal, which was contingent on getting back out on tour in August."

"Right. So, what's the problem?" Uncle Carter slowly folded his arms over his chest.

"I didn't tell Grace yet, and she somehow found out."

He shook his head. "Why didn't you just tell her? Of course, she found out. All a person has to do is look online and see the headline."

"She was going through a lot. I didn't want to add that to

the pile." I shrugged. "I obviously made the wrong choice."

"Men nowadays make things so damn complicated."

"I was trying to protect her," I explained.

Uncle Carter let out a howl. "You were trying to protect her? From what? Life has already handed her more mountains to climb than most. I think her tender little heart could handle your going on tour again."

I knew he was right, but I straightened and stared at him.

"It's not just about my going on tour again. It isn't like I'd be coming back to Buttercup Lake, and by all accounts, I think Grace and Izzy are planning on staying."

"What's wrong with sticking around here between whacking a ball now and again?"

There was no doubt that my family kept me humble.

"Nothing is wrong with it, but I only came here for the summer to decompress and help you out."

"I don't need any help and haven't for a week or two," he grumbled.

"I know." I nodded and thought about how angry I'd made Grace, and I wasn't sure I'd be able to fix it.

The thought killed me.

"I need to go talk to Grace." I glanced at the two tents and camping gear piled in the back. "And at least convince her to borrow everything. She doesn't have time to go buy it all."

Uncle Carter nodded and patted my bicep as more texts came over. "Good luck. It sounds like you'll need it."

I glanced at my phone. "Pray for me."

Uncle Carter waved and wandered toward his house as I climbed in the truck and pulled out of the drive. I stuck to the speed limit because I really didn't want to deal with Nate right now.

Running different apology scenarios through my head only made me more anxious. I'd really screwed up. She'd just found out that her husband kept things from her, and I did the same thing while not on the same scale.

Uncle Carter was right. I didn't need to protect Grace Henry.

I pulled into the drive, and a row of four women stared at me from the porch. None of them looked thrilled to see me. Even Pancake gave me the hairy eyeball as she sat on Grace's lap.

The one thing I learned as a member of the PGA is to never let them see you sweat, and I fully intended on sticking to that.

Getting out of the truck, I stood for a second and took a deep breath.

"Here goes nothing," I muttered, noticing no movement

from the porch.

When I made it to the house, I smiled at Grandma Millie.

She didn't smile back.

"I guess this means I don't get free lemonade any longer?"

Izzy's lip twitched, but Grandma Millie stood tall. I glanced at Grace, who looked like she'd been crying all afternoon, and my gut twisted into a million knots.

I did that to her. The thought killed me. I looked at Grace's red nose and tear-stained cheeks and felt like a complete jerk.

"Grace, I'm sorry." I waited for her to bring her gaze to mine.

She didn't.

Instead, she folded her arms across her chest and stared at the ground. Pancake kept her eyes on me, though.

Grandma Millie moved to Izzy and tapped her shoulder. "We should give them some privacy."

Grace snuck a look in my direction, and I kept in a chuckle, knowing what she was thinking.

There might be the illusion of privacy, but there certainly would be prying ears.

When the storm door smacked shut, I climbed a step and leaned on the porch post.

"Grace, I should have told you."

She raised her head, and her eyes met mine. "Yeah. You should have."

"You were going through so much, and it felt like I'd just add to your problems."

"Instead, you slept with me and decided to worry about it later." She pressed her lips together. "And then I get to hear from my grandma and daughter that you're headed back to work in less than three weeks."

"I made it so I'd still be able to come to Seattle with you when Izzy is at camp."

She shook her head. "No, thank you. I'm fine. We're fine."

Pancake lifted her lip at me, and I scowled back at her, so she put her head on Grace's knee.

I took another step up and knelt in front of Grace. "Grace, my intentions weren't meant to hurt you."

"But they did." Grace sucked in a breath. "I just want to be able to trust someone. Is that too much to ask? To have someone tell me everything that's going on in their life. That's not unreasonable."

I shook my head. "Not unreasonable at all, and I should have said something."

"You felt like the one person who'd always tell me like

it is."

"And I always have."

She shook her head. "Until keeping something from me worked in your favor."

"My favor?" I was shocked.

"You got what you wanted from me, and then you're going off on tour again."

She patted Pancake without looking at me.

"Never in a million years did I expect to sleep with you, but we got so wrapped up in each other that night . . . And yeah, I guess I should have stopped to tell you, but I couldn't." I glanced around the house, praying the windows were shut. "I needed you, Grace. And I know that complicates everything."

"It doesn't complicate anything." She brought her gaze to mine. "I learned my lesson."

I stood and shook my head. "Grace, I can't stop thinking about you. When I'm with you, I wonder what the point of golf is. I imagine what it's like to have a family. You make me realize that there's so much more in life."

"I'm glad I provided clarity for you, Jackson." She lifted Pancake up to her chest and nuzzled the puppy. "While you go about living your dreams, I will stay here and try to figure out what mine are."

Even though she intended to sound strong and angry, I heard a quaver in her voice.

"Grace, you already know what your dreams are. It's up to you to be brave enough to go for them."

Her gaze whipped to mine. "Do you have any idea how much pressure I have on me? Izzy is my responsibility. I can't just sink all our savings into something I hope will work out. Life isn't just exotic destinations and golf courses, Jackson. Some of us have real problems that need real solutions."

"And I want to be there for you. I want to help. I want to protect you." The moment I said the words aloud, fury filled Grace's gaze.

"Protect me?"

I nodded. "That's why I didn't tell you I was leaving right away."

She stood with Pancake. "Is that what Tim was doing too? Protecting me? Didn't want me to know he'd fathered another child while I was pregnant with mine?"

I let out a sigh, wishing I'd just told her the moment the ink had dried. "I realize now how stupid I was, but it's too late. You don't need protecting. I get it. You're strong."

"It's not about being strong, Jackson. I'm allowed to be weak, but I don't need to be sheltered or treated like I can't handle things." She shook her head. "What Tim did to me destroyed his credibility, even the credibility of our marriage. Not because he slept with someone before me. Not because he had a child. But because Tim didn't tell me any of it. He didn't trust my reaction to the news. Just like you obviously didn't either."

This summer had been perfect. Seeing Grace legs out, bicycle out of control, and zipping right by me made me feel like the luckiest man in the world. I had a second chance, and I blew it.

"Grace, please let me come with you to Seattle. I don't want you to go there alone."

"I still need protection?" Her brows rose sharply, and Pancake looked unimpressed.

"No. You don't need protection, but maybe a shoulder to lean on."

She shook her head. "No. I need to continue to count on myself."

I nodded, seeing her jaw clench. "I didn't mean to make you cry."

Her gaze met mine. "You didn't. These tears were about my parents and my late husband."

"Oh." I glanced toward the truck and then back at her. "So, not even one tear?"

Her lip curled slightly but dropped instantly. "Jackson,

there's a lot of history between us. You and I both know it. So I'm sure on some level, you're a little gleeful to find out that Tim was a jerk."

Her words stabbed me in the gut. I never thought that at all.

I shook my head. "Then you don't know me as well as I thought you did, Grace. Was I happy I lost the only girl I ever loved to my best friend? Hell, no. Was I angry? Yeah. But I created a life for myself and accepted it. And Izzy is worth my heartache. She was meant to be here." I let out a deep breath. "I'm just sorry I screwed it up by misjudging."

Grace nodded, and I finally saw a couple of tears, but I knew it was too late. I'd already screwed up my chances.

Chapter Thirty-One

Grace

The camping trip was exactly what I needed. Izzy's laughter drifted over from the campfire as Caleb hit together two sticks, trying to impress her with his singing skills. He was a likable kid, charming, cute, and charismatic.

Izzy had good taste in men.

Bonnie handed me a soda and sat in the lawn chair beside me while Pancake stayed securely snuggled on my knees.

Bonnie's husband Danny dashed off to the convenience store about ten miles away because the hot dog buns had been forgotten.

"How's everything going with Izzy and her first job?" Bonnie asked.

"She loves it." I smiled and rested my head on the chair. "But it just highlights once more that she's growing up."

Bonnie pointed at the teens and nodded. "This solidified

it for me."

I thought back to Jackson and me. We were inseparable. Summer after summer, we'd meet up and never part until we both had to leave camp. After camp, I'd lie on the kitchen floor with my feet propped up on the wall and the cord wrapping around my wrist as I talked endlessly on the phone with him. That was the only positive of having parents who were so checked out. They never told me to get off the phone.

Meeting Jackson felt meant to be, like he was my stable force in life, and then he never showed.

But Tim did.

In hindsight, Tim took delight in talking trash about Jackson. It always made me feel uncomfortable, but I was also pretty hurt.

"Does he like the school here?" I asked Bonnie.

Before we left, I'd scheduled a time to see a rental with a realtor. I really liked it. The house wasn't too big to manage but big enough to fit everything we had. Izzy would have her own room, and we'd even have an extra bedroom.

"Caleb loves it. Yeah. He's pretty much a social butterfly."

I laughed. "Yeah. I gathered that. I think Izzy needed that. She got sucked into some friends back in Chicago who weren't really friends."

"Well, here you get friends for life whether you want them or not."

I chuckled and nodded.

"Not to pry, but I'd be lying if I pretended that I wasn't fascinated . . ."

I took a sip of the soda. "About what?"

Her eyes lit up. "You and Jackson."

My expression fell.

"Oh, that doesn't look good."

I chuckled and shook my head. "No, there's no us. I'm not ready, and he has no intention of staying here. He's at the top of his career. It's just not the right timing."

"Oh, man." Bonnie shook her head. "We were all rooting for you. Even his cousin was dreaming up ways to get you two together."

"You mean Daisy?"

She nodded.

"I knew the book club was into some serious shenanigans, but I didn't think his cousin was in on it too."

"Oh, yeah. And she's part of the book club. She joined last week but told us she might not be coming to every meeting since she works late."

"Oh." I nodded. "That makes sense."

"I guess she'll be taking over a lot of what Jackson was

doing for Uncle Carter." She shrugged. "Not the handyman stuff, but just the errands and whatever."

"That's sweet of her." My tummy tightened, thinking about Jackson.

"Well, shoot. The other ladies are going to be really disappointed to hear that. It was so romantic. Young love, and then you meet again." She touched her heart. "I guess I just have to read about it."

I grinned. "Maybe that's the ticket. I'll just find my man in a sea of beautiful words."

That way, he won't lie by omission.

"Well, I thought something was up when he didn't come. Abby had told Mandy, who told me, that Uncle Carter had told her how he wouldn't stop talking about going on this camping trip. It didn't sound like he'd miss it for the world." She glanced around the trees and tents. "And I don't think our camping trip is all that special. It had to have been you."

My stomach clenched into a spiral of knots. Hearing that Jackson had been talking about looking forward to this trip made me sad.

Like really sad.

Maybe I'd misjudged Jackson. Perhaps he really had been trying to protect me.

He was right about that night we'd had sex. We'd gotten

pretty hot and heavy by the time we entered the hotel room. I really can't think of a moment where he would have been able to stop and relay that kind of news. I probably would have kissed his mouth shut.

I smiled at the thought and blushed, looking around, grateful that no one was watching me.

Maybe Danny didn't really go to get hot dog buns. What if he was just going to meet Jackson and bring him back to our campsite?

I sat up in the chair, kind of liking that idea.

No, that was utterly delusional. I shook my head and heard a truck's wheels touch gravel. My heart pounded as I glanced up to see the truck pulling next to the tents and completely plummeted when I realized I'd let crazy take over again.

Just like the silly idea that Tim had somehow put a building in a trust for me to open an antique store with.

Yeah, right.

I smiled and waved as Danny brought a bag full of more chips, hot dog buns, and some beer.

Caleb pulled out the chips and took them over to Izzy, who happily crunched on them while admiring Caleb.

My mind drifted back to Tim and the surprise he'd left me, and the one thing that bothered me the most was that he put me on the account. He didn't have enough guts to tell me about his son when he was alive, but why did Tim want me to know now? For what? For Izzy? I shook my head in annoyance, and Bonnie glanced at me.

"You okay?" she asked.

I smiled and nodded. "Yeah. Sorry. But this is probably why Jackson and I aren't together. I'm just not ready for that next step. I'm too busy enjoying conversations inside my head."

Bonnie chuckled, but she gave me a warm smile. "Give yourself time, Grace, and I'll gently guide the book club away from you and toward its next victim."

I laughed and nodded. "That might be a good idea. The crazy thing is that I kind of miss the guy."

Danny turned around. "Who?"

I laughed. "Oh, just Jackson Locke. We went out years ago before I got married, and I ran into him here in town." I eyed Bonnie. "Over and over again."

Danny laughed and shook his head. "He's pretty popular with the ladies."

Bonnie tried to kick him, but she missed and kicked dirt into the campfire instead.

"Er, I mean. So, I wouldn't know, really."

I chuckled. "We're not dating, so you're free to spill the

beans."

"He's rich, successful, and good at sports." He shrugged. "I just assumed."

Bonnie eyed her husband. "Tell us what you've heard."

Danny grabbed a beer and popped it open. "Well, he was getting some cheese curds down at the tavern."

Bonnie interrupted. "Which tavern? There are several around Buttercup Lake."

"The one that has the best cheese curds."

Bonnie nodded. "The Umbrella Tavern."

Not that the name told me anything.

"Anyway, I guess he was having a great old time there. He was getting his neck massaged by the ladies, and one woman wanted him to sign her boob. She wanted it tattooed."

I saw Danny's mouth moving, but just a blurry field of flames in his place.

Mr. Jackson Locke.

The guy who just wasn't interested in women much.

Too focused on his career.

I brought my focus back to Danny, turning him back into a man. "When was this?"

He frowned. "Ah, I think just a couple of weeks ago? Maybe?"

"Interesting." I nodded, sitting back in the chair. "Really,

really interesting."

Izzy came over to take Pancake for a walk. "What's interesting?"

"Apparently, Jackson loves cheese curds."

Izzy chuckled. "Who doesn't?"

I smiled and watched Izzy and Pancake trundle down the trail with Caleb, and against all my strength, I wondered what Jackson Locke was doing.

I shouldn't care. I should be even madder now, hearing that Jackson was out at taverns doing the one thing he swore he never encountered in between rocking my world. Signing women's boobs.

Chuckling to myself, I took another sip of my soda and let out a deep breath.

Things were going to be okay, but I needed to tell Izzy about her dad and the half-brother she never knew she had.

"Hey, Izzy. Do you mind if I tag along?"

She spun around, let go of Caleb's hand, and waved me over. When I got there, Bonnie was waving Caleb back to camp, and the teens shrugged as he took off.

"I guess it's just you and me," I told Izzy.

She didn't look disappointed, which was a nice change over the last couple of months.

We wandered deeper into the woods that edged along a

slow-moving river. "I wanted to tell you something I just found out, Izzy."

She slowed and picked up Pancake. "Should I be sitting?"

I glanced at a couple of fallen logs and nodded. "Actually, it might not be a bad idea."

Izzy took a seat, and I sat next to her. She was busy scratching Pancake's back as I tried to think of a way to present this bit of news.

"What's up?" she asked, studying me. "I know you're not into Jackson any longer."

I sighed. "Well, I'm still into him, but it's not the best idea right now."

"Why's that?" She cocked her head.

"I'm going through a little something. There are some trust issues."

Izzy scowled. "If it's about Jackson in a bar getting rubbed down by some lady, it's not true. Well, some lady was trying to massage his shoulders, but it was to get back at her boyfriend, who happened to be the bartender."

"What?" I shook my head. "How do you know all this?"

"I work at the coffee shop. I hear things. Anyway, I guess she wanted Jackson to sign her boob or something. She was totally wasted and tried to pull it out, but he told her to wait on that idea for a while. It sounded like she was a mess."

"And who told you?"

"The bartender. He was mortified," Izzy revealed. "It's weird. Abby is like half barista and half therapist. You'd be amazed at what people come in there and tell us."

"Wow. Okay." I nodded, feeling slightly less irked about Jackson.

Maybe I didn't need to send him nasty texts about that too.

"Thanks for telling me about that."

She nodded. "It didn't sound right when Danny was talking about it."

I shook my head. "No, it didn't. But it really shows you how sideways a story can go."

Izzy nodded. "So, what did you want to tell me?"

"Well, Izzy . . ." I bit my lip and thought about just saying it all at once or going slow. "Remember when I went to Chicago?"

She grinned. "And you wound up staying the night with Jackson."

I groaned. "I'm glad that's the message you got from that trip."

Great. This was why raising teenagers was such a delicate balance.

"What about it?"

"I went down there because your father had left me a key to a safe deposit box."

"Was it filled with cash?" she asked. "Or stolen jewels?"

I laughed and shook my head. "What kinds of books are you reading?"

"Good ones."

I smiled and patted Pancake, who was fast asleep on Izzy's lap.

"What I found led me to learn something I didn't know about your dad. He'd never mentioned anything about this, and I want you to know that."

"You're kind of freaking me out."

I shook my head. "Sorry. I'm not trying to do that." I let out a deep breath. "It turns out your father got someone pregnant right before he asked me out. He has a son."

Izzy's eyes widened. "What?"

"You have a half-brother. His name is Tracy. He lives a few towns over."

"Why?" Izzy shook her head. "Why didn't Dad tell us?"

I thought back to Jackson. "Maybe to protect us?"

"But he lied to us," she whispered. "And what about that poor kid? Why wouldn't Dad want to be in his life?"

"I don't know. I wish I did."

"Why keep it a secret from you and then tell you when he's gone?"

"I don't know that either." I shook my head. "Maybe he felt guilty, but he wasn't brave enough to—"

Izzy interrupted. "No wonder you broke up with Jackson."

My gaze whipped to hers. "I didn't break up with him over that."

"I wouldn't be able to trust anyone." She shook her head. "If Caleb wasn't with me all the time, I'd start thinking he was suspect."

"He's only fifteen."

She glanced at me. "Dad was a teen too."

"Why are you so observant all the time?"

"Just lucky."

I gave her a hug and pulled Izzy into me. "I know it's a lot to digest, and I'm sorry it's something we didn't know a long time ago."

She pulled away, but her eyes met mine. "Do you think I could meet him sometime?"

I smiled and nodded. "Absolutely. I think he'd like that."

Chapter Thirty-Two

Jackson

There wasn't any point in sticking around Buttercup Lake any longer. I'd packed my bags, readied my old pickup truck to be put back in Uncle Carter's garage, and sat at the local airport to take a shuttle plane out.

I swung by Millie's when they were all at the lake and picked up my uncle's camping gear. It was more difficult than I thought. Not really emotionally, but physically since Grace didn't fold anything up right or pack things where they belonged.

I figured it was payback.

Emotionally, I was already a wreck.

I'd left her a voicemail and sent her a text about leaving town, and I didn't get much in the way of a response.

I think her last text was something like *good luck*.

And judging by where my headspace was, I'd need it. I glanced at the nearly empty airport and jumped at the chance to load the plane early.

Nothing was keeping me here. My future was ahead, which I knew all along. But I kept hoping that the first misunderstanding that led to losing her wouldn't lead to a second.

I was wrong.

There didn't seem to be a time I wasn't wrong about love.

Love?

I rolled my eyes and shook my head.

Lust? Yeah. Love? No.

I pushed away the sneaking suspicion that I was lying to myself.

I grabbed my bag and walked to the agent. She scanned my ticket, and I headed down the corridor and onto the plane. A few people had already boarded before me.

Shoving my bag into the overhead compartment, I plunked down in my seat and closed my eyes.

If this was just lust . . . would it hurt so bad?

"Excuse me."

I blinked my eyes, wishing Grace were leaning over me, and stood to let the older woman sit next to me. Since it was a commuter plane, there were only two seats on either side of the aisle.

"You look a little glum," the woman said, buckling in.

I smiled, confessing, "I'm not sure I'm ready to be leaving."

"It's a special place. The only thing that gets me on a plane is to see my daughter, son-in-law, and first grandbaby. Although he's not much of a baby any longer. He turns five tomorrow."

"That's sweet."

"Do you have any kids?"

I shook my head. "Nope.

"Are you married? Available? I'm only asking because I have another very single daughter. She's a teacher in Nebraska."

I laughed, wondering if she was part of the Sunshine Breakfast Club. "I am not available, but I've never been married."

"Oh, really. That's interesting." She eyed me suspiciously.

"My job keeps me busy."

"Most jobs do." She nodded. "That's what my daughter always says too. But if you young people don't start making love a priority, what will come of our world?"

I nodded in agreement and thought about Grace.

About how much I loved hearing her run out the door with Pancake as Izzy is screeching in the background. How I loved hearing Grace's laughter on the back patio during Sunday dinner. Feeling her against me when we were making love. I glanced in the other direction and let out a silent sigh. It wasn't just sex. It never was with Grace.

I didn't realize my knee was bobbing up and down so quickly until the man across the aisle glanced at me.

"Nervous flyer?" he asked. "I always take a Xanax myself."

I grinned and nodded, noticing just how friendly the people of Wisconsin were. But I already knew that. It was one of the things I loved about the place. I secretly loved that Uncle Carter put his nose in everyone's business and that the coffee shop was the gossip mill for the Northwoods.

My pulse started racing as the pilot gave us his spiel and the plane took off.

I'd made a mistake, and there was nothing I could do about it.

I was leaving my heart behind and diving into a world that would be soulless because I'd found my person.

I knew she was meant to be mine all those years ago, but life had something else to say about it. And that was okay. Lots of good things came out of it.

But one thing I was determined to do was to win Grace back. I had to prove that my misstep would never happen again. That I was a man of my word, and I'd always give her my word. No more trying to protect her by keeping her in the dark.

The guy next to me pulled out a stack of magazines. The top was a golf magazine. He opened it up and started flipping through the pages while I devised a game plan. Then, I noticed he stopped flipping, turned to look at me, stared back at the page, and then narrowed his eyes at me.

"Hey, this is you," he said, chuckling. "I thought you looked familiar."

I nodded and smiled.

"You're one of the best," he continued. "I can't believe I didn't put two and two together right away."

He looked up and down the aisle. "I heard you took the summer off. Were contemplating retirement. Any truth to that?"

I shook my head. "No. I was just looking after a great-uncle of mine."

"Oh, good. You're a real pleasure to watch on the course. You move with such ease."

My mind flipped back to the golf course with Grace and Izzy and the debacle that resulted in Pancake. Yet, I couldn't help but smile.

"Oh, wow, and the sport still makes you smile like you're in love." The guy nodded. "Pretty incredible."

"It is, but I think this break was good for me. It put things in perspective."

The guy nodded and returned his gaze back to his magazine while my mind raced with longing. I needed Grace. She might not need me, but I felt it in my soul. She was my future. Somehow, we could make it work.

I grabbed my phone that was on airplane mode and opened up the notes section, where I started typing everything I wanted to tell her. Everything I tried to apologize to her about.

And that night. I wanted to tell her what had happened.

I wanted to confess everything.

I didn't fight hard enough for her that night so many years ago, but I'd be damned if I was going to lose her again over something like this.

By the time the plane touched down, I knew what I would do.

I just needed to get my agent on board.

I collected my bag and wandered to my connecting flight to California. The one thing I knew was that I needed to give Grace space. She needed to feel like she could breathe, even if I was suffocating.

I couldn't believe what I saw when I glanced down at my phone.

It was a text from Millie.

And then from Daisy.

Uncle Carter had a stroke and was being flown to Madison, where I already was.

I took a deep breath and shook my head while trying to get my bearings. With my bag over my shoulder, I darted through the terminal and waved down a cab, instructing them to take me to the hospital at UW Madison.

It didn't take long before the driver pulled up to the main entrance. I thanked him, grabbed my bag, and dashed through the spinning door, where a greeter asked if they could help me.

"My uncle was just flown here from Buttercup Lake. He had a stroke," I explained to the greeter.

The greeter nodded quickly and motioned for me to follow him down several corridors to a waiting room.

A nurse looked up from behind a plastic shield. "May I help you?"

"My uncle was just flown here. He had a stroke."

She smiled sympathetically and nodded. "A woman named Daisy is with him. He's stabilized, and they are waiting to run some more tests."

Relief spread through me.

"Would you like to see him?"

"Absolutely."

The nurse stood and pointed at the door. "I'll go around and open it up for you."

"Thank you."

The moment the door clicked open, I could hear Uncle Carter's voice echoing down the hall.

"That's him, alright. I'm so sorry."

"He's a little loopy right now," she said empathetically.

"Where the hell is the doctor?" Uncle Carter barked as Daisy tried to quiet him down. "I don't need to be in here."

"You've had a stroke."

"Like hell, I've had a stroke."

I rounded the corner as the nurse nodded in the direction of the room and dropped me off.

"Well, I can see your speech isn't affected," I said wryly but stopped when I saw the left side of his mouth drooped.

Daisy hopped off the chair, looking so grateful when she saw me. When Uncle Carter got on a roll, it was dicey.

"Thank you for coming," she whispered. "He's been a handful since the medics arrived, and you can imagine what happened once the helicopter landed in his front yard."

"Where's the doctor?" he repeated.

"The doctor has been in twice. He told me that the repetition can be part of things, but they're hopeful he got treatment in time."

I shook my head. "I just left his house. I can't believe it."

Daisy nodded. "He's lucky. Millie happened to be at his house conspiring when she saw him fall over."

"Conspiring?" I asked, shaking my head.

"Long story." Daisy glanced at Uncle Carter. "But if she hadn't been there . . ."

She didn't need to finish her sentence, but I knew.

I understood that the Sunshine Breakfast Club wasn't going to leave well enough alone, and for that, I was grateful.

Chapter Thirty-Three

Grace

The moment I heard about Carter, my mind couldn't stop spinning. Millie was at his house for some reason and thankfully saw him drop. She called the ambulance. I'd heard he'd since been transferred to a rehab facility down in Madison. There wasn't much I could do, but I sent Jackson a few texts. His replies were short.

I had my suspicions as to why Millie was visiting Carter in the first place. She wasn't thrilled that I didn't want to give Jackson a second chance, but I'd obviously overlooked some red flags with Tim, and I didn't need to start having to play Whack-a-Mole with truth bombs with Jackson.

"How do I look, Mom?" Izzy spun around in a pair of khaki shorts and a green polo with the Camp Buttercup logo on the front. *COUNSELOR* was in all caps and embossed across the back. She reached for a green baseball hat and slid it on, yanking her ponytail through the back.

And this was why I couldn't let myself crumble into a pile of tears even though I'd felt like it since I said goodbye to Jackson. Every morning, I thought I'd wake up feeling better. I didn't. I felt worse.

I winked at Izzy. "You look absolutely dynamite. So cool. So awesome. Definitely going to make an impression on the young kids."

Izzy rolled her eyes. "Mom. I meant for Caleb."

"Well, I think he'll be rolling up in the same outfit, so I think he'll like it better on you than him."

She chuckled and looked at me. "I really like him."

"I know you do."

"Is it bad to like someone so much?"

I smiled and shook my head as she stared at herself in the mirror.

"No, it's a wonderful thing. Treasure it."

She turned to look at me. "Did I tell you I beat him in swimming? My time for saving the dummy was faster than his."

"Nice work, Izzy. How'd he take it?"

She blushed. "Really well."

My arms went to my hips. "How well?"

Izzy laughed. "He picked me up and swung me around, telling everyone I was his girl."

"Seriously? That's like from a movie."

She chuckled. "I'm training him well."

"Does he know you refer to him like he's Pancake?" I teased.

"I think he's just happy I don't call him Ball Boy any longer."

I nodded in agreement as Bonnie's car pulled into the drive. I pulled the curtain a little wider and waved out the window.

"You ready for this?" I asked, and she nodded.

"Are *you* ready for it?"

I knew what she was referring to, and it wasn't her going off to Camp Buttercup. I'd made the reservations for Seattle to see my mom. I was scheduled to fly out late tonight and get there in the morning. I only booked the hotel for one night because I didn't know what to expect. They didn't exactly know I was coming because in the past, that often made them panic and flee. They equated visitors with interventions and rehab.

At this point in their lives, I wouldn't think that would necessarily be a bad thing.

"I'm as ready as I'll ever be."

Izzy nodded. "Are you sure you don't want me to come?"

"And miss your first year of being a camp counselor? I don't think so. Caleb would never forgive me, and I don't want to be on his bad side."

She smiled and nodded, leaning in for a kiss. "Okay, I'm ready."

Caleb was already on the porch, hauling her suitcase to the car.

"Thanks, Caleb," I shouted after him.

He gave a quick wave and kept trudging forward. I leaned and whispered to Izzy, "You know, he actually looks pretty good in that uniform."

She chuckled and nodded as we stepped off the porch toward the car. "I agree."

Even though the camp was less than ten minutes away, they still stayed in the cabins overnight and managed the campers who were fourteen and under, day and night.

I remembered some nights being so exhausted on my cot that I didn't know how I'd wake up at six the next morning, but somehow, Jackson made it all seem possible.

That was the problem with him. He always made me believe that the impossible was possible.

"I should have us all moved into the rental by the end of camp, too," I reminded her.

She spun around and looked back at the house. "I'm gonna miss staying here."

"I know, but Millie is spending less time with *her* Jackson, and I don't want to interfere. She's already been super generous, and we needed a permanent address to sign you up for school."

Izzy's mouth dropped open. "Wait. So, it's not a temporary rental like you thought?"

I grinned and nodded. "The realtor was able to convince the owners to let us rent it until at least next June."

Izzy squealed, and we gave each other a long hug.

"If you need me for anything, I'll be on the next flight back. You are the most important thing. Grandma Millie promises to keep her phone on and near her at all times too."

"I'll be fine."

I hugged her again. "I know you will, but I'm just saying."

"I'll look after her," Caleb hollered from the car, and his mom rolled her eyes.

Izzy and I chuckled as she walked to the car, and I knew a piece of me was going to hurt the entire time I was away.

How I was going to handle college in the future left me for a loop. I had no idea how that was going to work, and the thought was nearly paralyzing.

I watched Caleb and Izzy climb into the back seat before Bonnie pulled out of the driveway, and I made my way back inside.

Rolling my small carry-on to the front door made it finally seem real. I took a deep breath, glanced around my grandma's house, and contemplated whether or not I really wanted to go to Seattle.

What I actually felt like doing was climbing in the shower for a good cry.

The front door opened, and Grandma Millie stepped inside about the time I'd almost chickened out and opted for the shower.

"I was hoping I'd catch you," she said, nearly breathless.

"Is everything okay?"

"For sure." Grandma Millie looked puzzled. "I just wanted to know your flight numbers and arrival times."

"Uh, okay." I dug through my bag and showed them to her. "Do you have a pen?"

She whipped out her phone and took a picture.

"That works too."

My grandma nodded. "Have you told your sisters you're going?"

"I texted them."

"They just have no interest in seeing her," Grandma

Millie said softly. "But I understand. There's a lot of pain, hurt, and disappointment."

"Rejection," I added. "Betrayal."

Grandma's eyes connected with mine. "Are you planning on mentioning any of that when you see her?"

I chuckled and shook my head as Pancake came to see what all the ruckus was about. "I don't want to add anything to what she's already feeling."

"You're a good daughter, Grace Henry."

I smiled. "You're an even better grandma, even if you do turn the book club into a matchmaking competition."

She grinned coyly. "I plead the fifth."

"Hey, I've been meaning to ask you."

"Yeah?"

"What were you discussing at Carter's?"

"Just how stubborn you are."

I gasped.

"And how stubborn Jackson is."

I scowled. "We're not stubborn."

"What would you call it?" she prompted.

"Responsible."

Grandma Millie's brows rose. "We will agree to disagree."

"I have a daughter."

"True."

"I can't just have men going in and out of her life all the time."

"Last I checked, we were only talking about one man, and Izzy seems to like him."

She did, which made it harder every single time she asked if I was going to give him another shot.

"You know, I've been thinking about Tim's not being honest with you." She shook her head. "My guess is he thought what you two had was pretty perfect."

"It seemed pretty close with the occasional hiccup."

Grandma Millie nodded. "I'm sure he never expected to pass away so young, but maybe rather than focus on the betrayal of omission, focus on the imperfection of it all. Understand that nothing is perfect. Mistakes will happen."

My pulse rose, and nausea came flooding into my belly.

"I miss Jackson."

"I know."

"But I'm pretty sure I ruined our chances." I waved my phone in the air. "He barely responds."

"He has a lot on his plate."

"I know."

"And so do you." She gave me a hug. "Now, are you sure you don't want me to drive you?"

"I've got it, but I should probably leave now." The thought of seeing my parents made my feet feel like lead weights. I scratched Pancake's ear and forced myself to stand back up.

"I'm proud of you, Grace." She gave a tender smile as I pulled my bag to the car and made my way to the regional airport.

By the time I checked into the hotel early in the morning in Seattle, I was so exhausted and grateful they had my room ready. I crashed on the bed and started to cry, but it oddly wasn't just for my parents. It was for the man who let me dream a little, the one who reminded me that life could go on.

Chapter Thirty-Four

Jackson

I drew in a deep breath and knocked on the door. With everything I'd been through with Uncle Carter, I had no idea what I would be dealing with next. Things hadn't been going as smoothly as I'd planned since my first attempt to leave Wisconsin.

I'd flown back and forth between Wisconsin and California to get some shots done for the new advertising campaign while spending time with Uncle Carter. My life had turned into a whirlwind since my agent started the rumor mill about my getting back out on the course, and my parents finally decided to fly to Madison to help Daisy with Uncle Carter, and I kept him company in between everything.

I tapped on the door again right when it opened.

Grace took my breath away. She had a white towel

twisted on her head and the hotel bathrobe barely tied around her waist. She'd obviously just stepped out of the shower.

She looked like she was in shock, but she didn't close the door on me.

Baby steps.

"What are you doing here?" Her voice was hoarse, like she'd been crying.

"I couldn't let you do this alone." I shook my head. "I just couldn't."

"You don't have to protect me from the world," Grace said with her eyes staying on mine.

"I'm not protecting you, Grace. I'm supporting you."

Her gaze dropped to the floor, and when her eyes returned to mine, she was smiling.

She glanced over her shoulder, and I froze.

I played it off and laughed. "You've got a guy in there?"

She cocked her head at me and gave me a dirty look. "Really?"

"You could. You're single."

"Same with you." She smiled. "I heard you got a pretty good massage at some tavern at Buttercup Lake."

I chuckled. "Seriously? That got around?"

She nodded. "Seems like the perfect town to have a husband."

"Or a wife."

She licked her lips and glanced into the empty hallway. "I was just about to throw on some clothes and head out to see my parents."

I nodded, and she walked into the hotel room without closing the door.

Everything about Grace was even more enticing than I'd been fantasizing about the last several weeks. The mind had a way of fading the important details. It was the little things I'd forgotten, like the swish of her hips, the sweet smell of her, the way her mouth turned up more on one side than the other when she smiled.

All of her. I missed all of her.

"Are you coming in?" she teased, and I quickly made my way inside and shut the door.

I knew this trip was about her parents, but I wanted nothing more than to pull her into my arms and kiss her.

"I didn't want to presume anything."

Her right brow curved. "You hopped on a plane to see me, and you didn't want to presume anything?"

"When you put it that way, it sounds like a lot of presumptions were made, but I do have a contingency plan to get back home if you decide to slam the door on my face."

"Home." She nodded. "Where is home right now? I know

you've had so much happen with your uncle. How's he doing?"

"Uncle Carter is doing well with his rehab and therapy. He's starting to soften up a little, thankfully. He was pretty cranky in the hospital." I smiled, noticing Grace's gaze wandering along my arms. "And home is Wisconsin for now."

She nodded and rummaged through her small bag, pulling out some underwear. I glanced at the art over the bed as she put one leg in and then the other before pulling up her underwear into the safety of the robe.

Grace glanced over her shoulder. "It's not like you haven't seen all of me recently."

She reached for a bra, dropped her robe, and I swallowed hard as the softness of her back led my mind to the night we'd made love.

"Grace, I've missed you." I waited to hear anything.

A breath.

A sigh.

A grunt.

Still not facing me, she nodded as she fastened her bra. When she turned, a weepy smile looked back at me.

"I've been absolutely miserable knowing you weren't down the street." She sniffled and picked up the robe to use like a tissue. "But I don't know what to do. I'm scared. I don't want to be lied to again. I don't want to find out that the life I was living had secrets I wasn't a part of. Or be left to pick up the pieces myself." She sighed, and all I wanted to do was hug her and tell her everything would be fine, but I didn't know if that was true.

"I can only promise to make changes going forward. I can't erase the past. I should have told you that I'd signed some new contracts and what my plans were to leave Buttercup, but I just didn't . . ." I ran my palms over my face and sighed. "I guess I didn't really want to leave."

She nodded slowly. "I signed a lease for a rental."

I smiled, already knowing that. "You've decided to stay?"

"It's the best place for us. I've actually grown really fond of all the meddling. Sometimes, it comes complete with casseroles."

"Good deal."

She nodded, and I saw part of the wall start to crumble away. "There's so much I want to say."

"Me too, but I didn't come here to take away from what you have going with your parents. We can save it for another day." I pressed my lips together before adding, "But I do want to talk about it. I want to talk about everything."

She pulled on a floral dress and slid on a pair of sandals.

"I want to talk to you too, but I'm worried nothing will come out right, and we'll leave worse off than we already are."

"Grace, we're not together. It can't get any worse for me."

Surprise dashed through her gaze, but she winced. "Ready?"

I nodded, knowing neither of us was probably ready for what we were going to encounter.

We stepped into the elevator, and as soon as the doors closed, I could feel the energy rolling from Grace. It was right for me to come. She looked up at me and smiled, and my stomach finally unknotted a bit. I hadn't seen the relaxed Grace since that night in Chicago, but even then, her gaze was etched with worry, with the baggage of what Tim could have left behind.

"I was going to take a cab."

"I have a rental car. We could just drive if you want."

She looked at me and smiled. "I'd like that."

When we got settled into the car and I plugged in the address for the tent city, I let out a deep breath. "I really hope this goes how you want it, Grace."

She let out a little laugh. "Things rarely do, Jackson. I'm prepared no matter what."

I pulled out of the parking lot, and we were on our way.

As we drove on the freeway and merged onto a floating bridge taking us out of Seattle, I glanced at Grace before taking in the glistening water and mansions propped on the hillside.

She touched my knee, sending a jolt of electricity through me. "Before I forget, I want to tell you that I'm sorry."

Her words surprised me.

"For what?"

"Taking out everything I was feeling toward Tim on you."

"I don't think you did."

She shook her head. "I really did, and I'm sorry. At the time, finding out you were leaving felt so raw, and I felt so vulnerable and torn up from finding everything about Tim."

I nodded, looking at Grace and seeing the woman I couldn't live without.

"It just felt like once again, things were being hidden from me, and I never struck myself as someone who was fragile. I can take it."

I smiled and nodded, studying Grace. "You know what it is, Grace? I think it's the complete opposite. You've been so strong for so long. You've had to deal with things that most people haven't had to deal with, and the surprises keep coming." I gripped the steering wheel as her hand still rested on my knee. "I think it's because you're so strong that sometimes, the thought of lessening your burden drives some of what I did. I can't speak for Tim, but I know you can take care of yourself and Izzy. There's no doubt in my mind about that, but I guess I didn't want to add to your troubles or give you any extra. And believe me. I now understand to tell you everything. Forever. Always. Open book. That will be me."

Grace chuckled, and the sound calmed me. I hadn't felt calm for so long, the sensation was unexpected, but that was what Grace did for me. She calmed me.

"Damn right," she said, squeezing my knee, and I felt like progress was being made.

I followed the instructions and got off on an eastside exit.

"You ready? You want me to swing through a coffee drive-thru first?"

"Actually, maybe we could go to the grocery store, and I could pick up some flowers."

I smiled, thinking about Grace. She was just sweet and spice thrown together.

"Absolutely."

She spotted a market, and I pulled into the parking lot. "I'll be right back."

"You sure you don't want me to come inside?"

"What were we just talking about?" She opened the door

and laughed.

I winked. "I got it."

I watched her walk into the grocery store and turned on the radio, wondering if maybe Grace and I were on the road to recovering what we had.

There was so much I wanted to tell her about that night I lost her. There was so much I wanted to hear from her and learn from her.

But our time was limited. I was going on tour soon. I shook my head and watched her marching back out of the market with a bouquet.

When she slid back into the car, I held it for her while she buckled. "I don't know. Maybe this is a dumb idea. She lives in a tent."

"Keep staying with what your heart is directing, Grace. It's okay." I turned on the car and followed the directions, leading us to the parking lot of a church.

Temporary chain-link fencing circled the outskirts of the parking lot, and a multitude of colored tents dotted the pavement like a faded quilt. There were a couple of porta-potties near the back and a person sitting on a stool at the entrance to it all.

It wasn't the first time I'd seen things like this. There were tents propped on sidewalks in many parts of the city here and in Los Angeles.

"This wasn't what I was expecting," she muttered. "I don't know what I was expecting, but this wasn't it."

"Do you want me to turn around?"

She shook her head. "No, I got this."

I found a parking spot on the other side of the parking lot that wasn't fenced and turned off the car.

"Want me to stay in the car? Come with you?" I didn't like the look of this at all, but I knew now wasn't the time to look all macho. She didn't want a knight in shining armor.

"Okay. Let's do it." She nodded. "Maybe come with me?"

"Will do." I took the arrangement from her lap and climbed out of the car.

"Do you think we can just go in, or do we check in?"

I shook my head as she grabbed the flowers from me. "I don't know."

We slowed as we got to the entrance, and the man slid off his stool. "Visiting?"

I nodded, and Grace cleared her throat.

"I'm here to see Joe and Tamra Bailey."

He grabbed a notebook. "They're here."

"Right now?" Grace asked.

"Yeah. We have our residents check in and check out."

Grace nodded and glanced at me, looking painfully nervous.

"They're behind me, down the far aisle, in the green tent." He handed me a pen and a clipboard. "Please write your names down."

Grace shook her head. "You don't have to. I can go in myself."

And there she was again, trying to be the protector. This time, of my reputation.

I printed my name and Grace's and handed the clipboard back to the man.

She looked at me and smiled as I took her hand in mine. There were people waving at us as we walked by, their tent flaps open and sparse personal items inside. We spotted a green tent and a paper hanging on a window with Grace's maiden name.

"I think this is it," I whispered, and she nodded, taking her hand from mine to hold the arrangement better.

"Um, hello." She tried to tap on the door of the tent. "It's um . . . it's me, Grace."

I heard some faint whispering and then the zipper to the tent. Grace looked at me as the door fell open, and a very emaciated man stood in front of us.

"Grace, hello," the man said, glancing in my direction.

"Is this Tim? I don't . . ."

"No, Dad. Tim passed away almost two years ago."

"Oh, right . . . right . . ."

I pushed my anger down at the man who had so little interest in his daughter.

"This is Jackson."

Her dad smirked. "Ah, the kid you had a crush on."

Grace looked surprised that he remembered me, but I just assumed it was her dad's more sober of decades.

Slightly.

"Good to meet you," I said.

A woman mumbled from behind him, and I saw Grace crane her neck to see her mom.

Disappointment washed through Grace's fine features, and if there were ever a time I wanted to protect her, this was it.

"Is that Maya?" the woman asked.

"No, it's Grace," her husband responded.

"Ah, that's too bad. Maya sends money."

I ground my teeth when I saw the hurt dart through Grace's gaze as she turned to look at me with a shrug.

Grace cleared her throat, and I stepped next to her, snaking my arm around her waist. She moved her gaze to mine and said a silent thank you.

"I brought some flowers for you, Mom. I heard that you have fallen ill," Grace said. "I'm sorry to hear that."

The woman coughed as her husband stepped aside. "When have I ever been well?"

Grace didn't respond, but she stepped inside the tent as I dropped my arm from her. She handed her mom the arrangement, and it felt like the saddest moment I'd ever witnessed.

Her mom took the flowers from her and put them next to a dirty comforter and what I spotted to look like drug paraphernalia. There was a reason Grace didn't give them money.

"I just wanted to see you again," Grace said softly. "I know life hasn't been easy on you."

"No, it has not. And then I get to die."

Her mom's hair looked matted and her eyes dull, but it was her tone that struck me.

Complete indifference.

No reference to what she'd put Grace and her siblings through, or Millie. The dad stood looking about as out of it as the mom.

"I hope you change your mind about seeking treatment—"

Her mom looked like she was about to rage.

"For cancer," I interrupted, and Grace gratefully nodded.

"Yeah, for cancer," Grace added.

She shrugged. "What's the point?"

Her dad nodded in agreement.

Grace stood straighter, and I wasn't sure if she was going to try to hug her mom or her dad, but I saw something change inside Grace.

"Because you're worth it." Grace eyed both of her parents. "Both of you are worth living a life that is worth living."

Her mom snorted. "Yeah. I know that I'm really valuable. High-end merchandise."

I clicked my tongue under my breath and watched Grace's vulnerability ooze from her pores.

"I should get going, but please know that I know you both did the best you could, and I hope things get better for you. I hope some decisions on your part make things better for you. Whatever they may be."

I saw her dad roll his eyes, and it took a lot to restrain myself. So much came to mind that I wanted to say, but it wasn't my battle, and Grace was a class act.

"Thanks for the flowers," her mom said as Grace stepped outside the tent. "Nobody's ever given me flowers before."

Grace turned to see her mom and smiled. "I'm glad you

like them. Love you both."

Grace's dad nodded and smiled a toothless grin. "Tell our granddaughter Sammie that we love her."

Grace cocked her head and studied her dad. "Izzy is your granddaughter's name. There is no Sammie."

And with that, Grace spun around and looped her arm through mine.

Chapter Thirty-Five

Grace

We'd just landed back in Wisconsin this morning, and Jackson drove my car back from the airport. I was mentally and physically exhausted. Jackson and I didn't talk much. He didn't inundate me with questions. He let me have space. And who knew? Maybe he needed it, too, after what he saw.

As we pulled into Millie's driveway, my grandma came out onto the porch holding Pancake, who was trying to wiggle out of her arms.

"I love that dog," I muttered, shaking my head.

Jackson glanced in my direction, and an odd parade of butterflies marched through my belly. After what I'd just been through with seeing the absolute indifference my parents had for me, it was hard to reconcile that I'd just shown that side of me to a man.

I even kept the embarrassment and shame I'd felt hidden

from Tim. I'd read enough self-help books to know that it's not my fault and I shouldn't feel those emotions, but they still crept up now and again.

Turning in my seat, I smiled at Jackson. "I can't thank you enough for meeting me in Seattle, even with everything I put you through."

Jackson's smile melted me as kindness churned through his gaze. "You didn't put me through anything except from unrelenting agony about losing the woman I was falling in love with and making me question every single life decision I'd ever made up to meeting you, and . . ."

I chuckled, putting my finger to his lip. "I get it. I get it. You kind of like me."

He kissed my finger, and a wave of longing pressed through me.

"We're giving my grandma way too much to be able to report back to the book club with," I teased.

"Let 'em talk." He chuckled as I crawled out of the car.

Grandma Millie let go of Pancake on the ground, who darted right toward me as Jackson pulled my bag out of the trunk.

"Funny seeing you here with Grace," Grandma Millie said, winking at Jackson.

"So that's why you wanted all my flight info and hotel

reservations?" I eyed my grandma.

Grandma Millie feigned innocence, and I gave her a big hug.

"How'd it go?" My grandma eyed Jackson instead of me.

"Grace is an incredible human being." Jackson shook his head. "That's all I can say."

"Things haven't changed. They're pretty much wrapped up in the world they created, fueled by something I can't change."

Grandma Millie ran her slender fingers along my cheek and tucked some hair behind my ear. "You did your best, even though they haven't done theirs."

I smiled. "It's funny you said that because I told them that I understood that they did their best."

"But we know that's hogwash," Grandma Millie said. "Those two have put their addiction above everything else, but I've learned that's what addicts tend to do." She clapped her hands and rubbed them together like she was cooking something up. "The silver lining in all of this, if there can be one, is that it got you two stubborn kids talking again."

Jackson laughed and shook his head. "I'm glad everyone has kept their perspective on this situation."

Grandma Millie chuckled as I held Pancake in my arms. The little pup sniffed Jackson's hand and licked it.

I eyed Jackson and smiled. "I guess you're back on her good side."

"Thank goodness because I've had nightmares about that very thing."

I laughed and held Pancake up toward the sky, noticing that her tongue refused to stay in her mouth and her eyes were bugging out of their sockets. Thankfully, her extra moppy hair made it difficult to see that she looked like she'd stuck her paw in a light socket, but I loved her. She fit our crew just fine.

"Izzy called about an hour ago to see how things went with you."

Anger roiled through me unexpectedly as I thought about Tamra and Joe. Finally, what had happened to my sisters years ago had happened to me.

"Tamra and Joe didn't even remember my daughter's name, and they thought Jackson was Tim."

Grandma Millie gasped. "I told them multiple times that Tim had passed. I'm so sorry."

I smiled at my grandma and knew she'd been my savior all those years ago. My grandma and Buttercup Lake.

Glancing at Jackson, I knew he had been too. More so than he ever knew.

"I heard that Carter is coming home tomorrow. Your

parents are driving him up. I think they plan on staying with him for a few weeks."

Jackson laughed. "How do you know all this before I do?"

"Daisy. She's a real talker, that one."

Jackson snickered and nodded. "She really is."

"Well, I've ignored my boyfriend long enough. The house is yours. Pancake has been fed, and I'm ready to make the best of a beautiful summer night. I suggest you two do the same."

My cheeks flushed, and I hugged my grandma. "Grace, you're as transparent as an ice cube. Give that man the chance he deserves."

She let go, and I nodded. "I will."

"You will what?" Jackson asked as Grandma Millie trundled to her car.

I handed Pancake to Jackson, and she settled right in.

"I will give you the chance that you deserve." I smiled, feeling an ache deep inside of me from being away from him for so long. "More than deserve."

Jackson waved at Grandma Millie as she pulled out of the driveway before we slowly walked to the porch.

"Then we have to settle some stuff before we can make this work," Jackson said flatly, and I wondered if I'd guessed wrong.

What if he'd only showed up because he's dependable and that's what friends did?

"It's way more fun being dysfunctional," I teased.

Jackson laughed and sat next to me in a rocking chair when my phone rang. It was my sister FaceTiming me.

"It's Maya," I explained, and he nodded as I answered.

"Hey, sister," Maya's voice rang out. She was sitting on a deck with a margarita. "I heard you made the trip out west."

I nodded and shrugged. "Not sure why I did."

"You're a better person than I am, Grace. You always have been."

My phone wobbled, and Jackson came into the shot. Maya's eyes widened.

"Is that Jackson Locke?"

I chuckled. "Yeah. He met me there to go see them. It wasn't pleasant, but Jackson made it bearable."

Maya smiled and nodded. "It's nice to see Grace ask for help."

I snickered.

"If we're being perfectly honest," Jackson started, "she didn't ask for help. I just showed up."

Maya laughed. "That sounds about right. I'll let you two go. Call me when you have a free second, and you can fill me in."

I nodded and gave a quick wave. I didn't have the energy to talk to my sister about our parents right now. I was still trying to process it all.

A few minutes of silence passed between us.

"This looks good on you, ya know." I smiled at Jackson.

"It feels good too. I've been running around nonstop between photoshoots, meetings with my sponsors, and practice time, all in between caring for Uncle Carter."

I nodded, wishing I'd been there for him like he'd been there for me.

"What happened that night so long ago?" I asked, setting Pancake on my lap to curl in.

A warm breeze swept along the porch, and Jackson turned slightly so he could see us better.

"I—" He stopped himself. "I don't want to say something that will make you think worse of Tim."

I shrugged. "At this point, nothing would surprise me."

"He knew how much you meant to me, and he knew what I was going to ask you."

My heart stalled. "What do you mean?"

"You know how I had that scholarship to play golf at college?" he said softly.

I drew a breath and nodded. "Yeah. I remember."

"I had confided in Tim that I had planned on giving it up."

I gasped and shook my head. "Why would you do that?"

Jackson clamped together his hands and propped his elbows on his knees. "Because I wanted to be with you."

I opened my mouth and smacked it shut and did that two more times. "But I . . ."

"I was going to ask you to marry me." He drew a breath and shook his head. "My parents wanted to kill me, and Tim wasn't exactly keen on the idea either."

I nodded slowly, swallowing down my surprise.

"He never seemed to be interested in girls, so I just blamed his negativity on his not understanding." He shrugged. "But after meeting Tracy, I don't know what to think."

I shook my head. "I had no idea."

"No one did. Tim was the only person who knew my plans that night. I stopped talking to my parents about it. Anyway, Tim was the one who was supposed to get you in that boat and across Buttercup Lake."

"I don't understand."

"We took the skiff, and he dropped me off and rowed it back to the camp to pick you up when the time was right." He rocked a little faster. "It was all supposed to go according to my plan, and then you never showed up."

I stared at Jackson.

"And I was stranded on the other side of the lake with a tent, candles, and the whole deal."

Shock chugged through me. "You've got to be kidding me."

"I wish." He let out a deep breath and laughed. "Of course, in hindsight, I saw things clearer. He'd talked about how you'd flirt with him, and he'd been pretty busy planting those seeds that last summer."

"No way." I thought back to that night and groaned. "Wow. I had no idea, not even an inkling."

"I'd love to hear your version," he prompted.

"I'd love to tell you." I brought my eyes to his and let out a sigh. "I was hanging out at the dock that you told me to meet you at for what seemed like an eternity. When a couple of my friends saw me standing alone, they started hanging out with me, and a couple of hours went by. I was totally crushed because I kind of felt like something was going to happen between you and me."

I patted Pancake and studied Jackson. I knew he was telling me the truth and was now listening intently to my version.

"I kind of thought that you were either going to let me down gently so you could go have your college experience or you might give me a promise ring. I don't know. It all seems so innocent now."

Jackson nodded and licked his lips. He sat back in the chair and continued to rock.

"I think it was around ten or so at night, and I finally had to admit to myself that you weren't coming. I'd already been eaten alive by mosquitoes . . . and Tim showed up."

Jackson watched me and drew a breath. "At ten?"

"Tim told me that he saw you out with one of the older girls from college. Tim said he saw you with your arm around her, making out."

Jackson's jaw dropped. "Son of a . . ." He stopped himself.

"I felt so betrayed and rejected," I said softly. "He tried to kiss me that night, but I wouldn't let him."

"And he told me you kissed him," Jackson said, laughing. "Boy, we got played."

I nodded. "We did, but I wasn't completely innocent. I did kiss him before I left to go back home."

"Wow. He told me you never came to the dock, but you invited him to your cabin. He said you were going to break up with me since I was going to college."

"The tangled web Tim wove," I said, sighing and glancing at Jackson. "How'd you get back to camp without a boat?"

"I swam back in the morning." Jackson swiped his hands over his face and laughed. "I swam back, found Tim, and went to clock him when he gave me this elaborate tale of betrayal. Apparently, all that flirting you did with him over the summer paid off."

"Well, he was apparently a really good storyteller."

"Apparently."

"And yet I look back on it and wouldn't change things for the world." I looked at Jackson. "I have Izzy."

He nodded in agreement. "And it's almost sweeter to hear our stories now when rational thought and mature decisions have entered the picture."

I chuckled. "You don't think giving up a full-ride scholarship would have been the best move?"

Jackson grinned. "Not even a little bit," he confessed. "But at the time, I only wanted you."

"The whole thing is crazy. I remember when I got home, you only called a couple of times and my sisters intervened."

"Yeah, they did." He nodded. "Tim had told me you'd kissed, and your sisters filled me in on the rest."

"I'm so sorry." I rested my head on the chair and rocked slowly. "And here we are."

"I don't want to lose you again to a bad game of

telephone." Jackson stood and leaned against the porch railing, studying me.

The way his eyes swept over me made my entire body respond. He got me. He understood me. I couldn't ask for more than that.

"I have fallen so hard for you, Grace." Jackson slid his hands over his hair. "Not just you, but the life you have. It's so fun for me to hear Izzy in the background hollering about some teenage meltdown or listening to Pancake yap as you're running outside with her to go potty. I picture myself in those messes with you. I guess that's the thing. Since we've reconnected, I see myself with you in a house, making a home, blending a family. I just don't want to be without you any longer."

There was so much love inside me that I thought I might burst, but the moment Jackson's lips landed on mine, I knew we were home.

Chapter Thirty-Six

Jackson

Nothing was going to screw it up this time. I gave no tasks to anyone but myself.

Myself and Pancake.

She had a pretty big job to do, and I was counting on her.

But the majority of this was on me.

It was October at Buttercup Lake, and Grace had been so busy readying her antique shop to open that she barely registered that I was in town, which was a good thing. Before I left on tour, we made a schedule where either I flew back home, or she and Izzy came out to see me. It had been working flawlessly, except that I missed my new family tremendously.

But one conclusion that Grace and I came to was that Buttercup Lake needed an antique store, but not a typical one.

Grace was smart enough to know she didn't want to provide all of the inventory at once, so she created a booth system where different vendors would rent space from her to display their antique and vintage items. Plus, it gave Grace the perfect outlet to showcase her latest finds and her own projects. I was really proud of her. The space was in a small house down the street from Abby's coffee shop, so it should get a lot of foot traffic, and she purchased it flat out from the savings she'd had built up.

The idea scared her to death, but once the applications came flooding in to rent the space, she'd make her money back in three years. It was brilliant, and it felt like her personal dreams that she'd kept locked away for all those years were finally getting to see the light of day.

The Grand Opening was going to be October 31st, and thankfully, her sister came out here a couple weeks ago to help. I wasn't sure exactly what was going on with Maya, but it didn't sound good. Some sort of messy breakup. I didn't really know, but I was sure I'd find out soon enough.

What mattered now was making sure the chairs wouldn't blow away or the sunset didn't get interrupted by the storm that was due to arrive.

I glanced at my watch and smiled. I was picking Grace up in a couple of minutes from the shop. While I was kidnapping Grace, the Sunshine Breakfast Club, Maya, and Izzy would swarm the beach. They just thought it was a party for the antique store before I left town again.

Pancake started barking uncontrollably and spinning in circles as I sprinkled rose petals across the sand leading up to the water. Every time I sprinkled a few more, Pancake tried to eat them, and I realized I should have left her at home, cute or not.

I ruffled her fur and picked her up as I dumped the last of the rose petals on the beach.

"Hey, Jackson." Izzy waved from the parking lot with Caleb next to her. "This looks a little suspicious."

I held Pancake and laughed. "I don't know what you mean."

"Aren't you supposed to pick up my mom now?"

I looked at my watch and nodded. "Shoot. Yeah. Running late."

"Can we catch a ride with you?"

Not quite what I'd planned, but fine. I handed Izzy Pancake, and we started toward my truck when thunder rolled in the distance.

"Crap," I muttered.

Izzy held up Pancake and sniffed. "I don't think so."

Caleb laughed and squeezed Izzy before they piled into the cab.

I chuckled and rolled my eyes. "You're so much like

your mom, it's scary."

Izzy smiled and nuzzled Pancake as we drove to town.

I spotted the house and the glow of light from inside and pulled in front.

I did a double-tap on the horn, and Grace stuck her head out the door and waved us in.

"Not again," I muttered to myself, but Izzy chuckled.

"Are you a little worried about something?" she asked, piling out of the car with Pancake and Caleb.

Getting them rounded up was going to take forever.

I didn't have forever.

Shake it off, buddy. It will all come together. Grace wasn't going anywhere.

Izzy plowed ahead of us and opened the door, letting Pancake inside first. Caleb followed behind, and then I finally got the honors.

The moment I stepped inside the store, I knew something was different. Grace appeared from behind one of the false walls where she'd hung some of her artwork that repurposed vintage doilies.

"It looks fabulous," I said, looking around the store.

I spotted Maya in the back and waved as she motioned for Izzy and Caleb to go with her.

"Hey, baby," I said, picking Grace up and spinning her

around.

"Better enjoy that now," she whispered.

I shook my head. "What are you talking about?"

She bit her lip and held up a finger. "Sorry. I have to tinkle."

"Tinkle? Since when do you say tinkle?"

She grinned. "I'll be back lickety-split."

I chuckled, realizing Buttercup Lake had really rubbed off on Grace, and glanced out the window to see the dark storm closing in.

Grace rushed back with a quick apology. "Hey, I know we have to get to the beach for the party celebrating all of this, but I have something I wanted to tell you first."

I nodded and smiled. "Yeah?"

She smoothed her hands down the front of her dress and let out a deep breath. "I . . . uh . . . I'm . . ."

I glanced out the window. "So happy I'm here in person to celebrate?"

She nodded and then blurted two words I didn't understand.

"Huh?"

"I'm pregnant." Her eyes were wide with apprehension.

"You're pregnant?" I looped my arms around her and held her. I held her so tight, and I knew I'd never let go.

"I've been so busy with everything, I didn't really connect the dots when I'd missed a couple of months. I've been having to pee nonstop, and then I feel a little flighty."

My brows raised, and she laughed.

"More flighty than usual." She reached into a cubby and showed me the stick. Two pink lines.

"You've made me the happiest man in the world, Grace."

"Really? I thought you might think the timing was off."

I chuckled, reaching for her hand. "When has the timing ever been right?"

"So, you're happy?"

"I'm ecstatic. Like I can't even fathom it." I grinned, feeling terrified bliss running through my veins. "I love being there for Izzy, and I can't imagine what this is going to mean."

Grace smiled. "It's going to mean no sleep, lots of diapers, lots of squeals, and one more seat on the airplane."

Maya came walking toward us with Izzy, Caleb, and Pancake. "Should we head over to the lake before the weather says we can't?"

I looked at Grace to see if maybe her sister knew, and she smiled. "Izzy and Maya both know. Clumsy me left the stick in the bathroom. Maya panicked and thought it was my daughter."

Caleb's eyes nearly popped out of his head, and I knew

everything I didn't need to know.

"Okay, then. On to Buttercup Lake to celebrate your store's soft opening before I leave town." I squeezed Grace's hand, and she laughed.

I promised not to lie to her, but it was just this one last time.

"Honestly, I think it could wait until it's actually open, but I appreciate your level of commitment and excitement for my endeavors."

"Izzy and Caleb, you can ride with me," Maya informed them.

Grace and I climbed in the truck as Maya wrangled the teens into her car.

"So, a baby?" I couldn't wipe the grin off my face, and I hadn't even gotten to my part of the night. "I am so in love with you."

Grace chuckled. "That's good because you're stuck with us."

I smiled even wider at the thought as I followed Maya to the lake. We parked our cars, and Maya and the kids wandered to the beach. I spotted a few members of the Sunshine Breakfast Club and suddenly felt a wave of butterflies.

What if Grace said no?

"You okay?" Grace asked, sliding out of the truck.

"More than okay."

Izzy put Pancake down, and I called the pup over, lifting her into my arms. When Grace wasn't looking, I looped the box around Pancake's collar and whispered in her ear, begging her to follow what I'd trained her for.

This was her major break. Pancake looked up at me with such big doe eyes, I was pretty certain my hamburger trick had worked.

When I spotted Grandma Millie with her boyfriend and my parents, who were sitting under cover next to Uncle Carter, it suddenly felt real. Sure, there were all of our friends gathering around for this big moment, but seeing family solidified it. This was home.

Grace slowed when she saw the candles and rose petals lining a path to the water.

"Jackson, this looks a bit romantic." She eyed me, and I knew this was the last omission that would ever happen between us.

The crowd started lining up as they watched me hold Grace's hand as we walked toward the water.

I took a deep breath, seeing the sunlight reflect in Grace's soft brown eyes, and things became clear.

Without waiting another second, I knelt down and whistled for Pancake, who zoomed toward me. All of our friends and family quieted, and I sucked in a deep breath.

"Grace, you've taught me that my life was missing a lot. I'd barely scratched the surface of happiness, but you and Izzy made me realize what true bliss is. The thought of living another day without you being mine makes it hard to breathe."

Pancake crashed into me as I held Grace's hand, and everyone chuckled, including Grace.

"Grace, will you make me the luckiest man in the world? Will you marry me?" I held Pancake up for Grace to see the ring.

Tears welled in her eyes, and she pulled me up as I unfastened the ring from Pancake's collar.

"Yes," she murmured in between kisses. "Oh, yes."

Our foreheads rested together right when it started to sprinkle. Grace held up her ring finger and shouted, "I said yes!"

As she turned around, I realized her dress was tucked into her underwear, and I couldn't help but laugh.

This girl was my person, and I wouldn't want it any other way.

Dear Reader,

Where do I start? I LOVED writing Dash of Love! I came up with this series as I wrote the Cloudberry Inn Series, and I immediately fell in love with the idea of Jackson and Grace at the same time I fell for our new state of Wisconsin. When we moved here after living in Washington state my entire life, I had no idea how much I'd enjoy the adventure of it all. I was so excited when I started writing the first chapter Dash of Love, and the story just flowed!

It has been so much fun hearing how much readers have loved Grace, Carter, Izzy, Grandma Millie, and Uncle Carter and can't wait to see them in the next book. I feel the same and had to jump into writing the second book immediately. I don't want to give them up! So, thank you so much for reading the first book in the Sunshine Breakfast Club! I hope you enjoyed getting to know everyone and are looking forward to Pinch of Love! If you loved Dash of Love, reviews and ratings are always so helpful as is word of mouth!

Thanks again so much for reading. It means a lot to us (my family). It's a joint effort! If you're looking for another romance series to binge while you wait for more Sunshine Breakfast Club, I have the Cloudberry Inn Series, Silver Ridge Series, and Island County Series out that are fun to read and have been super popular. But with over sixty books written, keep turning the page and you can see if something else calls out to you.

I'd love to have you join my newsletter at karicebolton.com or hang out in my Facebook Group (Karice Bolton Book Buzz).

Hugs and warmest wishes, Karice

BOOKS BY KARICE BOLTON

THE SUNSHINE BREAKFAST CLUB SERIES
DASH OF LOVE
PINCH OF LOVE
SPRINKLE OF LOVE
CHRISTMAS OF LOVE

CLOUDBERRY INN SERIES
IMAGINING YOU
REMEMBERING YOU
LEAVING YOU
LOVING YOU

ISLAND COUNTY SERIES
FINDING LOVE IN FORGOTTEN COVE
LOVE REDONE IN HIDDEN HARBOR
TANGLED LOVE ON PELICAN POINT
FOREVER LOVE ON FIREWEED ISLAND
TEMPTING LOVE ON HOLLY LANE
CHANCE AT LOVE ON MYSTIC BAY
IRRESISTIBLE LOVE AT SILVER FALLS
LUCKY IN LOVE ON HOUND ISLAND
MISTLETOE MISCHIEF
ACCIDENTAL LOVE ON MEADOW COVE LANE
DISCOVERING LOVE ON CRANBERRY LANE
CHRISTMAS ON FIREWEED
IMAGINING LOVE ON WILLOW ROAD
CHRISTMAS CRUSH ON FIREWEED ISLAND
WAITING LOVE AT HAWTHORNE AVENUE
FOREVER CHRISTMAS ON SUGARPLUM LANE

BEYOND LOVE SERIES
BEYOND CONTROL
BEYOND DOUBT
BEYOND REASON
BEYOND INTENT

BEYOND CHANCE
BEYOND PROMISE
BEYOND the MISTLETOE
SILVER RIDGE SERIES
A HAPPY TRUTH ABOUT LOVE
A LITTLE SECRET ABOUT LOVE
A FUNNY THING ABOUT LOVE
A SURPRISING FACT ABOUT LOVE
A SIMPLE WISH ABOUT LOVE
CHRISTMAS AT SILVER RIDGE

LUKE FLETCHER SERIES
HIDDEN SINS
BURIED SINS
REDEMPTION
MIA

V MAFIA SERIES
BLAKE
DEVIN
JAXSON

THE WITCH AVENUE SERIES
LONELY SOULS
ALTERED SOULS
RELEASED SOULS
SHATTERED SOULS

THE WATCHERS TRILOGY
AWAKENING
LEGIONS
CATACLYSM
TAKEN NOVELLA (A Watchers Prequel)

AFTERWORLD SERIES
RecruitZ

AlibiZ
UprisingZ
BLOOD TORN DUET
BLOOD TORN
BLOOD CURSED